Authoring
Amelia

Lia Conklin

Dedication

To Dad, for reasons obvious to anyone who knows me and him.
To Mom, for reasons that are in many ways the opposite.
I love you both for making my journey what it has been and will be.

Table of Contents

Authoring

Amelia

Chapter 1

Amelia could no longer make out the landscape outside her window, though she had the vague sense they had passed through most of North Dakota. She looked at the other passengers mostly sleeping with their necks bent in various awkward positions—except for the man in the hat. She thought she remembered a hat like that tilted over her grandfather's brow. Had his been brown? The bearer of this days-gone-by black hat was clicking away on his laptop. A writer, she imagined, or one of those businessmen who prefer a computer to a high-maintenance wife. Not too successful at either, she mused, or why would he be here among the woebegone salesmen, pension-less elderly, and penniless adventurers of the Greyhound bus line?

She casually let her mind drift to the possibilities such a man presented. He had more than just glanced her way when she boarded the bus in Minneapolis. It was as if he had wanted to stare, but memories of his mother's pursed lips made him look away. A handsome man like that could surely save her.

Save her. Save her from what? From being completely alone in this world, her sole possessions a sack under her seat and the sixty bucks in her pocket? Except for her guitar, of course, squeezed between her knees like a security blanket. Or was he to save her from her destination? One she had chosen from a list of scrolling departures that flashed a hundred new beginnings, a hundred new lives.

Amelia imagined the man with the hat leading her from the bus to a taxi and from the taxi to his suburban home, perhaps in Seattle. And then what? Would she keep house for him? Would they have a dog? Two and a half children?

She shook her head as it dawned on her that above feeling lonely and scared, what she really felt was free. Free. Who would want to be saved from being free?

She was surprised she felt this way. She hadn't felt free as she watched them bury her aunt, looking over her shoulder to see if her father had finally arrived, careful to avert her eyes from the two mounds of fresh earth that after thirteen years now met the graceful contours of the hillside. She hadn't felt free when her uncle, not bothering to look up from his watch, asked if she needed anything. She had answered "No," but any answer would have been lost on him as he mentally calculated the timing of his trip back to Chicago. And she certainly hadn't felt free as she watched the Houston TSA agents lead her father's small, thin frame away. He had looked back at her from under his Honduran cowboy hat saying, "Go on ahead to the funeral. I'll catch the next plane."

But he hadn't caught a plane, at least not to Minnesota. He had never arrived at the funeral, even as she and her grandmother kept furtive watch. And he hadn't communicated why. In fact, she hadn't heard from him at all. What had the TSA agents wanted? Had they really detained him so long that he just skipped the funeral all together? Had he gone back to Honduras? She had lots of questions for him, but not so many that she would waste this great opportunity, the opportunity to be free of him. At last.

The man with her grandfather's hat shifted his head and caught her eye. He began to open his mouth as if to talk. That's when she realized it was he who needed saving. Amelia smiled at him and turned away, looking out into the passing landscape obscured in darkness. *Like my future*, she thought. And her past.

Chapter 2

Amelia wasn't sure how long she had slept, but when she awoke, there was a kink in her neck, and the man with the hat was gone. So, he wasn't going to Seattle after all, she thought. As she stretched and massaged her neck, it occurred to her that she had no idea where she was or how far she had come. Making her way to the front of the bus to check with the driver, she caught her first glimpse of the landscape through the expanse of the bus's windshield. Disfigured jagged buttes and juniper-spotted cliffs ascended on each side, the handiwork of the Yellowstone River that flanked I94.

"We'll be in Billings in a couple hours," the driver said glancing up at Amelia, his eyes lifting no higher than the lettering on her T-shirt. "You got family there?"

"Yeah," she lied, turning away. No need to delve into details with a driver more focused on the stretched lettering of her T-shirt than on the road. "Thanks," she called back with a quick glance over her shoulder, catching his eyes as they reluctantly left her backside to turn their attention back to the road.

Back in her seat with her forehead pressed lightly against the window, Amelia let the Yellowstone River and its earth child, the Badlands, toy with her, flitting away from her to hide within the landscape, only to curl back to accompany her upon her journey once more. She did not tire of this flirtatious game of hide and seek. In fact, when the Conoco-Phillips petroleum plant burst forth directly in her path, she discovered that two hours had passed within the few minutes of her playful musings. She lost sight completely of her meandering friends as the bus veered to the left of the towering smokestacks to reveal instead Amelia's first glimpse of Billings, Montana.

Billings turned out to be more picturesque than the Conoco-Phillips's smoke-stacks suggested, set in the foreground of what Amelia later learned to be the Bighorn and Pryor Mountain ranges. It also turned out to be more city than country with its hand-standing skateboarder statue bidding, "Welcome to Billings." She was momentarily disappointed by this bronze, baggy-jeaned teenager juxtaposed upon the tumbleweed town of her imagination, but looking towards the mountains nestled in the haze of the morning, she decided there was sure to be remnants of the Old West outside the city limits.

As she descended the bus steps, the driver offered to treat her to breakfast. She stood mute for a moment, calculating which was more distasteful, the driver or the roadside café, finally deciding they were both too greasy. Of course, she didn't say that to the driver but instead gave him a conciliatory smile for his gesture, quickly realizing the effort was lost on him as he never looked above her neckline.

Chapter 3

So, this is freedom, Amelia thought as she sat down on the curb a few blocks from the bus terminal. Her stomach growled, and she realized she wasn't so free that she didn't need to eat. She almost regretted turning down the free breakfast—almost—but remembered the sixty bucks she had in her pocket and knew she had made the right decision. It wasn't much, but it was more than she had had when she left her grandmother's house two days before. Her uncle had been too preoccupied with his own life to be concerned about hers, but her grandmother, even in her grief, had been kind enough to give Amelia fifty bucks. She had probably thought Amelia was going back to Honduras where fifty dollars was much more than a month's wage. Maybe she would have been more generous had she known the truth.

As it was, Amelia had made good use of the fifty dollars. She had bought a used guitar at a secondhand shop, having left her own in Honduras. Then she had sat down in the downtown Minneapolis Nicollet Plaza and begun to play.

It was at times like this that Amelia realized how lucky she had been to have learned to play guitar and sing as a young girl before her father had whisked her off to Honduras. In Honduras, she had continued to play, learning all kinds of Mexican and Spanish music. Honduras itself had been wiped clean of most of its culture, except for some Mayan fabrics that found their way to market. But music, in all of its forms, was still greatly appreciated, and for Amelia, it had been her salvation. Music had carried her through her grief, as well as helped her belong to her new community. It had also helped to put *frijoles* and *tortillas* on the table after heavy rains had washed away their crops. Now it would help her start a new life once again.

She had made over a hundred dollars that day in Minneapolis, as well as an impression on several Latino men who considered a fair-skinned, blue-eyed singer of Mexican music quite a novelty. Amelia was used to that. Being a novelty had made her a hit with the boys in her *preparatorio* school in Honduras, though only one stole her heart—among other things.

The loose change and bills scattered throughout her guitar case had given her enough for a ticket to Billings, the next bus to depart from the Minneapolis bus terminal. Besides, she had always dreamed about the West, and now here she was, sixty bucks still in her pocket and a guitar over her shoulder. The day was full of possibilities. But first, breakfast.

Chapter 4

Over breakfast at a Café that may or may not have been less greasy than the one she turned down, Amelia thumbed through the employment ads. She was excited to see that there were still parts of the old West in this twenty-first century city.

Wanted Ranch Hands. Exp. w/ horses & cattle nec. Willingness to work hard & long hrs. Weiland Ranch, S. of Billings. Ref. Required. Call (966) 342-5698.

Amelia carefully tore out the ad. It was exactly what she wanted. Sure, she didn't really have experience with horses per say, but she had ridden their burro more times than she could remember. It couldn't be that different. And sure, goats weren't exactly cattle, but how different could four-legged, hoofed animals be?

Looking at the phone number, she began to regret not buying the burner phone she had seen for thirty dollars. She hadn't considered that she would need a cell phone. Why would she? She hadn't used one her whole twenty-one years on the planet. But here she was contemplating a number she could easily tap into a cell. Or she could just ask to use the phone at the counter, she thought. Either way, on a cell phone or the antique counter phone, the result would probably be "Thanks, but no thanks." In fact, she mused, wouldn't going to the ranch in person be a better way to make a great first impression? Or maybe the only way to make any impression at all, considering her lack of experience, burro or no burro, and her inability to provide a reference.

The waitress at the café wasn't sure how far the ranch was but decided without looking up from her Glamour magazine that if it were in the Bighorn Mountains, it would be "a ways out." She motioned vaguely towards the mountains with a lazy hand that caught a cup of coffee on its way back. From the café's grease-smudged windows, the mountains looked like gentle pilings of fresh cut hay, a far cry from the lush green Honduran mountains that had been Amelia's home for the past thirteen years. She couldn't judge how far they were. Maybe it would take a few hours by bus in Honduras with all its stops and starts and give or take a flat tire, bottoming out on a rutted mountain road, or waiting for a lazy Brahman bull to cross. She thought that a bus from here would possibly take over an hour…with maybe only a dawdling cow or two to prolong the journey.

Distances appeared to be deceiving in this new territory as Amelia soon discovered. The ranch was at least two and a half hours from Billings, the city bus driver said, and there was no public transportation.

"You'll have to take a taxi, but I warn you, they'll charge an arm and a leg. Or, you could take an Uber" he added, "but still pretty pricey. Of course, you could hitch it. Safer in these parts than most, but not the most desirable option for a young, admirable lady such as yourself." He winked down at her from his perch in the bus. "Then again," he assured her grinning, "you wouldn't have much trouble hitching one. Your thumb alone's prettier than the cattle the men in these parts are courtin'!" He laughed at his wit and Amelia responded in kind, feeling her encounters with the folk on her trip were gradually improving…very gradually.

Amelia wasn't so naïve that she didn't know the dangers of hitchhiking, but her remaining fifty-five dollars assured her it was the only way. She thought one last time about making a phone call to the ranch and protecting herself not only from the danger of the trip but also its unknown outcome. Yet, what was freedom, she thought, if you couldn't pursue your own options and create your own possibilities? She felt sure that once she got to the ranch, her efforts would be rewarded. What could hitching a ride with some chatty townsfolk hurt anyway?

Chapter 5

Reservation folk were who they turned out to be: four young Crow Indian men in the back of a battle-worn Chevy S10. Three other Indian men sat in the cab, jabbing their heads through the missing partition with an occasional look at the road ahead. Amelia had just reached Interstate 90 and was positioning her thumb appropriately when this crazy, tan-gray-green pickup came skidding to a stop a few yards ahead. As she looked at the dark, shiny-haired heads that jerked forward and careened back, she felt like she was home. These were Honduran boys. She had only seconds to contemplate how odd it was that she would feel that way. During the thirteen years she had lived in Honduras, she had felt like a prisoner—a prisoner of gender, culture, religion, and most of all fate. And now here she was, running with winged thumbs to this jalopy whose tailgate hung open-mouthed, inviting her to her old home and new freedom.

As she reached the tailgate, four dark hands reached forward to secure her wrists. She was comforted to look up into four pairs of deep, dark eyes. This was familiar. So too was the pickup that sputtered forward, tossing her like an untethered chicken on a flatbed truck. She righted herself just as four brown hands once again came forward to help. She loved those hands. She sat back on the tire hub that had been vacated for her and laughed. As the pickup ground into third gear, the wind lifted her blond hair from her shoulders and carried her poignant notes of glee and relief across the plains. Three heads jabbed back through the cab window to join four pairs of quizzical eyes already observing her upturned laughter and yellow, dancing mane.

"Oh," she finally gasped, freeing one hand from its firm grip on the pickup box to wipe tears from her face. "I'm just so relieved!" She said.

They looked at her with a mixture of curiosity and amusement. She wondered if they had ever known how she felt at that moment and decided they probably had.

"I'm Amelia," she said offering her free hand to all the hands extended her way. The three heads nodded from the partition, and she waved and nodded back. "I'm heading towards the Bighorn Mountains," she explained, "to a ranch called Weiland. Do you know the place?"

They all nodded and passed with their glances the ancient story of land lost and annexed.

"How close can you get me there?" she asked when their eyes returned to hers.

"Close enough," replied the young man with the "Caught Dead in Billings, Montana, 2016" T-shirt, the outline of a tomahawk appearing from behind the gold lettering.

"Maybe too close," grinned another, showing even, white teeth in contrast with his dark recessed eyes. They all laughed at some hidden meaning that Amelia could only guess.

One of the heads that poked through the window, having somehow caught the conversation over the rumble of the engine and rattles and thuds of each unabsorbed bump and rut along the highway, asked, "Why ya goin' there?"

"Applying for a job," Amelia shouted back. "Thought it'd be cool to work on a ranch for the summer. I've always dreamed of living out West. Such a sense of freedom out here."

"As long as you're the cowboy," grinned the toothy one. They all laughed heartily, albeit good-naturedly. Amelia found herself reddening. Not only did she know a lot about native history, she thought her own past somehow connected her to the disenfranchised, the forgotten. She was embarrassed to discover that in spite of her own history, she spoke as white as her skin.

"I'm Darian," said the tomahawk T-shirt kid after he finished laughing.

"And I'm Paul," the other grinned with his perfect teeth. She realized they were much quicker to forgive white-speak than she was, and soon they were introduced all around. She couldn't help but be disappointed by the absence of their last names that surely were as poetic as White Wolf, Smiling Bear, or Dancing Pony. There was that white mind of hers again, she scolded herself. Well, who was to say they weren't assuming her last name was as boring as Jones or Smith?

They had a good two hours more to talk about life on the Rez, outings to the city, children that came too soon, girlfriends that came too late—or not at all, they admitted sheepishly. Other than references to the Rez, Amelia recognized these conversations. She had heard them before from the backs of school buses in Minnesota, her first home, and the backs of flatbeds hauling workers to coffee and banana plantations a thousand miles away. It was comforting to know that wherever there were people there were such conversations.

And silence too. Amelia had shared many silences in the past and had learned enough about silence to hear its story. The silences between the jarred memories and spontaneous thoughts of these young men told Amelia the story of camaraderie, of loyalty and acceptance, and of stilled passions. She was not part of the same silence, but they generously shared with her its intimacy.

It was during a silent story of these young men's kinship with the surrounding landscape that Amelia first met the Bighorn Mountains. They barely resembled their distant Honduran cousins. Here, levels of wispy green foliage were intercepted by upsweeping lands of coarse vegetation, crumbling outcroppings of yellow and gray shale, and wall faces of barren red, yellow, and gray stone. Fissures of spindly, green pines and red chert took turns crisscrossing the coarse yet gentle ascending landscape. Amelia could feel Destino, her Honduran burro, move beneath her, negotiating the new and hostile terrain. Destino would acclimate easily, she was sure. She only hoped she could too.

Destino came to an abrupt halt. The five pickup box occupants jolted forward and fell back against one another.

"Weiland Ranch is that way," the driver said craning his head through the back window.

"You'll have to go the rest of the way on foot," Darian explained. "It's a rough trail, mostly for ATVs and horseback riding."

"We'd go with you," grinned Paul, "But I hear they get bored just shooting coyotes." They all laughed again.

"How far is it?" Amelia asked, wishing she could decide whether or not to use the cafe's phone back in Billings based on their answer.

"I'd say close to five miles," one of them answered.

Miles. How far was that anyway? She had gotten so used to distance measured in time that she had no idea what it meant, other than it was "a ways."

"How long will it take me, do you think?" she asked.

"We could use some Indian magic and send you as the hawk flies," Paul said, wiggling his fingers as he raised his hands upward. The others laughed. At first, Amelia felt it was at her expense. Then Paul placed a hand on her shoulder and as she looked into his eyes, she realized they were laughing at themselves. They had no Indian magic; they had only an ancient past, a confining future, and this dilapidated pickup truck.

"I'd go with ya," he said, serious for the first time. "My great-grandfather would love to see the day our family set foot on this land again. But it won't be today. These guys," he gestured to his buddies, "got girlfriends at home ready to show them how much they been missed.

"And Paul's got his Shepherd mutt in heat!" This time the joke was on him, and Amelia left them as they continued chuckling after goodbyes were said and thanks given. She was alone with the land and the echo of these men's conversation…and silences.

Chapter 6

Amelia soon discovered "How far?" or even "How long?" was not the right question. Time and distance became irrelevant as she topped another brittle crest, or rounded another jagged bend, each revealing an immense panorama of emergent green, stubborn brown, and receding sun-sparkled white. "How much?" was the true question. How much air could she breathe? How much silence could she bear? How much depth could she explore? How much more could she know by the time the first bark of the ranch dogs penetrated her eardrums and the first glimpse of the "Weiland Ranch" sign arched above her trail? She wished she would have known what to ask. Maybe her Crow friends would have prepared her for the answer.

She had not traveled terrain like this before. Yet the crunch of her feet on the loose shale was as familiar to her as her heavy breathing and the lean bulges of her thighs. How often she had climbed from the village road to her mud home. How often she had felt her heart growing heavier with her breath as she climbed, each bringing her one step closer to a home that held no comfort, a father with no warmth, and a mother and brother who were not her own.

Each day that she opened the door to step onto the earthen floor of her mountaintop home, she stepped into servitude. The few schoolbooks she had were placed upon a banana crate by the bed she shared with her younger stepbrother to be opened by candlelight while the others drifted off to sleep. Homework was a luxury. Her new life meant fetching two five-gallon pails of water each morning and evening from the spring downhill, combing their deforested mountainside land for the day's firewood, grinding the maize and preparing the dough for the evening tortillas, gathering vegetables from the garden, and tethering the goats to graze on overgrown pasture.

There were also chickens to tend, to rear from squawking chicks to scrawny molting hens whose necks would be wrung with a quick crack of the wrist and skinny bodies plucked and cleaned to become boiled chicken bits floating in *sopa de pollo*, chicken soup. And there were clothes to wash with cold spring water against a granite slab, faded fabrics slid back and forth to reveal a sudsy façade, then rinsed, wrung, and haphazardly hung, ready for the sun to take its turn in preparing them for their next day's toil. Each shirt, each skirt, each sock and slip went up and down, up and down, up and down, until Amelia's brain rode the monotony of her hands like an abandoned swing in a colorless breeze.

Each time she reached her mountaintop home, the extravagant blanket of descending mountain foliage with its patches of hand-sewn plots at her back, her soul yearned to breathe. The beauty around her offered her no inspiration…no respiration. For how could her soul breathe if it had already died? Been burned and buried with all that she loved?

Her heavy breathing and the pumping of her legs as she climbed may have dragged her into the caverns of her past, but as she crested the ridge of this new mountain, no door to exile appeared. Rather, the sweeping view of the tumbling mellow to piercing green slopes lay opened at her feet. This time her soul breathed in and refused to exhale.

Chapter 7

About the same time that Amelia saw the ranch buildings below, she heard the first excited yet wary bark of the ranch dogs. She remembered a dog once that had barked like that. She remembered all his different barks—wariness, warning, excitement, and welcome—as she jumped off the school bus to embrace his furry torso in her book-laden arms. Then she suddenly wondered what his last bark sounded like, before everything turned inside out and upside down.

The dogs below continued to bark as she made her way down the trail. In Honduras, there had been no jovial border collie to welcome her home, only a scrawny mutt with oversized ears that yipped and whined at her heals and rubbed his scaly skin against her calves. He offered no comfort from her torment at school or concern for her sadness or shame. His was not a cry for affection but rather a desperate plea for reprieve from his hunger and the singe of his parasitic bowels and skin. How funny that everything about her life in Honduras was a cruel parody of her life before, including that diseased mutt.

The only constant in her life, she realized, had been her father. She realized how little she missed him; how thankful she was to have her lungs filled with this fresh, Montana air untainted by his insistence that she breathe more from her diaphragm or equally from her chest, or hold it longer than she had or maybe somewhat less. She caught a whiff of sweet vindication as she entertained the idea of his being detained, while today she was breathing free.

Once through the gate, the dogs waited no longer to investigate her approach and came barking towards her. They were not menacing and quickly took to sniffing her jeans and outstretched palms. A man stepped out onto the ranch house porch. Even from a distance his legs appeared uncertain whether to descend from the porch or wait where they stood. They did finally make their willowy way down the steps towards her, knees bowed outwards as if preferring to turn back.

Amelia waved, extracting a hand from the tangle of fur she was caressing and cajoling forward. This time the man's arms seemed uncertain what to do. They decided to move slightly upwards from the body and hang there just above his hips. Amelia lowered her hand and continued slowly forward. She was wary of the sun that would surely catch the polished sheen of his badge and blind her aim when the time came to draw. Her periphery vision offered no assistance, yet she was sure her Crow friends were crouching just behind the rocky ridge, in black and white film, ready to come to her aid. A blue heeler snout to the crotch later, "Take one" of her Wild West debut snapped to a close, leaving Amelia just time enough to stifle a nervous giggle before offering her hand to the pistol-ready one that now hung before her.

He was no Clint Eastwood, not even the over-aged one. In fact, there was little to redeem his cavernous, jowly face. Not even a smile. Amelia had enough smile for the two of them, and though contagious, this anti-Eastwood had a hearty immune system.

"Hello. I'm Amelia Kingston," she offered, undaunted. "I've come to apply for the ranch-hand position. I've had a lot of experience with animals," she said, hoping she had not emphasized the word *animals* too much and given away the fact that they may as well have been hippos or kangaroos for all the good it would do on this ranch. "And I'm very strong and not afraid to work hard and long hours. I think you'll be very pleased with my performance if you give me a chance."

She felt once again embedded in a Western film, this time playing some young tomboy dying to prove herself equal to a man—not to just any man—but to this man that stood before her, bronco-beaten and nature-worn, his humor scraped away by wind and rain, like the earth of his surrounding landscape. She became aware that her outstretched hand no longer showed evidence of Honduran labor and hoped he would not notice.

She realized she had nothing to worry about as he dismissed her hand entirely and instead nodded at the guitar slung over her shoulder.

"Do ya play that thing?" he asked.

"Ah, yes, I do," she replied, wondering who would carry it upon their back for five miles if they didn't. "I sing too. It's a nice interruption to a hard day's work to sit back and listen to some music. I'd be happy to play for you anytime you'd like."

"Do ya know any Marty Robbins?" he asked.

"Uh, no, not really…though I could learn it quick enough."

"Come back when you do then, and I'll think about taking ya on." With that he gave in to his knees and turned back towards the ranch house, leaving Amelia to contemplate her return to Billings.

"Take Two" was over, and Amelia's good first impression was lost to the wind.

Chapter 8

The five-mile hike gave Amelia time enough to contemplate who the hell Marty Robbins was and to go through a list of other singers that may or may not have been Country icons. She was less interested this time in the lay of the land than in the waning sun and her equally waning energy. The greasy breakfast and two granola bars she had eaten on her way to the ranch were now joined by another granola bar and washed down by the last of her water. Her dinner did little to raise her spirits and even less the sun. She worried that she would not make it to the highway before dark.

When she finally saw the highway, her legs shakily bore her weight upon the loose shale of the final descent. She laughed to see four hawks sitting upon the barbed-wire fence. They had waited for her after all! And now they would return her to Billings upon their magic wings. A few trickling streams of shale later, they flew off. How fickle her new friends were.

It was night, but darkness never came. The dark mountain to her side rose up to send sparks from its summit campfire into the heavens. This was not new to Amelia, who often in the past, upon tethering the last goat or making her final trip of the day to the outhouse, was serenaded by this heavenly mariachi of glimmering brass. Here, however, the sky seemed turned around, or maybe she was walking upside down. The Big Dipper ascended to rule the sky with Polaris, her dear old friend, offering her guidance once again like so many years ago. Looking up at him on his heavenly throne, for the first time since his descent to the milky Honduran horizon over a decade ago, Amelia thought suddenly that maybe they had risen with him. Maybe she would round the next bend to see her mother, silver in starlight, and her brother, swathed in the same blue filter of heavenly light, nestled in her arms. Their faces would be upturned, following her mother's dazzlingly blue finger in a path to Polaris. But the only blue finger Amelia was to see that night was her own as it wiped silver tears from her face. Polaris had risen alone.

Chapter 9

She was rescued from her lonely journey on foot by a middle-aged truck driver. But it didn't take Amelia long to realize that "rescued" was a rather loose interpretation. As it was, the truck driver was not driving his Peterbilt truck, but rather his Ford Ranger SL pickup, he offered up as a way of apology.

"I live out here near the Bighorns," he announced. "I'm on the last of my five days off and about to start my ten days on. But don't you worry none," he said planting a beefy hand on her thigh, "My little wife gives me enough lovin' those five days to last me twenty!" He gave a hearty laugh and a wink at Amelia who took the opportunity to adjust her seatbelt and dislodge the large hand that showed no signs of leaving her thigh. Unperturbed, he continued, "And now a pretty young gal such as yourself, ridin' shotgun, I could probably go thirty!" He winked again, his sweaty hand rediscovering her thigh, this time just a bit further up. Amelia winced at the contact and wondered what had ever possessed her to think hitchhiking was at all an option, even "in these parts." By the time she saw the truck stop lighting up the outskirts of Billings, she had lost count of how many times her seatbelt needed adjusting.

"I'll get out here," she announced, with no attempt to hide her relief.

"I'll join ya for coffee," he declared, announcing no attempt was necessary.

"I can't drink coffee this late," Amelia responded, and upon remembering the existence of decaf added, "and anyway, my boyfriend will be showing up any minute to pick me up." It was an easy lie since he had not asked her anything about herself during the entire trip.

"Lucky guy," he said. "Though my Cynthia's a hot one, I'd imagine even a bucket of cold water wouldn't put out your fire!" She had already jumped down from the pickup but wished she had slammed the door a few seconds earlier to avoid the crawlies that now crept up her spine. She slammed it now, not an ounce of remorse that she hadn't offered him money. She walked to the gas station without a look back, her butt conspicuously naked in the fluorescent beams of the Exxon station.

Around 11:00 after eating an egg salad sandwich and drinking a Coke, Amelia caught the ladies' restroom door as the woman inside exited. She gestured the key away and slipped inside. Wrapped in her coat she fell asleep on the cold tile floor. As it was, her slumber was interrupted only three times during the night. Each time the key turned in the lock, she jumped up, startling the woman who entered, but in time to hide the fact she had been sleeping there.

She woke up to the turn of the key in the morning. This time her rebellious legs, angry from their ten-mile hike and tile bed, barely allowed her to stand before the door opened. She hobbled past the startled, elderly woman and stretched her cramped legs as she walked into the truck stop for some breakfast. She returned to her suite later, this time key in hand, to wash away some of the dust and sweat from the day before. She was ready for her next challenge.

Chapter 10

"Marty Robbins?" the librarian repeated. "I'm pretty sure we don't have any sheet music, but I can set you up with some of his recordings and some headphones."

The library was a hobo's haven as Amelia came to find out. She spent the next few days hunkered over a CD player listening to Marty Robbins, Johnny Cash, Dolly Parton, and some Garth Brooks and Faith Hill who the librarian assured her were favorites around here for the older folks. Amelia left the library each afternoon nauseous from Country overload but came back the next day to listen again.

In the evenings, she sat outside the tent she bought at the Salvation Army for twenty dollars (even a charity in America wouldn't go down to fifteen), and with the help of the lyrics and musical notations she had scratched on paper, she hammered out the songs on her guitar. The young caretaker of the campground often came around to listen. Kevin was a nice enough kid and sang a decent rendition of "American Bar Association," making Amelia's least favorite Garth Brook's song somehow palatable. It was nice to have his company, even if he mostly sat and listened. Somehow, it made Polaris, who still beckoned from the sky, easier to ignore. Within a week, she had some thirty songs within her grasp, ten of which, the most she could stomach, were strictly Marty Robbins. She was ready to go back to Weiland.

The night before she left, Kevin showed her the guitar he bought earlier that day.

"You've inspired me," he said, "Every night I come over here and listen to you work out a song. At first, I don't recognize it, and then you gradually make it into something beautiful and all your own. I think I could do that."

When he left her that evening, he left her to lie upon the hard, canvas-covered earth, hammering out another song. This song too, though carved from tragedy and misfortune and not yet recognizable or beautiful, was all her own.

Chapter 11

This time the dogs were actually excited to see her, remembering her from the previous week. The man swaggering towards her seemed less so. Amelia wondered if he would even remember what he had told her. Deciding that action spoke more than words, at least to this man, she took advantage of a large rock along the path and sitting upon it took out her guitar. She had already started strumming the first few chords when the man approached.

> *As I walked out in the streets of Laredo,*
> *As I walked out in Laredo one day,*
> *I spied a young cowboy wrapped all in white linen,*
> *Wrapped in white linen as cold as the clay.*

"Not my favorite," he said when she had finished. "I like *El Paso* better." She began to strum the intro.

"Yeah, yeah, yeah," he said waving her off. "I get it. You'll be wantin' that job as ranch hand. Go up to the house. The missus will get you acquainted with the place. After you've eaten," he shook his head a bit after a quick once-over of her thin body, "I'll have Russ get ya started. I don't manage the work much anymore. Leaving that to younger, lighter bones."

"Thank you," was all Amelia had time for as the man, who she soon learned was Jack Stanton, turned away from her and headed towards the house.

The missus was anything but the missus Amelia had imagined for Jack Stanton. An elegant, lean woman, her slightly grayed hair cut in a wispy modern fashion, welcomed her warmly as she stepped through the door.

"So, you're the young lady who walked five miles through the mountains to be turned away by my cranky, curmudgeon of a husband. And you came back to try again!" she said, as she hustled Amelia into the house, stripping her of backpack and guitar all the while continuing to speak. "I could see this time you were ready for battle! Couldn't catch the sound of it from here, but from the fact my husband stood listening for so long, I'd say you're a pretty good songstress! Good for you." By now Amelia was in the dining room. "I had to resist the temptation last time to run out and welcome you in! Jacky would have been furious—not that I don't know how to handle him, —but I'd just as soon avoid the fury when possible. I've had five children, all of them boys and none of them married. I think you can understand why a young lady on this property would be so welcomed!"

Immediately at ease with this woman, Amelia laughed.

"I'm not quite ready to get married," she said with a grin, sitting down on the chair that had been pulled out for her, "though I'm sure your sons would make great husbands."

The woman's momentary puzzlement was soon replaced by a laugh.

"Oh no! I only mention that they are not married because I have no daughters-in-law yet, so no female company." She paused. "That still sounds like I'm marrying you off! Anyway, only one of my sons still lives here, and he's not exactly what I'd call marriage material! The others all prefer city life to this. I like the city in small doses: a little shopping, a good haircut," she said tossing her wispy locks. "But this," she exclaimed spreading her arms wide, "lets me breathe."

By this time, a bowl of salad and a heaping plate of lasagna lay in front of Amelia. Breadsticks followed and a bottle of wine.

"Are you twenty-one?" she asked, uncorking the bottle and beginning to pour it into the two awaiting glasses.

"Yes," Amelia answered. "Just turned twenty-one a month ago."

"Not that that really matters anyway," Mrs. Stanton laughed, placing a half-filled glass of red wine by her plate. "I already ate," she said, sitting next to Amelia at the table, "but haven't had my taste of wine for the day. Most people prefer it in the evening, but I prefer it just about any time! In small doses, of course. Just like the city!"

Amelia had had hardly enough time to take in her surroundings before this whirlwind of a woman had whisked her into the dining room. What she had seen had dispelled any unpleasant ideas of the place that Jack Stanton had invoked. It was a large house. The living room she had glimpsed had two different sitting areas, each with its own fireplace. And now this dining room, cramped as it was, fit a heavy, wooden table that sat at least fourteen. The walls held several large rustically framed prints of cowboy and Indian scenes that she later learned were prints of Frederic Remington's work. There was also a curio cabinet that housed what appeared to be Indian artifacts, animal bones, and fossils. The "missus" followed Amelia's eyes to the curio.

"We've collected some artifacts through the years, including a few arrow heads, as well as some buffalo bones, some of which show evidence of scraping. There are even a few eagle feathers—the Golden Eagle feathers are the ones displayed. It's illegal to keep bald eagle feathers, though I couldn't just leave them where I found them, so they're kept inside the cabinet if you ever want to look. How's the lasagna?"

"Great!" Amelia exclaimed, and it really was, in spite of the fact that anything she had been served would have been better than the food she had eaten over the past two weeks…or was it thirteen years?

Over the next few minutes and bites of lasagna, Amelia learned a lot about "the missus." Her name was Pamela, not Pam, since she wanted to retain something of her civilized Seattle upbringing. John Stanton was actually her second husband, her first having left her in Billings with a two-year-old son. After two years struggling on her own, she met Jack. They were married a year later and she'd lived here ever since. She had four more sons, one of whom had died two years ago while bull riding in Billings.

"Nothing romantic, not like the movie *Eight Seconds*," she said. "The bull simply went down on him coming out of the chute. Anyway, romance isn't anything to cling to when your heart is ripped away. I hope you never have to understand that," she said glancing at Amelia and quickly looking away.

Jack appeared at the door, a grimace on his face as he took in the scene of his wife and Amelia chatting at the table.

"What's she still doing in here, Pam? She's supposed to be out with Russ taking care of things. Don't you go ruining the hired help. I brought her here to work, not to sip wine and reminisce about better days."

"Reminiscing about worse days, Jack. Worse days. It kind of takes your mind off the time," she responded sadly. Amelia saw his eyes soften. He couldn't argue with that. Time meant nothing when death had once visited.

"Either way," he finally said, "it's time for her to help out Russ. Lord knows he needs a helpin'.

"Thank you for the wonderful meal, Pamela," Amelia said, endowing her name with all the dignity she could muster. As Pamela beamed, it became clear to Amelia that no one ever called her as such.

Chapter 12

Once in the stable, Russ came over to greet her. He was a thin, young man, perhaps even frail, his blond hair swept in a silken wave across his forehead. Even with his piercing blue eyes, something kept Amelia from finding him handsome. When he shook her hand with a graceful flourish, she thought that maybe she understood what it was and why his mother said he was not marriage material, at least not before the Supreme Court ruling.

Although gentle from his girth to his gate, he was anything but weak or lazy. Amelia followed him around that afternoon as he went from shoveling manure to bedding down stalls, from feeding an orphaned calf to chaining its dead mother to his ATV and rolling her into the manure pit. He brought out oats for the horses and took time to brush down six of them before he motioned to Amelia that it was time for supper.

"The cows just started calving two weeks ago. We'll go out after dinner to see if any have calved or are having trouble." Russ began scrubbing his hands at the stable sink and handed her the lava soap. "The next few weeks will be pretty hectic as we prepare for our first round of guests. We're a working dude ranch, you could say. We have a few cattle drives for guests at the beginning and end of the summer and some ranch weeks in between. We'll be going out to bring some horses in so we can tame them down from this winter to be ready for the first cattle drive in June. We also have to get the guest rooms and bunkhouses cleaned up and ready for the guests and staff." He dried his hands and offered Amelia the towel. He continued to look at her as he said, "I'm glad Dad hired you on. Up until last year, he used to help me out. Last year I nearly killed myself doing almost everything on my own. I told him I needed help this year. He said one man was good enough for the job." Russ laughed as if to himself. "Then he looked me over and said, 'Yeah, I better hire someone on.' He's probably pretty proud of himself now, thinking between the two of us he's got one man for the job!"

Amelia wasn't sure whether to smile or comfort him. She decided to do both, placing a hand on his shoulder, she smiled up at him.

"Well, if he's right and it takes just one man for this job, we're going to have an awful lot of free time on our hands!"

Russ chuckled gratefully.

"Let's go to dinner," he said, patting the hand that still lay on his shoulder. "No matter what Dad says, can't ever leave this place 'cause no one cooks like Mom!"

Chapter 13

The next few weeks were a blur of activity, and either Jack Stanton was right to believe they were ill-suited for the task, or he miscalculated the manpower needed. Either way, Amelia's repertoire of Marty Robbins grew rusty as she worked from dawn to far past dusk. Her hands soon resembled again the hands of her past, but this time the work was satisfying.

There was little that resembled routine since the cows' birthing refused to follow a schedule. Amelia made frequent ATV trips out into the mountains to bring in each mother and new calf or to come frantically back for Russ's help in birthing a breach. The calves they brought in were penned with their mothers; the mothers fed on hay while the calves suckled. The cows and their newborns that had drifted far into the mountains would be brought in on the cattle drives. Some would be lost to failed births and coyote kills, so it was vital that the ones within their reach were saved.

The guestrooms and bunkhouses were cleaned and thoroughly supplied with fresh linens and accessories by the time the rest of the summer staff arrived two days before the guests. There was the middle-aged woman, Loni, to help with the food and the thirtyish Mexican-American, Raymundo, to help along the trail. The four of them worked together on last-minute preparations: preparing the horses, tack, and provisions, and tending to the new calves and the late-birthing mothers.

Finally, it was time for the first group of guests to arrive. The Stanton's rented a shuttle once a week to transport the guests to and from the airport. Once at the trailhead, they mounted ATVs that brought them beneath the arch of "Weiland" ranch. Amelia remembered her first trip from Billings to the ranch and felt sure the guests would have been disappointed to know they had not gotten the authentic Western experience. Maybe she'd suggest to Jack Stanton that her Crow friends provide the transportation.

This first group of tourists showed Amelia another reason why Russ stayed on at the ranch. It was apparent from the moment they stepped up to board the shuttle that Russ was in good company. Out of curiosity, several groups later, Amelia got the courage to ask Raymundo why so many of their clientele were from the LGBTQ community.

"My first year at the ranch three years ago, some queer from California came on the cattle drive. Turns out he was the editor of some homo magazine. He got Russ a good deal on advertising, and now nearly a third of the guests are queer. Lucky thing too, because we were light on tourists. Now we're just light in the loafers!" Amelia was almost sorry she had asked. At least Raymundo, having this laugh at their expense, was respectful to their faces.

The first cattle drive was fun. The tourists were eager and boisterous. They were up for anything and complained about little. Russ catered to the gay clientele, while Raymundo and Amelia tended more to the others. They enjoyed the casual pace and the occasional gallop. They "oohed" and "aahed" from the backs of the trail horses as they perched at the edge of steep drops with breathtaking landscapes. They gulped down the meals Loni prepared over an open fire from the provisions she hauled in a small wagon hitched to her horse. They listened attentively, sung uproariously, and applauded gregariously as Amelia revived her country repertoire, including some Mexican music as well, not entirely out of context. Raymundo, having up to this point refused to speak Spanish with Amelia, sung along when caught off guard. They groaned good-naturedly and rubbed their buttocks—or someone else's—before they bedded down for the evening under the stars or within the supplied tents. The summer was off to a good start.

Russ warned her that the cattle drives seldom went that well. But Amelia was little prepared for Bull. They all were.

Chapter 14

Amelia and Raymundo, along with the dogs, greeted the second group of guests as they rode up to the ranch house aboard the ATVs. Russ was in the lead as usual, but this time a young woman clung to his waist. As he dismounted and approached her, Amelia shot him a questioning glance. He nodded toward a large bulldozer of a man extracting himself from one of the ATVs.

"Wanted to ride alone," Russ shrugged. "And he," he smirked, cocking his head in the direction of a young man sporting a tea-green polo shirt, "wanted to ride with his partner. So here I am with her." This time he nodded towards the young woman who upon removing her helmet tossed her red curls and walked towards him.

"This is bomb!" she exclaimed, fixing Russ with a radiant smile of berry lips and gleaming teeth. "So much land!" she exclaimed, her arms swooping wide to follow her feet in a grand pirouette. "Just bomb! But I couldn't live this far from civilization. How do you do it? You must get so lonely out here." The gentle smoothing of his lapel with her ornately manicured hand triggered Russ's dormant sense of humor.

"Well," he said with a flip of his wrist, "You got that right girl! That's why we got to get ya'll," he flipped his head towards the young men who stood nearby, "to come by and see us!"

The woman retracted her elegant hand and coy smile instantly. She mumbled something about how glad she was to have come while backing away and scanning the crowd. She smiled suddenly again, her gleaming teeth lighting upon Raymundo. She was at his lapel in an instant and stuck there throughout the week.

Through stifled laughter, Amelia managed to throw a pouty smile in Russ's direction. He feigned a gasp and turned away haughtily. He walked away chuckling to himself.

The bulldozer man, however, turned out to be the perfect antidote for laughter. "What kind of outfit is this?" he said gesticulating wildly at his surroundings. "When do we get to eat around here? You send us on a ride through hell, and then you sit around chitchatting while we all die of hunger?"

"Mr. Goldfield, just bear with us, please," Russ responded. "The grub will be served at high noon, which," he added, glancing at his watch, "is in fifteen minutes." Russ now turned to address the entire group. "We'll show you to your quarters now. Then when you hear the dinner bell in fifteen minutes, just head over to the mess hall over there," he said, pointing to the large rectangular building to their right.

The bulldozer man mumbled and grumbled to himself as he and the rest of the guests followed Russ to the bunkhouse. His bad attitude didn't keep Amelia from smiling, though, as she noticed an extra sway to Russ's walk. Nothing like a gay cowboy dressed in traditional duds, speaking of grub, quarters, and mess halls, to give an authentic feel to the Wild West.

There was little to sway or smile about over the next few days as the crew realized that the bulldozer man, aka "Bull," had only begun to make waves across a terrain that had not received significant amounts of precipitation in years. The crew established a secret *flash flood* warning whistle within the first five minutes of the following day's cattle drive to deal with the constant crises Bull managed to create. Somehow under Bull's direction, horses scattered, hearts fluttered, and somewhere in the mountains boulders rolled.

Within the first five minutes of the drive, Bull broke formation to complain of a too-small saddle and a gassy horse. The horses behind him stopped, confused, and the ones he rode up alongside of skittered off the trail. What the crew already knew and what the guests came to understand was that once a rider broke formation, the trail horses, used to a certain order, became startled and confused, and the peaceful cadence the riders were enjoying became a stressful derailment.

The group would soon get used to such derailments, but the first one had everyone unsettled. Amelia would have happily explained to Bull that all saddles ever made would be too small for his large pompous ass, and that he'd be gassy too if a bulldozer was straddling him.

Russ handled it more diplomatically, however, apologizing for the saddle that unfortunately was the largest saddle they owned and explaining that it was quite natural, however unpleasant, for horses to pass gas, especially when carrying weight. He assured him that all cowboys had withstood such unpleasantries and welcomed him to the fraternity. He then politely gestured toward the derailment and asked that Bull please not break formation in the future as the horses were not accustomed to such breaks in routine. He, himself, would ride back to check with him periodically to make sure everything was fine.

Thus, the *flash flood* warning came to be, and, true to his word, Russ returned to Bull's side to deal with his complaints the moment the low whistle reached his ears. Unfortunately, a warning is only as good as its forewarning, and Bull's disruptive intentions often defied detection. On one particular occasion, Bull rode past the carnage to where Russ, who had reined in his horse, sat looking back at him, the brim of his cowboy hat hiding most of his disgust. This time it was the young man in front of him who didn't make the mark.

"I think he's queer," Bull confided to Russ. "And I can't stomach watching his backside any longer and listening to his high-pitched girly prattle and 'oohs' and 'aahs.' I need a new place in line. Maybe behind her," he said pointing back toward the buxom redhead who was currently enlisting Raymundo to calm her frazzled nerves.

"Listen," Amelia said riding up to them after overhearing his request, "if you ride behind Betty, then you got Jordan riding behind you. Would you rather watch his backside or he watch yours?" It wasn't diplomatic by any means but it did the trick. Bull took up his position again, looking over his shoulder throughout the next half hour or so to get a good take on the graying, college professor who rode behind him. Said professor spent most of his time gawking at the scenery and calling out observations to his wife behind him. No danger there, presumably.

Somehow, they made it to the first camp, only an hour off schedule, which considering the number of derailments was pretty good. Although there was no formation from which Bull could break in this setting, he managed to inflict as much damage as ever. From complaints about the grub that might as well have been grubs—provoking the only laugh from him all day— to complaints about the scenery that was nowhere near as beautiful as his trip to New Mexico had been the year before. Even the sky was not immune to insult, for it had the audacity to be cloudy on a trip for which he had paid hard-earned money.

Chapter 15

Throughout the week-long cattle drive, the essence of Mr. Goldfield, who—he assured them—was anything but Jewish, unfolded like a gangrenous confederate wound, opening as it festered to ooze and squirt its green puss onto the nurses who tended it. For the first few days Mr. Goldfield may have kept his comments restricted to complaints, insults, and the harassment of others, but by the fourth day, with the help of some brandy (that thank God he brought along to dull the boredom) he journeyed into more personal territory. Turned out that he worked for the Terrorist Screening Center in charge of integrating terrorist intelligence from the CIA, FBI, Homeland Security Department's National Security Agency, and local law enforcement agencies. But having been originally employed by the former INS in Texas, where they had in his words, "their hands full of Spic terrorists pouring over borders under-funded by the bleeding liberal bastards in Congress," he had a unique perspective on the war on terror.

"It's the A-rabs that get most of the attention when it comes to talking about terrorists," he confided to all as they sat roasting marshmallows—highly untraditional cowboy fare—Russ had laughingly admitted. "Now don't get me wrong. They are a scary lot, not to be trusted, green card or no, but we're overlooking another threat! We've got millions of illegals flooding into this country, filling our streets with drug dealers and rapists, and you know I'm not the first to say it! I think it's time ICE got some balls!"

"They hired you, didn't they," quipped Amelia. "Obviously they've got more than they can handle."

"Yeah, missy, you're right. Problem is they don't let me at the border! A wall? My ass! Taking away a few lil' snot-nosed brats from their mommies and daddies? Child's play! Get it? Child's play? Hah! No, I'd nip it in the bud. Just give them patrols the permission to fire at will. A little machine gun action at the border would put an end to that threat. Or better yet they could send me to Gitmo! In case you're ignorant, that's Guantanama Bay."

"Yes, that would be a better option," Amelia agreed.

Bull missed the point and rampaged on. "I'd interrogate those A-rab terrorists better than they've been doing it."

"Haven't they shut that place down?" Amelia interrupted.

"For the most part the liberals got their way, but there's still a few dozen terrorists for me to get my hands on. Hell with naked pyramids. I haven't seen a man yet who is willing to give up an ear or a finger. Or for that matter, who's willing to eat the shit they feed us on this trail!" Here he stopped to laugh uproariously, slapping a meaty thigh with his colossal hand. The pause gave several people the chance to make a break for it. Loni left first with several guests following her away from the campfire, obviously assuring her that the food had been wonderful and appreciated by everyone else. For some reason, Raymundo stayed. He had heard his countrymen and women fired upon at will, but still sat transfixed, his large dark eyes never leaving the puffy, contorted lips of the man who sat laughing in front of him.

"Phew!" Bull finally said, wiping tears from his face. "I gotta let them know that one down in Guantanama. You could make a killing exporting this grub to them. But seriously," he said, straightening up and looking them all in the eye, "we've got some serious threats to deal with. 9/11 was not an isolated incident. It could happen again at anytime and anyplace. It's my job to make sure that doesn't happen. We've got to be vigilant. VIGILANT. So now we've got the National Counterterrorism Center coordinating efforts between all agencies vested in national security. With my department's terrorist watch list, we can inform even local law enforcement of known and suspected terrorists. Not to mention that airport security can now catch terrorists before they board a plane and hijack it with box cutters."

For the first time during Bull's rampage, Amelia was more interested than disgusted. "How exactly do they do that?" she asked. "I mean keep suspected terrorists from boarding a plane?"

"They compare the passenger's name to our 'no fly' list," Bull willingly informed her. "In minutes, airport security's got a hold of them and the FBI's not far behind. Talk about brilliant."

Amelia couldn't shake the image of her father, his look of resignation beneath his Honduran cowboy hat as airport security led him away. She had gone on without him, sure there was some mistake. Later, when he failed to appear at his sister's funeral, she believed he had returned to Honduras, perhaps because there were no flights to Minneapolis that would get him there on time. Now she wasn't so sure. All this talk of terrorists and government watch lists made her suddenly uneasy.

"So, if this suspected terrorist were a citizen, how would he get on that watch or 'no fly' list, whatever it's called?" Amelia queried.

"Follow the money! And their phone calls and travel itineraries. If they lead to a terrorist group, well then, we've got a live one."

Amelia felt more than a little unsettled. Having been out of the country so long and only eight when she left, she hadn't been aware of all that had taken place in her absence. A new department, new intelligence surveillance systems, and even new laws she hadn't heard of. Had her father known about any of this? Could he have somehow gotten mixed up in this new era of security? It made sense, his being a journalist and all.

"Take the CIA for instance," Bull continued, undeterred by her silence. "Officially, there's a ban on assassinations, but unofficially they've taken care of our national security throughout history and continue to do so. Smart bombs and Predator drones are par for the course for 'targeted kills' in Afghanistan and for preemptive manhunting' in Iraq. Now the NSA and the FBI employ their own tactics on the home front, secret surveillance, infiltration, and intimidation giving those bastards what they deserve. Or better yet, 'preemptive manhunting' if you can get away with it! Now that's a gig I could sink my teeth into. 'Ka-boom!' Blow that terrorist's house to bits. Blast him and his whole family to hell! Now that's my kind of barbeque…charred terrorist ka-bobs! Family brisket!"

Kaboom. The word, the sound, reverberated in Amelia's head, drowning out Bull's heaves of laughter. *Kaboom.* Charred…Ka-bobs. Suddenly, an aching tightness gripped her chest. She tried to breath, but with each attempt to inhale the tightness deepened, burning into her chest like the glowing coals of the campfire before her. She realized the coals were inside her, burning through her, absorbing her. *Kaboom.* There was no longer reason to breathe. No longer reason to fight. There was nothing left, just embers and ash.

"Amelia? Amelia, *estas bien*?" It was Raymundo squeezing her shoulder. She turned her face toward his. Was that a helmet he was wearing? And were those ash smears across his face? His second squeeze relinquished her from the fire's smoldering grip, and she gulped in air. After a few quick coughs and a few more intakes of breath, her vision cleared and she was looking at the clean face of the Raymundo she knew.

"You speak Spanish," she said in a daze.

"*Si*," he said smiling. "*Ven*. Come. Let's get you away from this *pendejo*." He led her from the campfire to her tent. "Amelia," he said, as he unzipped the flap, "I don't know what happened to you over there, but are you sure you're okay?"

"*Si*, Raymundo. I'm fine," she lied. Even if she wanted to tell him the truth, what would she say? What the heck was going on?

"Okay, then. Get some sleep. We're almost free of that arrogant ass. *Buenas noches, amigita.* Good night, my friend."

As she climbed into her tent, her confusion enveloped her as tightly as her sleeping bag. What had happened? Was it the image of her father being detained at the airport or something else from her past that made Bull's talk of blowing up terrorists so upsetting? She couldn't shake how she had felt succumbing to the fire, letting it burn her alive. Or the image of the smoke-stained firefighter she saw transposed upon Raymundo's concerned face. Firefighter? What? Her brain had obviously been starved of oxygen, she assured herself. Yet, no matter how sure she was of that, she was equally sure that something was terribly wrong. And even here, in this pristine place, she was not immune to its fallout.

Chapter 16

The final two days of the trail ride were an improvement. Amelia wasn't sure if it was a massive hangover or something more sinister that kept Bull in quarantine. The day after his fireside rant, he kept to himself, his only interaction his seemingly paranoid attempts to catch others watching him. Amelia felt something of a secondhand hangover. She had given up trying to explain her uncommon reaction to the events of the previous night and turned her attention to something more satisfying, like easing Bull's discomfort.

"Now don't get me wrong," Amelia said as she sat next to him as they settled in for their trailside lunch, "I'm grateful for the information you shared with us last night, but I have to say I'm surprised they allow you to speak so freely about such delicate homeland security issues. I would have thought they'd make you take some kind of oath or something."

Bull's only response was a puckered mouth, and although Amelia added a few more comments of the same sort, his eyes remained averted, his focus instead on the sandwich that was far tastier than previous provisions, apparently, as it disappeared behind puffy lips before Amelia even took a bite of hers.

"Nice chattin' with you, Mr. Goldfield," Amelia called after him as he walked quickly away.

Fortunately, or perhaps unfortunately for Amelia, who had enjoyed her last interaction with Bull more thoroughly than she cared to admit, Bull maintained near perfect self-control over the remaining two days. Only once did he forget and begin to make some remark to Russ about the queers being the real threat to national security, infiltrating even the highest offices and spreading their diseases and immorality.

"You know, Mr. Goldfield," Amelia offered, sidling up to him in a confidential manner, "from everything you've said, it sounds like fascinating work you do. Really fascinating. I might be interested in a national security position myself. Could you pass along your supervisor's name? I'd love to get even more information from him, if I could."

That bought them all another Bull-free day, and another day brought them to the end of the trail.

Chapter 17

The weeks that followed the second cattle drive were "ranch weeks," where guests participated in ranch activities such as branding, castrating, dehorning, and vaccinating. Not as picturesque as the cattle drives, but these activities gave guests, and Amelia too, a real feel for ranch life. Here the calves were baptized into the cult of reality. No more suckling from the teats of innocence; pain was their real brand of existence. Like the calves, Amelia and the Stantons wore their own brands, not upon their skin but within their hearts. Amelia wondered if theirs still seared as hers did. Pamela's distant eyes often told her it was so.

During one of the lighter ranch weeks, Jack sent Amelia out on the ATV to run the property line and check for broken or weak spots in the fence. She was grateful for the opportunity to get away from people for a while and experience the land on her own terms. The hum of the ATV kept her company as she followed the reaches of the fence that unrolled in the morning sun, settling at odd angles to creep from ridge to ridge. She had been riding for a few hours when she saw three figures on the ridge ahead of her, their bodies opposite the barbed wire that stretched across the fenceposts where they stood.

Three heads looked up as she drove towards them. She could see that they were Indian. Positioned in front of them just outside the fence was a surveyor's tripod. She cut the engine and hopped off the ATV. No one said a word to her.

"Hello," she said. "I was just out checking the fence line. Looks in pretty good shape."

The three Indian men looked at her but said nothing.

"That your land?" she asked nodding to their side of the fence.

"That's ours too," said the oldest of the men, breaking his silence and nodding toward her side.

"Wouldn't doubt it," Amelia said, conciliatorily. "Is that why you're surveying, then?"

The old man gave a nearly imperceptible shrug and turned to look back through the tripod. The other two took his cue and turned away as well. She was about to get back on the ATV when she saw another figure climbing towards them. When he came closer, all she could see was his gleaming teeth.

"Amelia," he said as he reached the ridge and came face to face with her. "Imagine seeing you here! Dad, this is that girl I was telling you about."

The man looked up from his tripod with new interest.

"Is that so," he said, eying her curiously. No tripod needed to see into her soul. "You're just as he said. An Indian in sheep's clothing."

All four of them laughed. Amelia looked at Paul.

"It's nothing, really, just that you struck me as being more Indian than white, and I told my dad about you."

"Well, I'll take that as a compliment, then," she said smiling at all of them. "So, what are you doing out here?" she asked. "If you don't mind me asking," she added hastily.

"Well," Paul began, glancing at his father and taking his disinterest as a cue to continue, "after giving you that ride out here, I got to thinking about what my grandfather said about this land. Not only did he say that it was bought illegally but that the property line...how did he put that? 'Was overly generous,' he said. I talked to my dad about it, and he said we should check it out just to see. So here we are."

"Any verdict?" Amelia asked.

"Not yet, though it appears that this ridge was used more for convenience than by actual measurement. We'll file a report with the county surveyor but it'll be a battle before this fence ever gets moved."

"I've got the equipment right here," Amelia rejoined with a nod towards the back of her ATV, "if you just wanna take care of it now and avoid the battle."

Paul laughed.

"Ha!" His dad harrumphed turning his attention away from the tripod. "That's probably the only way it *would* ever happen. But where's the fun in that without the battle?"

Amelia saw both the humor and the truth in his wry smile. The battle surely would be the prize. She smiled with a small nod of acknowledgment and then shifted her gaze to the land that sloped off behind them.

"Which direction is your home?" she asked.

Paul pointed south, then turned suddenly towards her. "That gives me an idea," he said. "We have our annual Crow County Fair in August. It's got a pretty amazing powwow and rodeo. My sisters are in some of the dance competitions and ride in the parade. Would you like to go? I could pick you up at the trailhead in the morning, and you could spend the day, or the whole weekend if you wanted. I mean, whatever you want...I mean, if you want..." suddenly embarrassed at his effusiveness.

"Yes!" Amelia responded without hesitation. "That sounds like so much fun. I mean, if they'll let me have the time off. How can I let you know?"

"Smoke signals, of course," he said deadpan. Then he laughed seeing the red rise in her cheeks. "No. I got one of these," he said, pulling an iPhone from his pocket. "Dad says I've sold out." Then in a whisper, "But he always finds some reason to use it."

"I heard that, Paul," his father said sounding affronted. "Then again, I can't argue that Satan's messenger has his advantages. All that building a fire and sending up those S's and O's takes some time. And then you can't even keep it in your pocket."

Amelia laughed. "I'm sure they're both equally effective," she offered, "just one more efficient than the other."

A few minutes later, with Paul's cell phone number securely in her own pocket, Amelia followed the "overly generous" fence line back to the ranch. She could already feel the Earth's drumbeat calling her.

Chapter 18

Pamela had no problem giving her permission to go, but Jack thought it was the last place on the planet a white girl should be. Amelia almost took his adamant refusal as concern. Eventually, Pamela won him over. Amelia wondered how Jack would feel once the county surveyor visited him with the survey results. She was sure there'd be no more staff going to the Crow Indian Reservation.

She left early in the morning, taking an ATV to within a mile of the trailhead. As she walked, she realized how different this trip back to the highway was compared to her first. Before, when she had emerged from the trail, she had encountered only an empty expanse of highway. This time, once she crested the last ridge, Paul would be there. And this time, he would not fly off at her approach.

As she made her final descent to the highway, she imagined what the powwow would be like. She had been to one in Minnesota as part of an elementary school multicultural experience. She remembered the flurry of vividly colored regalia and the dancing chorus of the jingle dresses as they swooped and spun in their revolution around the throbbing heartbeat of the drums. She remembered the drum pulsing in her veins, urging her from her seat in the bleachers. Somehow, she had denied its urgency, but today she would not.

Even her daydreaming of pounding drums, wailing vocals, and jingling dresses could not mask the sounds of the approaching vehicle. It was obvious to Amelia from the cacophony that grew louder that Paul's iPhone came at a great expense to his transportation options.

The oxidized metal dinosaur roared and clanked to a stop just as Amelia stepped onto the side of the highway.

"Hurry!" Paul motioned frantically from his window. "Get in before Ole Betty dies!"

Amelia opened the passenger door, letting it scrape along the asphalt as its dislocated hinge settled out of socket. Once inside, she heaved the door up and in and eased herself back into the cracks and scales of the green vinyl seat. No need to look for a seatbelt that may or may not have still existed, for two tons of metal between her and anything else on the highway made her feel safe enough.

"Hey, Amelia! How was the walk?" Paul shouted over the engine.

"I had some help this time!" She shouted back. "Mr. ATV is parked a short way up the trail."

"Yeah, I remember dropping you off the first time. We all had a good laugh on the way home wondering if you'd get there before dark. I put my money on you. Looks like I get to collect."

"Well, I made it there before dark but not so much luck on the way back."

"You had to walk back?"

"Yeah, I got turned away the first time."

Amelia proceeded to fill him in on all that had happened since their first meeting. She told him about the slimy truck driver who picked her up and took her back to Billings, about her time at the library and the campground, her second meeting with Jack Stanton and first meeting with his lovely wife. She told him about Russ and Raymundo, the trail rides and the ranch work. Though she spoke of many things, she was aware it was the unspoken things that told her real story—the words between the lines, the silences between the uttered thoughts. She wondered if Paul understood silences as she did.

Chapter 19

The reservation town was more dismal than she had imagined. Everywhere she looked, gray and dilapidated, one-level houses stood guarded by metal dinosaurs heaped in backyards. As Amelia took in the gray surroundings, she began to fill in the missing colors of the familiar Honduran village she saw upon the pages of this uncolored coloring book. Only the children offered the vivid splashes of color she remembered as they sat on stoops, played catch, and tossed rocks.

Then the color outside her passenger window suddenly increased as small groups of brightly colored dancers and visitors straggled towards the powwow grounds. The Chevy climbed a steep slope and rounded a final bend in the road, and that's when she saw it. Lewis and Clark couldn't have been more awed than she felt now when they, when she, saw their first tepee encampment.

"Welcome to the Teepee Capital of the World!" Paul announced cheerfully as Amelia looked down at the thousands of teepees that permeated the valley like white triangular brushstrokes upon a large, grassy canvas. Sprigs of willows, scrawny pines, and scraggly junipers interrupted the clusters of white teepees, adding rough texture to an otherwise soft landscape. Only the rumble of Ole Betty reminded Amelia that she was not sitting bareback upon a painted pony, looking down upon her ancestors...*his* ancestors, she corrected herself.

As they descended into the encampment, the Dance Arbor came into view, and the color and activity of the big day burst forth like a patch of Indian paintbrushes twisting in a wind-worn field. They drove past the vendors, busy setting up their tents and stands. Then past the early arrivers who quickly scooped up the first batch of fried bread and stood chomping it down with honey as their young children, aflame in dance regalia, began testing the steps of their grandparents, feeling the hardened earth through hand-me-down moccasins and listening to the drumbeat that already flowed through their veins.

As Paul and Amelia finally stepped out of Ole Betty, who knowing that she was now supposed to die decided instead to choke and sputter, Paul filled Amelia in on the events that were to come. The primary event, the powwow, would start around seven that evening, featuring drummers and singers from different tribes all over Montana, the Dakotas, and Minnesota.

Their first stop was the fried bread stand. They arrived just in time to sample the next fresh batch. Paul assured her it wasn't as good as his mom's but pretty close. Then they walked around looking at the artwork and crafts that over the next hour gradually spilled onto the tables that unfolded in front of them. Amelia was amazed how her coloring book had so quickly changed from stark outlines of colorless forms to this technicolored bustle of activity.

The day passed quickly with so much to see, hear, touch, and experience. At 7:00 p.m. exactly, the Grand Entry of the powwow began. Under a sun that showed no mercy even as it tilted toward the western horizon, the painted and bedecked dancers filed into the Dance Arbor one by one in a flurry of color and bustle. There were male Grass dancers with their multicolored streamers blurring into a kaleidoscope of colors with each rapid, swirling turn; male Chicken dancers mimicking the prairie chicken with its floating steps, sharp jerks of the head, and craning body and neck; female Fancy dancers with light, lilting steps—two steps forward, one step back—shawls spread like playful wings swooping and swaying above the earth; female traditional dancers in elk tooth and Plains traditional dresses, prancing forward in prim elegance; and girls in jingle dresses spurring the whole procession forward with melodious bounces upon spry, moccasined feet. The unbridled energy of the earth flowed and fluttered before Amelia, transfixing not only her gaze, but also her breath. *Breathe*, she had to remind herself, momentarily dizzied by the hypnotic swirl of sensations before her.

By 8:00 p.m., the first beats of the drums announced the beginning of the dance competitions, and impatient children took to dancing more seriously while their parents and grandparents on the periphery began, themselves, to ease their stiffened joints into the ebb and flow of the dance. By that time, Paul and Amelia had managed to reassemble the original pickup occupants and they all stood around on the outskirts of the dancers, talking, laughing and commenting on certain dancers who really knew how to dance and others who were no more than cocks strutting their plumage before a fight. They filled Amelia in on some of the history of the dances and what made for well-executed steps and moves. They enjoyed watching the children the most, untainted by the arrogance and artificiality of some of the adult dancers.

"Look at that guy, for example," Darian pointed out. "See how he looks at his heel each time it touches down and then back out at the crowd. He knows the dance is good, but that's not good enough for him. He needs to know that we know it's good. That's fake dance. Real dance is when you feel the music, let it flow through you. You don't notice your foot and definitely not the crowd watching it. It's just you and the rhythm…and the earth."

"Don't listen to him," Paul said. "For him it's all about getting the girls! Now he's the one being fake."

Paul earned himself an elbow to the arm.

"When will you dance?" Amelia asked them as the next set of drummers set up their equipment.

"We'll wait 'til the competition is over," Paul said. "It'll be another hour or so, especially since they've got another giveaway or two."

Several family groups were gathered on the periphery of the Dance Arbor, heaps of blankets laid out before them ready to be given away to those who had helped the family achieve honor, success, or good fortune. Paul explained to Amelia that it was not only their way of giving thanks to their community but also of "keeping things even" among tribesmen.

"Keeps us from getting our heads too big and our pockets too full at the expense of others. Anyway, what we get is only lent to us, blessings from the Great Spirit. We can't really take credit for it."

Amelia glanced up at him, surprised at his uncustomary display of spiritual wisdom. Caught off guard himself, Paul blushed and flashed his even, white teeth.

"Hey. Even we 'me-generation' Indians are sometimes afflicted with ancient wisdom! Don't be so surprised!" Then quickly changing the topic he continued, "Anyway, after they finish these boring giveaways, they'll open up the Arbor to the real dancers! Then you can show us what you've got!"

"Now that's what Paul's been waiting for all night!" Darian chided, nodding to his buddies around him. Instead of paying him back with an elbow, Paul wrestled him to the ground, where they rolled around a bit until one of their friends kicked Paul in the rump and whispered, "Cops!" They untangled themselves and managed to stand up, dusting themselves off by the time one of the reservation officers arrived.

"You boys doin' alright?" the rez cop asked, putting his face in close to theirs to subtly sniff. Not catching any scent of alcohol on their breath as they uttered various versions of "We're fine, sir," he continued on his way through the crowd. In a matter of seconds, Darian was back on the ground, and this time Paul had him immobilized as the rest of them shouted a three count.

Darian may have been down for three, but coming up he was back in the game. "Bet you're impressed, Amelia. Paul's always had a knack for rubbing up on other guys." This time Darian took refuge behind Amelia, and all Paul could do was promise with a grin and a wagging finger that his would come.

The next two hours passed in much the same way. And in spite of the giveaways that dragged on and on, interrupting the intensity of the dancing and drumming, for Amelia the fabric of time became warped by the weight of this new friendship. In a single evening, she had spent a lifetime with these young men who baptized her into their fraternity with a stranglehold and a knuckle rub to the head.

As the last of the blankets were distributed and the first drum group began, they made their way into the Arbor. And somehow Amelia, without knowing the right steps, felt as if she had spent her life practicing this dance that took her deep inside herself and deep into the Earth. She drifted around the circle, more and more inebriated with each pulse of the drum and wail of the men, whose voices came from somewhere within the Earth's bubbling core: violent notes spurting forth like lava spears to burst through cold mantels prehistorically formed; molten notes ascending in fire to cool in the fertile soils of the sprouting roots that formed the great trees and sod paths of the birds and beasts that marked their patterns upon the Earth.

To Amelia, the sky seemed to grow darker. In her mind she was sure they made their way around an ancient campfire, its sparks flying upwards to join the stars, its flames stretching heavenward like dragon's wings. The drums grew louder, the voices hotter. Sparks and flames and drums and voices pulsed around her, within her. She heard the high pitches go higher, saw the red flames in her mind grow redder until their wailing and flashing reflected back at her from every point in the sky.

Then she smelled it in the air. She tried not to breathe but could not resist. It filled her lungs in one horrifying gulp. She tried to cough it up, dispel it with a single heave, but it caught in her throat. As she fell to the ground, she saw their bodies in front of her, cauterized corpses looking back at her through molten eyes. In one cannibalistic gulp, she swallowed the odor of their burnt flesh. Then she lost consciousness.

Chapter 20

Amelia was not sure how much time had passed, only that it was not enough before the memory came back to her. She clenched her eyes shut then flung them open desperately with the hope that the memory would retreat with her eyelids. Instead she saw them everywhere, their charred bodies bouncing off the myriad of faces that hovered over her. She sat up, almost knocking heads with the man that leaned over her. She had to get out of there. She pushed him from her as she rose to her feet. The people around her with their hideous reflections drew back as she stumbled forward. Someone caught her arm from behind, and she yanked it away. She teetered for a moment, blinking away the swirling red lights in her head that swam across the faces all around her. She felt again a pull on her arm, and this time as she yanked it free, her knees buckled. Amelia was vaguely aware of a strong arm that caught her waist before she eagerly succumbed to the blackness.

This time her name, spoken softly yet urgently, reached through her blackness. Wanting the voice to stop, to leave her to her darkness, she shook her head brusquely. Instantly, her head exploded in pain. Her eyes popped open to see her name formed upon long, lean lips that partially concealed strong, even teeth. They weren't Paul's teeth. They belonged to a different nose. And to eyes that were wider, darker, deeper. They held her own that pulsed with the throbbing pain of her forehead. The eyes blurred, reflecting back her pooling tears. Then a gentle finger traced the path of tears as they spilled down her temple. Eyes still locked, she let her tears fall, and somehow it was better than the blackness.

With the return of consciousness came the return of other senses, and Amelia could no longer block out the urgent calling of her name. She broke her locked gaze and found Paul's face leaning toward her from behind the broad shoulders of the man who currently cradled her head in the crook of his arm. Catching her eye, his signature teeth broke into a smile with relief and bewilderment tugging at its corners.

"Amelia," he said. "Can you hear me? Are you okay? Do you need anything?"

She tried to shake her head, but the pain in her head detained her, and her only movement was a wince.

"Don't try to move," the voice above her soothed. "You've got a pretty good cut on your temple. The ambulance will be here any moment. You'll probably need a few stitches, but you'll be just fine."

The deep resonance of the voice seemed familiar. Looking again into his wide eyes, she realized his voice echoed the vibration of the drums that still rang in her head. She willed him to speak again and pull her into the magnetic earthiness of his voice. He seemed about to comply when the sirens that had lain masked by the buzz of the crowd reached the unmistakable pitch of arrival. He turned his head and motioned with his free arm for the crowd to part.

Seconds later Amelia was being hoisted upon the gurney and jockeyed through the crowd to the awaiting ambulance. Pushing through the throbbing pain in her head, she searched the faces above for his face. She did not see it. Instead, she found Paul's, and though somewhat disappointed, she was relieved to have his company as the ambulance door enclosed them.

Chapter 21

Six stitches later and a diagnosed concussion, she lay in a reservation hospital bed for an overnight observation, waiting for the painkillers to take her into oblivion. The throbbing in her head had eased enough that her memories were returning. She could not bear to face them, yet she did not have the strength to deny them either. Now that Paul had gone, she was left with little alternative but to remember or to be saved by sleep. She focused on her grogginess and watched its waves lap at the cadavers appearing before her until the waves enveloped them completely and she mercifully succumbed to sleep.

She awoke in the morning to a nurse checking her pulse and to the pain that had returned at full tilt. She gratefully swallowed the painkillers the nurse handed her and for the first time forced herself to speak.

"When can I leave?" she asked the nurse.

"Anytime now," she said. "But let's have the doctor check you over before we say for sure."

The doctor came minutes later. After asking Amelia a series of questions, he determined that she was ready to be released.

"We want to release you to someone, however," he said. "I don't recommend that you leave by yourself, and you certainly are not allowed to drive. Is someone coming for you?"

"I don't know," Amelia answered, wondering if Paul would come soon and if so, what she would do once she was released to him. "I think my friend Paul will come for me."

"Well, as soon as he arrives, you should be fine to leave, but I don't recommend any physical activity for the next few days. I'm writing you a prescription for some painkillers that you can take every four to six hours when the pain gets too much. Once the prescription runs out, the pain should be at a manageable level, but let me know if its intensity continues and we'll have another look."

The doctor handed her the prescription and wished her a fast recovery. He was about to leave when he turned back towards her.

"I know this is unorthodox," he said, "but I get the feeling there is something much deeper than that cut going on in your head. You might want to take advantage of the fact that you are on an Indian reservation to see our local medicine man. I'm very good at healing cuts and broken bones, but he heals the soul. His name is Martin Real Bird, just in case you're interested. Ask anyone in town where you can find him, but mention that Dr. Blacksmith sent you. They're pretty protective of their medicine men when it comes to outsiders. Take care."

Amelia thanked him and watched him leave. She was surprised that she was so transparent. She realized the evening's events had stripped her of her protective shell. Even her eyelids could no longer hide the horrifying truth that now surfaced in her eyes.

The horrifying truth. It had begun as a vague mirage the night Bull had introduced her to his anti-terrorist methods, and now there was no denying it. How would she go on? Now that she saw them not within the moonlit glow of Polaris but as the grotesque remains of melted corpses?

She knew by the sudden appearance of a concerned nurse that her agonized wail had not been internal. As the nurse came forward, Amelia dissolved into desperate sobs. Though the nurse did her best to comfort her, only a sedative was skillful enough to turn her wracking sobs into gentle hiccups and finally into a quiet doze.

She awoke several hours later under Paul's soft gaze. He smiled, too concerned to even show teeth.

"Amelia. I've been so worried about you. I'm so sorry you're hurt. I wish I could have done something, but you were too far away. And when you fell...well... it happened so fast that I didn't even have a chance to respond until there you were, bleeding on the ground. I couldn't believe it. It was just so fast. Are you okay, now? How do you feel?"

Amelia smiled weakly at his apparent concern.

"Paul, it's not your fault. I just fainted. I guess maybe too much heat and too little water." *And sirens and lights and burnt flesh singeing my lungs*, she thought, fighting the urge to scream it out to the world. She closed her eyes to block out the images that seemed to be as immediately present as her own breath.

"Amelia? Are you okay?" Paul said drawing closer.

"Just the headache, Paul. I think it's time for another painkiller. Then what do you say you get me out of here?"

Within an hour, they were walking out of the hospital. Paul had offered that she stay with his family for a few days until she felt she could make the trip back to the ranch. She had almost forgotten entirely about the ranch and had to make a quick call from the hospital to tell them what had happened and that she wouldn't be back for a few more days. Pamela had been very concerned and offered to pick her up immediately. Amelia assured her that she was in good hands and preferred to make the trip when her head was a bit steadier. And now here she was walking tentatively down a heated sidewalk towards Paul's jalopy.

The rest of the day was sufficiently occupied with family introductions and friendly banter so that Amelia was able to successfully stave off her encroaching memories. She dreaded the moment she would be left alone and hoped the painkillers would knock her out quickly. That night she was lucky.

Chapter 22

The next day, a deafening horn blast awakened Amelia at 5:30 a.m. Muffled shouting, presumably in the Crow language and amplified by a bullhorn, followed, gradually fading into muted shouts until it stopped all together some ten minutes later. By that time, Amelia had quickly, yet gingerly, lifted herself from Paul's bed and made her way to the living room couch where Paul lay still asleep.

"Paul," Amelia said urgently shaking him, "something's happening."

Too tired to even smile, Paul motioned her away. "Go back to bed, Amelia. It's just the camp crier."

She returned to bed puzzled and remained so after being awakened yet again the following hour and the hour after that to the din of the same camp crier. Finally, on the crier's fourth round, Paul was awake enough to explain.

"It's just a tradition," he explained. "The camp crier walks through town announcing each hour leading up to the parade."

"What's he saying?" Amelia asked.

"Hell if I know," he grinned, looking up as his dad came into the living room stretching his lean frame. "I leave Crow to the old birds like my dad."

Said Dad shook his head sadly. "That's the trouble with youth, nowadays. No respect for the old ways. On that account, I can't say I'm much better. But pretty sure he's saying, 'Get the hell up!'"

"Well, it must only work on white people," Amelia offered. "You both slept right through it!"

Both Paul and his dad laughed.

"Well, the girls woke up on his third time around," Paul's dad replied. "So as long as he's persistent, at least someone will be in the parade, and at least someone will watch."

"Are you feeling up to it, Amelia?" Paul asked. "I mean it's not the world's greatest or anything, but my sisters prepare for it all year and get pretty excited about it."

"Absolutely," she responded in spite of her throbbing temple. Not only was she excited to see the parade she had heard so much about the day before but also realized she didn't want to be left alone.

Within the hour, Amelia and Paul sat with Paul's mother at her fairground stand which displayed the beautiful beaded clothing, regalia, accessories, and jewelry she had for sale. Amelia enjoyed her role as a spectator as the parade wound its way past the stand, an endless display of timeless regalia, spirited horses, and proud, elegant people. Paul's younger sisters rode past on painted horses, each displaying a priceless sample of their family's legacy: ancestral elk tooth dresses and Crow saddles of wood covered in buckskin with traditional high pommels and cantles displaying beaded bags and cradleboards. Draped across the saddle of his eldest sister lay a spectacular mountain lion skin with an underside of red wool, which Paul's mother explained symbolized the father's prowess as a hunter and protector of his family. The other sister displayed across her saddle an elk hide robe, which, according to Paul's mother, was traditionally a wedding blanket.

"You can barely see the beading from here," she explained, "but each robe has thirty rows of tiny beads. That one was my grandmother's."

As the painted hindquarters of the last horse and the swaying feathers of its rider drifted out of sight, Amelia turned her attention to Paul, who was just taking a turn at managing the stand. She helped him attend to customers until the late afternoon heat and the bustle of the crowd set her head to pounding, and when another dose of codeine did little to lessen it, she took her leave from the stand to head back to Paul's house.

Chapter 23

As Amelia left the festivities, she kept her head low and her eyes nearly shut in an attempt to alleviate the pounding in her temples. She was just turning from the main road when she nearly collided with the broad chest of an Indian brave in full regalia. Before her eyes drifted up to his, they noticed the intricate beading of his breastplate and beneath it the swell of his smooth adobe skin, its wisps of soft hair tipped with tiny beads of sweat every bit as intricate as the beads of the necklace he wore. She was already inhaling the soft scent of sweet grass mingled with hot skin when her eyes made their way up past his bold chin to meet the depths of his eyes.

Her sharp intake of breath was audible as she recognized him. She felt as one must feel realizing she has breathed her last breath. She felt the poignancy of her past within her lungs and the sadness and helplessness of her mortality. And yet, with this last gulp, she felt too, the glimmer of a new life beyond the bounds of her mortal skin. When she breathed again, she knew she had crossed over, and her story would never be the same.

By the time she realized he was speaking to her, she had already missed his first few words.

"...happy you are up and around. I hope you are feeling much better." He cocked his head and looked at her bandaged forehead. "It looks like it took more than a few stitches."

She wanted to respond but just as his skin held her mute so too, did his voice.

"So, how are you doing? We were all very worried about you."

Finally finding her tongue, she managed a shaky reply. "I-I'm, um, fine. Thank you so much for asking. I'm so glad I've run into you ...

literally, because I was hoping I'd have the opportunity to thank you for helping me out the other night. I don't know what happened. I guess I was dehydrated or something like that."

"Yeah, something like that," he said looking into her eyes with knowing skepticism. "You know, your stereotypical Indian would say you had some sort of vision." He paused, taking in the surprise of her expression. "I guess that would make me pretty stereotypical."

Amelia wanted to look away but stood transfixed. Then she found herself responding in a nearly inaudible whisper.

"No. Not a vision, a memory." She gulped and pulled her eyes from his, sure that they were saying too much.

"A memory within a vision. Some memory, to knock you down like that. In our culture, we'd say you received a gift."

She shook her head in disgust. "No!" she nearly wailed, backing away from him. "This is not a gift! This is anything but a gift. You don't know anything about me, anything about this. This is some grotesque celestial joke. That's what this is." She paused and closed her eyes. "I...I'm sorry. I'm tired. My head hurts. I've got to go."

She tried to brush past him, but he caught her arm. She was sure it was the same hand she had shaken off two nights before. Again, she could feel herself crumpling, but this time it was not her knees, it was all her insides falling in on themselves, an internal black hole pulling her in.

"Amelia," he said. "You don't have to do this alone. I know someone who can help you. "Amelia," he repeated, this time gently grabbing her chin with his free hand and forcing her to look into his face. His cheeks were flushed with color, and his eyes more intense than ever. "Come with me."

Chapter 24

Amelia wasn't sure how she was moving, but somehow, she was floating after him, his hand tugging lightly at her arm. She followed the bouncing feathers of the roach that adorned the top of his head as they traced waves in the blue of the overhead sky. Soon the feathers brushed across a low doorframe, and she found her pupils adjusting to a darkened room. It was a face that came into view first: weathered, wrinkled, and wise. Then the face's bottomless eyes captured hers in earnest entreaty.

"Uncle Martin, this is Amelia. She had a powerful vision the other night at the powwow. I was hoping you could help her."

The old man did not smile as he broke his stare to look at his nephew. "Donovan, you did a good thing bringing her here. She is being called. But fear surrounds her, prevents her from answering."

"Young lady," he said, turning back towards Amelia, "let them come. Let them take you with them. It will be alright. You will see."

Donovan helped her sit upon a tattered chair facing the old man who now closed his eyes in concentration. Had she been coherent, she would have laughed at the surreal nature of it all. As it was, all she could do was grip the chair's arms as if to keep from falling into the gathering abyss. Any moment she would topple. Maybe that was what she wanted.

"Donovan," the old man called. "Please brew some peppermint tea."

As Donovan left the room, the old man reached for a braid of sweet grass that lay in a basket within arm's reach of his chair. With a lighter he produced from his pocket, he lit it, and blowing on it softly, he rose from his chair. Amelia watched him through dilated pupils, seeing him weave in and out of her view as he waved the smoking sweet grass around and mumbled incoherencies. She felt her eyelids growing heavier, and even as she gripped the chair arms harder than ever, she felt the back of the chair fall out from behind her. And following it backwards, she crashed into darkness.

Falling through the darkness, she began to discern streaks of light that flew past her at dizzying speeds. Then she realized it was she who was in motion. The air through which she was falling began to grow heavy, and soon it pressed against her like a gelatinous soup, slowing her down until she came to a complete stop. The streaks of light had become stars, but as she looked closer, she saw that they were within her grasp. She reached up her hands, wanting to catch their brilliance like so many fireflies on a dark summer's night. As she did so, she heard music. No, it was not music but voices. What were they saying? She had but barely thought the question when she heard them answer,

"Seek the truth, then let us go."

Amelia looked at her hands and saw she held a speck of light in each. As she looked, the lights grew brighter and brighter until her eyelids popped open from the force of their intensity.

She was lying flat on the sofa, looking into the face of the old man who now was lifting her head and applying a cup of steaming tea to her lips. She slurped it in, not aware of its scalding heat nor minty, bitter taste, only of the cozy nest it formed deep within her that radiated heat from its epicenter.

She began to sit up, and the old man helped her. She was aware for the first time of the dim cluttered room she found herself in. Everything in the room was as gray as the braids of the old man who now crouched before her. Only a few parcels of drying plants that hung from the ceiling had retained something of their original color. Yet it was not a dismal place. It appeared to be a place to rest before the beginning of a long journey.

"You feel better, am I right?" The old man asked her.

"Yes," Amelia replied, surprised that she was so coherent.

She remembered why she had come. She remembered the desperation she had felt, the memory of their charred bodies that had threatened to swallow her whole. She saw them now with sadness, but the anguish did not come. Instead she saw their light on her palms and felt their warmth within her.

They had called to her. There was a truth they wanted her to learn. How odd to suddenly have such clarity after such profound confusion. For the first time since she began her journey to freedom, she understood that the previous chapters of her story were incomplete. She understood that to go forward in authoring her own chapter, she needed first to discover the ending to the one already authored without her consent. But, she thought as Donovan suddenly appeared in the doorway, maybe she would continue writing a bit more of this one first.

Chapter 25

Donovan showed her to a small bedroom adjacent to the living room. She gratefully lay down upon the bed whose fluffy pillow pricked lightly at her neck with its protruding feathers. Now that she had weathered her internal storm, she felt calm but exhausted. Donovan looked down upon her. She almost laughed at how surreal he looked towering above her—his long, shiny, black braids crowned by a vivid roach—set against the gray background of the room, as if he were a Charles Russell portrait of an Indian brave hung upon the wall. She must have smiled, for Donovan's stoic face relaxed.

"I see you're feeling better," the portrait spoke. "I want you to rest here as long as you like. I need to return to the powwow. I'm sure my drum group is wondering where I am. I'll let Paul and his family know that you're here with Martin."

"Will you come back?" Amelia asked before she could stop herself.

"I'll have to," he laughed. "This is my room! Martin is my uncle."

Amelia laughed too, feeling for the first time the vibrant texture of the wool blanket beneath the length of her body. When she drew the cover up over her as Donovan left the room, it wasn't a blanket that covered her but Donovan's warm, sun-seared skin.

She awakened several hours later to stars staring in upon her. After taking a moment to smell the blanket she had gathered around her chin, she got out of bed and went to the window. She remembered the stars in her dream and reached longingly towards the ones that now looked in. She hoped that they would settle again upon her palms. Yet, she knew it could not be. What she had instead was the beautiful memory of them emanating from her outstretched hands.

"I miss you so much," she whispered softly. "I love you so much."

She cried silently then, consoled by stars that held her in their luminescent embrace while her mind rolled the film she had refused to watch for so long. She wore black that day, a dress her grandmother had bought. Too big, she remembered now, swallowing her little body in its folds, so like the impersonality of her fate. She watched as her father's elbow supported that hollow garment into the church. She felt her leaden feet sink with each step forward toward the hundreds of vibrant standing sprays of flowers scattered upon the sanctuary; toward the scent of longiflorum lilies and chrysanthemums that shrouded the altar; and toward the two caskets, one large, one small, both shiny as the toes of newly polished boots.

Then she was in the cemetery, watching as the caskets were lowered into the earth. She heard for the first time the echo of grating rocks upon their surface as her father tossed in a shovelful of dirt, first on one, and then on the other. He handed her the shovel. She did not touch it. Her grandmother pried two roses from her hand, and she felt now for the first time their barbs tear her skin. She saw their red plumage soar through the air as her grandmother tossed them one by one into one grave and then the other.

Amelia finally saw the hundreds of mouths that had formed the words "I'm sorry." Heard the cracking of their voices, their grieving whispers. She witnessed the tearstained faces of strangers who at some level shared her agony: an elderly woman who kissed her forehead with trembling lips; another, who clutching her, sobbed into her shoulder.

She hadn't noticed until now the man who stood beside her. Her father's face was pale, corpse-like. Only his eyes were alive, and they screamed for mercy—for some kind of answer to his pain, for some kind of truth in this chaos. He caught her eyes. She would have seen it in his eyes before if hers had been opened. She saw it now: his need to hold her. Then he turned away and wrung his hands. Here, bathed in starlight, Amelia cried silently for that missed embrace.

"Amelia," she heard the voice in her ear just as she felt the hand upon her shoulder. She turned her startled face towards his, starlit tears tracing paths across her cheeks. She quickly wiped at them, intercepting a hand he raised to do the same.

"You Indians are stealthy after all," she giggled nervously. "You know, we whites prefer at least some creaking floorboards if you can't master the heavy-heeled approach."

"Didn't mean to scare you," Donovan replied, "but didn't want to interrupt either. You looked so peaceful. Sad, yes, but peaceful too." The starlight played across his breastplate and danced upon the damp skin beneath. She barely dared to look into his eyes. When she did, she saw starlight reflecting back at her from every corner. She couldn't look away.

Chapter 26

"Amelia," he said, taking her hand, "you don't have to keep all that sadness to yourself. I'm an excellent listener, if you think that would help."

"I haven't kept it to myself. Tonight, I shared it with the stars. They, too, are excellent listeners."

"Yes," he smiled, "I know they are, but a little aloof, don't you think? Come sit down," he said, leading her to the bed. "Tell me what you saw the other night. Tell me why you are crying now. You know, I'm training to be a medicine man like my uncle."

"Then shouldn't you know already?" Amelia chided him.

"Well, as you can see, I need more practice. Give me a chance to develop my Indian intuition."

Amelia had her own intuition, and though undeveloped as well, she found herself leaning towards him, her gaze drifting to his long lips. Not even the sliver of a moment passed before she felt his lips on hers. They touched hers softly, testing her resolve. She parted hers slightly to feel his more deeply. He responded by drawing her lower lip into his. His hands responded as well, sliding up her neck to cup her chin. She lifted her hands to put them over his, feeling with her fingertips the texture of his fingernails, his knuckles, the back of his hands. By the time her fingers found the crook of his elbows, his arms were cradling her, lowering her backward upon the coarse wool of his bed and prickly softness of his pillow.

Amelia's lips and fingers faltered suddenly, her mind recalling someone else once lowering her in a similar fashion to the grass. She had opened up to him, sharing for the first time her painful past. At least what she had remembered. She had responded longingly to his first kiss that promised to restore all she had lost, not realizing where it would lead. By the time she had understood what was happening, she had felt a sharp pain inside her and then the brittle grass imbedding into her skin with each rough thrust. She winced at the memory.

"Amelia?" Donovan's face hovered above hers, a mixture of desire and concern. "We can stop, Amelia, I just…"

Amelia answered him with an urgent kiss. Donovan took the signal and lowered himself more fully on top off her, his pelvis pressing down between her legs. His strong hands untangled her small ones from around his neck and lifted them up over her head, capturing them there in the iron grip of one large hand. His free hand found her shirt buttons and opening them one by one made way for the trail of hot kisses he blazed to reach her upturned nipple. She lay tortured by sensation, writhing beneath him, trying to free her wrists that he pressed more firmly then ever into the mattress.

Then his mouth was back on hers, biting her lower lip, responding to the urgent pressure he found there. This time his roaming hand found the lip of her shorts and panties, freeing a button and then a zipper. She wriggled her hips to aid their downward progression as his hand guided them past her trembling knees to her ankles, where her toes took over to free them entirely. Donovan's mouth left hers for a moment, and she followed his eyes as they looked down at the starlit skin of her belly that disappeared into the dark curls between her legs. He exhaled deeply.

Amelia took advantage of his loosened hold to free her wrists and reach for the ties on the trousers of his leather costume. Donovan, his knees straddling her, was momentarily still, watching her fingers untangle the leather ties, loosen them, and slide his pants from his hips. She half expected to see boxers but was not disappointed to find him fully exposed. She felt unsure what to do with her hands and chose rather to look up at him. He was watching her, and she blushed, knowing she had just exposed her insecurity among other things. He didn't seem to mind but held her in his steady gaze. Was that a question in his eye? Was he asking her something?

She didn't have the chance to find out for suddenly he was upon her, tearing her shirt and bra off over her head, his mouth once again finding her exposed nipple, this time nipping it with his teeth, sending her chest arching toward him. She wanted him to inhale her, gulp her entire length into his hot, moist mouth. He seemed to want to do just that as his mouth journeyed across her skin to taste every inch of her neck, shoulders, belly, and to breathe hot kisses into the curls of the lowest reaches of her torso.

She realized her hands were inactive and busied them with finding his ears beneath the silken lengths of his freed hair. When his mouth journeyed back to hers, her hands lowered and traced the taut muscles of his shoulders, back, and buttocks. She held him there for a moment, pressing him down upon her. She could feel his solid, damp, heat between her thighs. She squeezed her thighs around it. He groaned into her lips and lifted his head slightly.

"Amelia," he whispered, "I don't have anything. Tell me to stop. You need to tell me to stop," he pleaded, yet at the same time pressing himself more urgently against the soft folds between her legs.

"No, don't. Don't stop, please!" she urged throatily, pushing his buttocks down as hard as she could and spreading her legs beneath him.

He was inside her in a second, so swiftly that his entrance was announced only by the hot pressure that welled up inside her. She could feel him probing her internal boundaries, pushing against them in a circular, rhythmic movement. Then he was out, and his mouth was teasing her nipples, her neck, her ears. His lips met hers just as he pushed himself into her again, this time a thrust, nearly violent, that made her gasp. He held her bottom lip in his teeth as he pulled back and thrust forward again, sending a sweet ache traveling up her torso. His thrusts became rhythmic, alternating from slow to quick, tender to harsh. Amelia met his rhythms and intensity hungrily.

He tortured her this way until the tingling between her thighs produced a moan. Donovan responded to his up-until-then silent partner by pulsing rapidly within her, his pelvis pressing into her throbbing skin. Then spasms ripped through her, arching her back and sending shivers through the length of her body. As she lay quivering, she felt his warm, throbbing release within her. She heard a groan form at the base of his throat and followed his face upward, into the quiet stillness.

Chapter 27

Donovan rested Amelia's head on his shoulder and stroked her hair and cheek. Amelia still throbbed with the memory of him inside her, but soon she began to relax into his shoulder, smelling the bitter purity of his sweat. *Something like dandelion milk*, she thought.

They lay quietly like that for some time. As Amelia felt their breathing fall into a mutual rhythm, she realized that she had never felt this close to anyone, not even her mother who had never tired of cuddling and caressing her. It occurred to her that before this moment ended, she had to make the most of it. Once past, maybe she'd never have the chance again to absolve herself of her painful, secret past. She inhaled deeply then broke the silence.

"It was the evening of my choir concert. Even my dad decided to come since I was singing a solo." She hesitated a moment, remembering more or less the melody. Her mother had been so proud and even her five-year-old brother had said, "Good job, Sis." Her father came close to complimenting her.

"Overall, well done," he said, "but your vibrato was shaky here and there." Donovan caressed her cheek, encouraging her to go on.

"Mom and Dad had come in separate cars since Dad was working late that night. He was the editor for some political newspaper in our town and usually worked late. He had to go back to his office after the concert to finish up some last-minute things. I asked if I could go with him, which I did." She had always loved to watch him work, even when there wasn't much to watch, him pouring through articles, books, internet sources, typing with the "Columbus-method," making phone calls. She liked when he made phone calls the best.

"Robert Kingston here. I'm a freelance writer needing some information about–"such and such. He never said the name of his paper, for being an alternative news source it had a low readership and got its own bad press for being "leftist." She admired his tenacity as he called the same people time and again seeking information they didn't want to give.

"In a half hour, he had finished what he needed to do, and we were on our way home. But within a mile of our home we heard sirens. Dad pulled over, and we watched two fire trucks fly past. Just a few minutes later, an ambulance passed and then several police cars. We were within blocks of our house and were horrified to see that they were headed down our street." Amelia paused, remembering how she had looked over at her father and saw him leaning forward, craning his neck to see where the caravan of emergency vehicles was headed. It was one of the few times—perhaps the only time—she had ever seen him scared.

"He sped after them. I think if we had really known what awaited us, we would have taken more time, driven that last block at a snail's pace, lingered in that moment before our lives changed forever.

"It was dark, of course, so all we could see were these red lights ricocheting off of everything. He pulled up behind the police cars." Amelia remembered seeing several policemen unwinding a yellow ribbon across the street. It had almost clotheslined her as she ran.

"There was smoke everywhere. Somehow with all the flashing lights I hadn't seen it until then. I could no longer deny that it came from our house, or rather where our house used to be. I ran toward the smoke and the debris that still seemed to be settling. I felt someone grab at my elbow from behind. I tugged free but heard him say, 'No! Don't go there!'

"We had gotten there so soon after the emergency vehicles that they hadn't had time to secure the scene. I ran forward and tripping over something, I sprawled face down in the dirt. When I lifted my head, I was looking into my mother's face, melted into some gelatinous goo from a horror movie. I only knew it was her because I recognized the patch of red hair that hung from her skull. That's when I smelled her. I understand now what those concentration camp victims experienced standing outside the crematoriums, or, for that matter, in them. It is an ungodly smell. I imagine if evil had a smell it would smell like that.

"I was trying to rise to my feet, just as someone grasped me from behind. 'Get someone over here to cover them up!' she yelled. She was turning me away when I saw him. My little brother, sprawled a few feet from my mother. That's when I began to scream.

"I always knew they had died in some kind of accident, but I hadn't remembered that I was there, that I saw them. Not until the other night at the powwow. Something in the music, the heat, and the dance reminded me. I never wanted to remember, and then my blinders came off.

"I couldn't get away from that horrific picture. It was like someone had painted it over my eyeballs. Until your uncle helped me. I still see it, but I've been given a more recent one in a beautiful dream, and that one I conjure whenever the other starts to appear." She paused, breathing in deeply.

"You were right, by the way, you medicine-man-in-training. It was not only a memory but also a vision. They want me to do something for them. 'Seek the truth,' they said." She paused for a moment and shook her head. "Now's your turn to laugh, like a normal person would do, I mean like a non-Indian, non-medicine-man-in-training would do."

For a moment there was only silence. Then shaking his head Donovan answered incredulously. "Laugh?" he exclaimed. "At which part? Your pain? Or do you mean the part about your hope? There is not a laugh anywhere inside my body, only a knot in my chest that wants to burst."

He pressed her head so tightly into his chest, she couldn't have twitched if she had wanted to. He paused a moment before saying, "I can't believe my luck that you are here with me and not locked away in some loony bin. How did you make it all the way here, Amelia?" he asked, raising her chin to look into her eyes. "How did you get so strong?"

She didn't feel strong at that moment, looking into his questioning eyes, seeing his thick lower lashes kissed with tears. She wanted to crumble into him, be absorbed by him—replace her existence with his. How strong was that?

"See, I don't have any medicine for you that you don't already have," Donovan said, shaking his head and ruffling her hair. "I guess all I can offer you is something every recovering patient needs, a good bowl of Jell-O. Can I be your Jell-O?"

"Second helpings, please," Amelia replied climbing upon him. Somewhere inside of him, Donovan did find his laugh. It echoed around them as they embarked anew on another intimate journey.

Chapter 28

Donovan lay by her side, and Amelia could hear his breathing become heavier as he succumbed to sleep. Then suddenly he jerked awake.

"I can't stay in here with you," he exclaimed. "My uncle would kill me. Not that he won't figure it out anyway," he said as he scrambled out of bed, "but at least for appearances."

He dug some boxers out of his dresser drawer.

"I'll sleep on the couch," he said as he leaned down to kiss her, "but I'll be dreaming of you."

He left then, and Amelia felt a knot form in her stomach. She hadn't expected to feel afraid, but here she was, ready to vomit. Her first time, and only other, she had vomited, after seeing him the next day at school. She had pushed through the kids in the schoolyard and made it to the bathroom just in time to heave her breakfast into the toilet. She wished now that she hadn't taken the trouble to run all the way to the bathroom but had heaved all over his navy blue and white uniform instead.

It was lunchtime, and Amelia had just turned down the second guy to ask her to the park for that evening. She told him that she already had a boyfriend, Rigoberto.

"You mean that Rigoberto?" the boy asked, pointing over to a lanky boy hovering over a girl, a lock of her hair in his fingers.

Not bothering to respond, Amelia made her way over to Rigoberto.

"Rigo," she said, "aren't we going to eat lunch together today?"

He didn't look at her.

"He's eating with me today," the girl said haughtily.

"Yeah," Rigoberto agreed, finally looking down his long, straight nose at her. "Don't get me wrong, it was fun and all, real fun, but I'm really not into *putas*, sluts. Especially a puta gringa like you."

The girl laughed, and Rigoberto went back to fingering her hair. Amelia had stood for a moment before running for the bathroom.

The knot in her stomach grew tighter as she remembered the days and weeks that followed. Within days, she was known schoolwide as *Puta Gringa*, white whore. Though she had always been excluded because of her color and her imperfect Spanish, she became a leper to even the teachers in the school. It wasn't long before her family, too, became tainted.

She had just reached the summit of her climb home when she heard the argument raging within the tiny house. She had heard her father and stepmother fight before, but she realized quickly that this time it was about her. Before she had the chance to turn and flee, her stepmother opened the door and dragged her in.

"You brought her into this family, like a disease! Now I must lower my head before my neighbors, and she is not even my daughter. I tell them now she is not my daughter—that she will never be. But she is yours, and I hold you responsible for our disgrace!"

"Yes, she is my daughter," her father replied.

For a moment, Amelia thought he was going to stand up for her.

"But I will not take responsibility for her. She has been under your care, so don't blame me that she's gone wild. Where were you when she was out with that boy? I'll tell you where I was: I was at work. You want her pristine, you keep her pristine! I don't want to hear another word about it!"

Her father didn't look at her as he shoved his way out the door, but that wasn't unusual. Amelia couldn't remember when he ever really looked at her. Yet, the fact that he wouldn't defend his own daughter—or even give her a chance to defend herself—made his indifference even more painful.

That evening, she lay awake, replaying the past few weeks: Rigoberto's smile, his flirtations, the roses and poems, her secret confession, his promising kiss that led to that horrifying act in the grass, the repercussions. It was all so unfair.

Unfair. That little word suddenly brought her clarity. How trivial a word, after all she had been through. To be shamed and wrongfully judged in the scheme of her life was just as trivial as that word. Poor baby wrongly accused, condemned to wear a scarlet "P" for puta. Who really cared? She had survived the loss of a mother and a brother and already bore a "P" for "pain." So what if it had taken on added significance? She smiled at her own joke. Had she only had that clarity back then.

But she hadn't. What she did have was a relentless stepmother, determined to never again be shamed. For the rest of her adolescence following Rigoberto, Amelia was never left without a chaperone. Her stepbrother kept his mother strictly informed of all of Amelia's encounters and doings (and many fabricated ones). Gradually, conditions at school improved, but even so she never had more than a few girlfriends to speak of, and the boys continued to hound her for walks in the park, counting on Rigoberto's luck.

The memory wasn't a pleasant one; however, it gave Amelia once again the clarity she needed to push through her fear. The knot in her stomach dissipated and was replaced by an expanding chest, filled with the knowledge of her strength and determination. If Donovan scorned her in the morning, she'd vomit all over him and then move on, this time without a chaperone. Once again, she smiled at her wit and gradually drifted off to sleep.

Chapter 29

The smell of pancakes or maybe her grumbling stomach awoke her the next morning. She suddenly felt excited to start the day. A day that began with the scent of pancakes was a day filled with possibilities.

She heard them in the kitchen and saw Donovan's elbow through the doorway, obviously flipping pancakes on the stove. She stole to the bathroom and sponged herself down as well as she could before sliding back into the same clothes she had worn for the past two days. Looking a bit wrinkly and disheveled, she excused herself from the mirror and headed for the pancakes.

They were heaped on a plate in the middle of the table, their steam still rising when she entered the kitchen. Donovan almost flipped a pancake on the floor when he saw her but caught it with his left hand as it glanced off the stove.

"Good morning, Amelia," Uncle Martin said. "You look much better today. I believe you slept well."

"Yes, sir," Amelia replied. "I'm feeling very well. Thank you for helping me so much yesterday. Whatever it was that you did, it has made all the difference."

"I believe my nephew helped you somewhat as well," he said, "His medicine-man training must be paying off."

Amelia turned red but managed to sputter, "Oh…oh yes. He's been very kind."

From behind his uncle, Donovan shrugged his shoulders and shook his head smiling. It was hard to know for sure how much this wise man knew, but they both assumed just about everything.

Throughout the course of the meal, Donovan took it upon himself to be as attentive to Amelia's needs as a manservant. She laughed as he poured maple syrup on her pancakes.

"Could you cut them for me too?" she requested smiling.

She had seen dark skin blush before. Nothing obvious, just a heightened color along the check ridge. She saw it now in his skin as he sat down across from her. She loved that she could make him blush.

"How did you sleep?" he asked.

"She already answered that, son. Try something more original," Uncle Martin offered.

"Okay, then," Donovan said quickly recovering from his second blush. "Was the bed soft enough for you?"

"Yeah, that's a good one," Uncle Martin laughed.

"Not quite," Amelia played along. "After several hours of tossing and turning, I discovered a pea under the mattress. But after that, it was quite comfortable, thank you."

"Looks like our little princess fits right in with our lot!" Uncle Martin proclaimed.

When Amelia looked across at Donovan, he looked proud. He caught her eye and smiled. She felt a tingling sensation begin in her groin and travel up to her throat. She looked down at her pancakes.

Suddenly there was a knock, and Paul's voice called through the door.

"Martin? It's Paul White Clay."

"Come on in, young man. We're in the kitchen," Uncle Martin shouted.

Amelia looked over at Donovan and found him already looking at her. Was that jealousy in his eyes? Her own showed the guilt she felt, not having clarified her relationship with Paul to Donovan. Or to Paul.

Paul stepped into the kitchen, teeth gleaming as usual. Amelia's guilt washed away as she remembered how genuinely she liked him and valued his friendship.

"Looks like my timing is perfect!" Paul exclaimed.

"Sit yourself down, my son. There's plenty for us all," Uncle Martin assured him.

"Hey, Donovan," Paul said, moving towards him with an extended hand. "What's up with you, man? You're looking good in your boxers and undershirt this fine morning!" he kidded.

"Yeah, well I've got a young lady here to impress," Donovan grinned back, as he clasped his hand and completed a brotherly three-part handshake. Amelia was proud to realize that the sequence of five she had learned must have been reserved for Paul's inner circle of friends.

"Thought I'd come by and eat some pancakes before heading over to the Spur to put in my time," Paul said, loading a few on the plate Donovan slid over to him. "And as an added bonus, check on this lovely lady to see how she's doing. You look better, Amelia," he said grinning over at her.

"Feeling much better, thanks. It's this Indian hospitality," she replied smiling, unintentionally glancing at Donovan. Paul appeared not to notice, though Donovan blushed for the third time, but she wasn't counting.

"When are you heading back to the ranch?" Paul asked her.

Amelia laughed. How quickly her life had changed. It hadn't occurred to her that she was supposed to be anywhere but here.

"I forgot about that!" she exclaimed. "I suppose I should have been back yesterday!"

"Looks like that fall did a little more damage than we thought," Paul said, addressing Martin and Donovan with a shake of his head.

"Either that, Doc White Clay, or it was the aftermath of our Indian hospitality," Uncle Martin suggested.

"I guess a little of both," Amelia confirmed laughing. "I better make a quick phone call. Don't let on that I'm feeling better. I'd like to stay one more day, if that's okay with you."

She had looked over at Uncle Martin for his permission but was answered by a chorus of "Yes!" in three-part harmony.

She laughed. "I'll take that as a 'yes' then." She got up from the table and took the phone Donovan handed her.

She got her additional day off from a very concerned Pamela and made a commitment to see Paul after he got off of work in the evening. After waving to Paul as he walked away down the street, Amelia looked up at Donovan,

"Do you need to be somewhere today?" she asked.

Taking advantage of the fact that Uncle Martin was still in the kitchen, Donovan gathered her to him whispering, "Yes. With you." Her body ached for him.

"Let's help Uncle Martin in the kitchen and then send him on an errand for milk or something," Donovan suggested. Amelia laughed but secretly wished Uncle Martin could be so easily tricked.

Chapter 30

Uncle Martin didn't go out for milk, so Amelia and Donovan headed towards the powwow grounds. There was no more music, but the powwow didn't officially end until that evening. They walked through the booths, and Donovan proved very knowledgeable in Indian arts and crafts.

"Maybe I will have a booth next year," he said, "but I'm not sure my art would go over very well here. It's a bit untraditional."

"What kind of art do you do?" Amelia asked, surprised to learn he was an artist.

"Mostly painting and pottery," he said, "though I've been working more with metal lately. Pretty untraditional for a native artist. But it seems to fit what I want to say."

"What you want to say? What's that?" Amelia probed.

"There's just some things you can't say with words, or at least I can't, anyway," he said pausing and looking into the distance. "I guess I'm trying to show the coarseness of life, the complications. You know, the crossing of cultures, classes, generations. And the contradictions too, like strength and fear, hope and despair. You know, pretty much what you get from reality TV."

Amelia laughed at this, in spite of the fact she had little firsthand knowledge of reality TV.

"Really though, I think we all struggle with these things, and I think art helps me work through them. Does that make sense?" he implored, finally looking into her eyes.

"Yeah," she answered. "It does."

He took her hand, and they walked thoughtfully to the bleachers of the Dance Arbor.

"Do you make a living at it?" Amelia asked as they settled themselves on the aluminum that had begun to absorb the heat of the day.

"No," he laughed. "Hardly. I work at a casino. Decent money, nothing too difficult. I deal some cards and watch poor bastards lose their shirts. Sometimes I'm happy about it—if their shirts are too white, their checkered shorts pressed too neatly. Other times I feel sick to my stomach as they beg a cigarette off the guy next to them. All in all, in spite of the downside of gambling, it's done incredible good for our reservation."

"I didn't know there was a casino here," Amelia remarked.

"Well, there is one just down the road, but that's not where I work. I work up near Kalispell on the Blackfoot reservation. That's where I really live, with my mother's tribe. I'm just here for the summer to promote some native arts organization I'm a part of. I'm trying to get a chapter started here and give some folks a chance to promote themselves as artists."

"You're not Crow?"

"Half. My father was Crow. He was an artist too. He met my mother in Helena at an art festival. They lived here for a time, despite the scorn of the Crow tribe. You see, the Crow and the Blackfoot are traditional enemies, and even today intermarriage is frowned upon. Things didn't work out for them, so later my mother took me with her back to the Blackfoot reservation. My father died a few years later. They couldn't tell if his liver gave out or if he froze to death. Either way, they found him in a snowbank between the bar and home."

"I'm sorry," Amelia consoled, aware of the inadequacy of such a response.

"Don't be. I never really knew him that well, and anyway, my mother still has a collapsed nose to show for that relationship. I've always considered Uncle Martin to be my father anyway. It's easier to do that when your real one is gone."

"So, you're a Blackfoot Crow," Amelia mused.

"Yeah," he laughed, "they used to call me that in the old days. It hurt at first but really became a badge of honor later."

"Kind of like *Puta Gringa*, I suppose." Amelia laughed.

"*Puta* what?"

"Never mind. It's a long story, but I'm sure I'll share it with you one day!"

They spent the next couple hours sitting on the bleachers and then walking around with little awareness of anything or anyone but themselves. They bought lunch at a stand—Indian tacos—which made Amelia smile at how things always came full circle, a thousand miles away and Honduras was still as present as ever.

Now that Donovan knew the most tragic moment of Amelia's life, she gradually filled him in on what came before and after.

"Say something in Spanish," he insisted.

"*Aunque te acabo de conocer, te amo como si fueramos amantes de otra vida.*"

"What did you say?" he asked.

"Even though I just met you, it's like we've known each other from another life," she replied, careful to leave out the translation of *te amo*, I love you, and *amantes*, lovers.

"My mother taught me a little Blackfoot, but I hardly remember any now. Languages are just as fascinating as art. I guess they're all translations of the same thing: the human experience." He grinned. "Deep...right?" he chided himself. "But you know, I do think art gives us the freedom to express things we can't in language. We say we don't have the words sometimes, but I think it's more like the words have been taken from us. We just don't get to talk about certain things. Art gives us a way around that."

"Like a code," Amelia suggested.

"Yeah. Like a code," he nodded. "And what about you?" he asked, gently sweeping away a lock of her hair that had fallen across her face. "What are you interested in?"

"Music," she replied. "I play guitar and sing, but I'm self-taught and probably not too refined."

"Now why doesn't that surprise me?" he said taking her face in his hands and kissing her brusquely on the lips. "The more I learn about you the more I am amazed that we stumbled across each other...or rather that you fell into my arms and later stumbled into me!"

"You just had to remind me, didn't you," Amelia moaned. "Will I ever live that down?"

"Never." He replied matter-of-factly. "Seriously though," he said looking at her directly with a slight frown. "I have always believed in all that Indian 'hocus pocus.' I've seen strange things...amazing things have happened in my Uncle's hands. But it never really happened to me. I've always been an observer. Until now. But somehow, I'm still caught in that observer role. I see myself from above, looking down at myself talking to you, touching you...amongst other things," he waggled his eyebrows. "But really, it's weird, like a disassociation. I don't quite understand..." then catching himself, "and I really don't understand why I'm even talking about it!"

"A disassociation, huh? Maybe it's a flight response. I scare you so much that flight response meets out of body experience," she laughed. "Seriously though, it sounds like you're trying to rationalize something that doesn't work that way. I mean, does anyone ever really understand this?" she said gesturing between them. "I think this is one of those times we make a choice to let go and go with the flow."

"Listen to you teaching me how to be an Indian!" he laughed shaking his head. "Whoever heard of an Indian pitting rationality against authentic experience? A sign of the times, I guess." He continued shaking his head, and Amelia could tell it troubled him to have internalized so much of Western culture.

"How about we make a pact?" she suggested.

"Oh no!" Donovan retorted. "No more pacts with the white man!"

"First of all," Amelia interrupted, "this is a pact not a treaty. And second, I'm a woman not a man. Women are more trustworthy, of course. Things would have been a lot different in history if women had been in charge. Anyway, I say we not second-guess our connection anymore and enjoy it fully for the rest of this day. What d'ya say?"

He answered her with a bear hug that brought her off her feet. As he lowered her, his lips brushed a path from her chin to the top of her head.

"Let's go see if Uncle went to get some milk," he said.

Chapter 31

Uncle Martin was gone. They were excited to know that later there'd be milk to drink. In the meantime, they discovered that the previous night's passion had not been a fluke. The warm-up, though unnecessary, was every bit as new and intoxicating to Amelia as their first time, maybe even more so now that she knew what awaited her at the end. When they could not put off their gratification any longer, Donovan reached for his discarded jeans and pulled something out of his pocket.

"Pick a color," he said, displaying a row of colored condoms. Amelia had been pretty sure gum was just an excuse for going into the convenience store.

"Red," she answered, "Cherry Jell-O has always been my favorite."

An hour later as they still lay naked next to each other, lapping up each other's attention, unwilling to let even a cotton sheet come between them, Paul's voice called from the door.

"Shit!" whispered Amelia roughly, "I forgot all about him!"

"Well, I should hope so," Donovan said, grinning through the jealousy Amelia was sure she caught in his eyes. "I'll be right out, Paul," Donovan yelled towards the door.

"Come with us," Amelia begged, as she quickly jumped out of bed to put on her now sordid clothes.

"Never one for a threesome," he replied. "At least one where I'm not in the minority."

The pillow she threw at him hit him square in the face. He toppled her to the bed as she was trying to hook her bra. She fell giggling beneath him.

"Let's pretend we're not here," she pleaded.

"Too late. Remember I already told him I was on my way out."

"Well, then you better get off me, you oaf, and get some clothes on."

Donovan sighed, taking care to slide his skin across her body as much as he could as he reluctantly removed himself.

Moments later he was opening the bedroom door.

"I'll distract him, and then you can come in from the bathroom or something, if you'd rather not have him know."

Amelia was grateful for his understanding. She'd explain to him later how she needed to tell Paul in a more graceful way.

"That would be great," she agreed.

Minutes later she was greeting Paul in the kitchen, from his easy show of teeth apparently oblivious to the situation.

"What's the plan, Stan?" Paul asked her still leaning against the table.

She matched his lean with her own against the doorway.

"Don't know, Flo," she countered.

"How about some burgers and some pool at the casino?"

"Sounds great."

"What about you, Donovan. Up for some pool?" Paul offered.

"I'll pass this time, man. This young lady distracted me from some things I should have done today. You guys have fun. Maybe I'll catch up with you all later."

"We'll be there awhile," Paul responded. "You know us!"

As Paul and Amelia headed out the door, Donovan called after them, "Hey, Paul. Tell Darian I'm expecting to see some of that artwork he promised me tomorrow. He's also got a grant proposal he's supposed to show me."

"Tell him yourself when you see him later, man. Darian don't listen to me!"

Amelia waved back at Donovan, hoping he caught every nuance of her wave and smile. She already missed him as she turned away to follow Paul down the street.

Chapter 32

Over greasy burgers and onion rings, Amelia was drawn up once again in Paul's fraternity. Nearly all the gang was there, two of them with their girlfriends. Amelia seemed to meet hostility from one of them, but the other, Laura, was every bit as warm and gregarious as the fraternity itself.

"I saw you fall at the powwow," Laura said, lightly fingering the bandage on Amelia's temple. "How are you feeling?"

"Really great, actually. The doctor gave me enough painkillers for a week, but I only used them two days. I think Donovan's uncle worked some magic on me because I haven't had a headache since."

"Donovan's uncle?" the other young lady piped in. "You mean Martin Real Bird. We call him *Martin Real Bird* around here, not *Donovan's uncle*. Donovan's not even from around here, really."

"No, I suppose not," Amelia replied confused at her defensiveness.

Laura laughed. "Don't mind Brenda. She's still a bit put off by her rejection. You see, she and Donovan dated earlier this summer."

"Yeah, whatever," Brenda spat. She pointed over to her boyfriend playing pool. "Anyway, he's a better man than *Donnie* will ever be."

Amelia could tell by the way she stressed the "Donnie" that she wanted her to know how intimate they had been. Amelia was not sure if she was more jealous or disappointed that Donovan would have been with such a woman.

"Speaking of Donovan," Laura chimed in, "how is he? I haven't seen him for a while since he broke it off with Brenda. He's a little too serious for me—the tortured-artist type—but gorgeous to look at. Kind of miss having the scenery around, if you know what I mean. Don't tell my boyfriend that!" she laughed, poking Amelia in the arm.

Amelia felt an odd mixture of pride and jealousy to know Donovan was such eye candy to the ladies. She, too, had found him good looking but had never separated it into a quality in itself. He simply was unbelievable in his entirety. Obviously on the surface as well.

"So, are you and Paul an item?" Laura queried, unimpeded by the decorum governing first acquaintances.

"No," Amelia laughed, "we're just good friends. But…" she added, figuring this conversation would make it back to him and give him some consolation if he had hoped for something more, "if I wasn't going back to Minnesota after the summer, I could see he'd be a pretty good catch. Not a good idea to start a new romance, though, when I'll be leaving in a couple weeks." Sounded plausible, even to Amelia who planned to continue flouting her own advice.

The evening passed quickly but as the sky outside began to darken, Amelia caught herself checking the entrance again and again for Donovan.

"Do you think Donovan will come?" she finally asked Paul, casually looking at him over her pool stick.

"Doubt it," he replied. "He's not much for bars, being a recovering alcoholic and all. He came out a few times when he was dating Brenda, but they didn't stay long. Seems they had more important things to do," he added, unaware of the pang his joke caused.

She was just creating excuses in her head as to why she had to leave when Donovan strode through the door. She was unprepared for her reaction and had to keep herself from running towards him and flying into his arms. Her whole face was flushed and her hands clammy as he came over to the pool table to greet everyone. She was the last person he greeted, other than Brenda who had stalked away, and when she surprised him with the signature handshake, he pinched the corners of a smile that threatened to erupt over his face.

"Looks like you taught her well," he recovered, addressing the gang, but Amelia saw his hand was shaking as he wiped its clamminess upon his jeans.

Invited to join a game of pool, Donovan accepted with reservations. "Just one. I promised my uncle I'd have Amelia back to the house soon. He's still concerned about her." Excuse provided.

They bought it and after Donovan and Amelia were handily whupped by Paul and Laura, they said their goodbyes.

"You got a way back to the ranch?" Paul asked Amelia. "'Cause I got to work tomorrow."

"Don't worry, Paul." Donovan answered for her. "My uncle asked me to drive her back."

"Then I guess it's goodbye," Paul said, this time not smiling.

"I guess so," Amelia agreed. "I can't tell you how lucky I am to have met you. You're the best!" With that she gave him a strong hug that he returned, adding a knuckle rub to her head.

"Back at you, baby," he said.

Then Donovan and Amelia were out in the open air under the starry skies of another clear night.

"So, now you know," Donovan conceded.

Amelia wasn't sure if he meant Brenda or his alcoholism.

"Never was much at pool."

She laughed.

"I tried to save it for us," she said squeezing his hand, "but you kept putting it out of reach. Best you stick to other things you're better at."

"Amelia," he pleaded, stopping her in mid stride to look into her eyes. "I don't want you to go. When you left this afternoon, I felt like you took my life with you. I tried to do a few things, and I couldn't even function. I've never needed anyone before, but you take my soul when you walk away."

She knew what he meant but could only nod her answer.

They continued their walk home, hand in hand. When Donovan saw that the lights at home were still on, he said, "My uncle's still up. Come with me."

He pulled her quickly along after him and several minutes later they were looking over the Little Bighorn River, its basin empty but for a trickle of a stream that meandered through.

"When you leave, I'll be as the Little Bighorn in August. Look how sad she looks. How thirsty. I'm already thirsty, and you're still here."

"Hmmm. A poet too," she chided.

"I mean it though. And I don't really like it."

They looked at the river in silence. After a while, they sat down upon the bank and Amelia leaned back against him with a sigh.

"Up until the other night at the powwow," she began, "I was a free spirit; I had nowhere to go but forward, no direction but the future. But now after remembering, and after seeing what your uncle showed me, I have to go back. They told me to find the truth. I have no idea what that means, but I know I must go back to Minnesota to find out."

"I'll wait for you, like the Little Bighorn waits for water, if you say you'll come back." Although she could barely make out his eyes in the darkening night, she was sure of his sincerity.

"As soon as I can. I can't think of anything better to come back to than you."

"Then that'll have to do," he said, tilting her head backwards to meet his lips. He was thirsty, but the kiss was enough to at least ebb a thirst they both knew was insatiable.

Chapter 33

He drove her back to the ranch the following day. They tried to keep the trip light with plans for the future, but the inevitability of their separation brought moments of tortured silence. They would see each other before he went back to Kalispell and she to Minnesota. Then she would call him as often as possible, keep him abreast of her search for the truth—whatever that meant—and he would her about his art.

Instead of climbing up the embankment to look over her shoulder as he left, she chose rather to sit upon it and watch as he drove away down the gray highway to be swallowed by the encroaching mountains. Even then, she sat there for several more minutes before trudging up the embankment and mounting the ATV that still waited below on the other side.

After being treated to a thorough once over-by an anxious Pamela, Jack gave Amelia a list of chores that would keep her busy 'til spring, even when they all knew she and the rest of the staff would be leaving after Labor Day. Amelia was thankful for the distraction, for she was ill-prepared for her intense longing and desperation.

There would be one more cattle drive to drive the cows back into the mountains for the winter. This drive was not entirely necessary, but it was a good draw for the close of the tourist season. On the eve of this last cattle drive, Amelia could no longer bear the separation. Her hand shaking, she dialed Donovan's number.

"Hel—" she heard, and then the phone was dropped on the floor, but it was enough for her to realize it was a woman's voice. "Oops," the voice said giggling, "I dropped the phone!" She continued to giggle uncontrollably until Amelia found an opening to interrupt.

"Could I speak to Donovan, please?" she asked, a bit disconcerted.

"Oh Donnie!" She knew the voice instantly. "Some little bitch wants to talk to you!"

Brenda again erupted into giggles, dropping the phone again. This time when it was picked up, Amelia barely recognized Donovan's voice.

"Hel...lo....oh?" He crooned in a singsong voice. Amelia stood with the phone frozen to her ear. She couldn't breathe, let alone answer.

"Hel...loo," the voice repeated, singing into the receiver.

"Just hang up, Donnie baby," Brenda cooed from the background, "and come back over here." Somehow Amelia pried the phone from her ear and placed it clumsily into its holder. Then she ran to the bathroom.

She stayed there for hours. Tucked back in the far corner of the ranch house, she sobbed and retched undisturbed until the sky began to lighten. Then she slunk back to the bunkhouse and waited until the others stirred.

"You're sick!" Russ proclaimed when he saw her that morning. "We'll have to start without you. You could catch up with us tomorrow."

"Yeah, I feel pretty lousy," Amelia managed to say, "but I think if I just get moving I'll feel better."

"It's up to you," came Russ's reply.

Amelia managed to perform her pre-trail duties: arranging the tack, the horses, the grub, and first aid supplies. She focused on each detail as if it were her last breath, and somehow, she was soon guiding the others down the trail.

Once on the horse, however, she had little to distract her but a barren landscape that echoed her longing and loss.

"Clarity," she whispered to herself over and over, trying to bring back that strength she had found in herself those times before. This time there was no relief. This time the pain was too much like the pain she had thought she would never again have to endure.

She reasoned with herself as she led this anonymous group of tourists through the nondescript views of the trail. Berated herself for her pain after such a brief encounter with a stranger as she collected a few straying calves bewildered by the horses, the riders, the new terrain. He did not deserve this pain.

She felt awash with guilt. How dare she bestow upon him this pain that she had reserved for her mother and her dear little brother. What had he done to deserve that depth of emotion? Some good sex? Some corny analogy about the river? The river be damned. May the whole thing dry up and shrivel in misery. And while she was at it, she shriveled it up as well. *Have fun with that, Brenda darling*, she thought.

Relief had come, this time through anger and not clarity. But that was good enough for Amelia. And so, she took it out in various ways that week along the trail, certain that anger was better than falling apart on the saddle.

She was in the middle of scolding an eight-year-old boy for being a spoiled rotten baby, when she suddenly saw his face. Not his face, but her brother's.

"I'm sorry," she said suddenly, filled with remorse. "I didn't mean that. I'm just frustrated to be behind schedule. Listen, I promise if you get up in the saddle that your bottom will feel better, and you'll barely notice that it hurts. And, if you show me what a brave cowboy you are, I'll make sure we get you something extra special for dessert tonight. What d'ya say, pardner?"

"Ice cream?" he asked.

"We don't have ice cream on the trail," she laughed. "You'll get some of that when we get back. But, I can make sure Loni cooks you up something really special that I'm sure you'll like. Deal?"

"Okay," he said, putting his foot in the stirrup. Amelia helped him up. Now she had clarity.

This time when they got back from the trail they had a regular party awaiting them. A group of local musicians were there to play country music into the night. It was the Stantons' way of thanking the summer staff. Amelia took out her guitar for the first time in weeks and within minutes, her rusty fingers took on the shine she was used to. She played and sang off and on with the group, and without realizing it, she was happy.

She took turns dancing with Russ and Raymundo, and mother of all surprises, a turn with Jack! An old country fiddle tune had Jack eating up the sun-scorched ground with his well-worn heels and tossing Amelia about like the many calves he had roped and thrown in his day. They even set off a few fireworks. Then Jack sent Russ out to make sure nothing was smoldering. The evening was wonderful, and Amelia realized if anyone deserved her tears, these people did: Loni, the gourmet chef that never got the chance; Raymundo, torn between two cultures; Russ, a cowboy yearning to be free; beautiful, sophisticated Pamela juxtaposed upon this coarse landscape; and Jack, its mirror image. She would miss them. But not as much as she missed him. Such banished thoughts were never truly banished.

Chapter 34

Two days later, she was in Billings waiting for the bus. It was the day they had planned to meet in Hardin, a little town outside the reservation. She wondered if he'd be there waiting for her. She hoped he would and that his disappointment would be overwhelming. She doubted it, though. He had so quickly turned to another. Why would he bother to wait for her?

When the bus pulled away, she felt her loss well up inside her. As she choked it back, she tasted the bitterness of bile. She leaned her forehead against the window and sobbed quietly into the distant outline of the mountains where he waited. Or didn't. Another chapter of her life closed. No, not closed, she realized, but ripped from her hands like all the other chapters of her life. At least she was on the road back to reclaim the others.

Chapter 35

"How wonderful to see you, sweetheart!" her grandmother cried, drawing her into her pudgy arms. "Two times in a year after not seeing you for so many! I'm blessed! Let me look at you! You put on some weight! How great! You were really too skinny the last time I saw you. Meant to speak to your father about that, had he shown up for his own sister's funeral. But it looks like he took care of you after all."

Amelia's grandmother had been nearly dancing around her as she looked her over front to back, top to bottom.

"And how brown you are! That Honduran sun has almost made you Hispanic, or is it Latino or Chicano that they say nowadays? Anyway, took the Minnesotan right out of you! So glad you're here to stay awhile. We'll have you whitewashed in no time!"

She pointed to a chair. "Now, sit sweetie. You must be starving. I made a nice turkey hot dish for you, new recipe I found in the *Better Homes and Gardens*. They put a little blue cheese in this one, so I thought it sounded interesting. We'll have to see if it's a keeper." She flew into the kitchen and began extracting plates.

"Can I help, Grandma?" Amelia asked, rising from her chair.

"No, no, dear. You sit and relax. I have everything ready. It'll just take a minute. What was I going to say? Oh yes. Your father used to love being a guinea pig for my new recipes. If you plan to stay awhile, you better get used to it too!"

"It sounds great, Grandma," Amelia replied enthusiastically. Loni had been a good cook for what she was given, but Amelia was looking forward to a change of menu.

"Now tell me what you've been up to," her grandmother said, applying the finishing touches to the evening's offerings and taking her place at the table, "in that far off abysmal place your father whisked you off to. Do you have a boyfriend?"

Amelia hesitated on both accounts. She hadn't decided how much to tell her grandmother. She didn't want to worry her needlessly about her son yet didn't want to lie either. And she certainly didn't want to tell her about her recent heartbreak, which to remember for just an instant awakened the dull ache inside her. She decided the truth without the fixings was the best course of action.

"Actually grandmother, I didn't go back to Honduras. I went to Montana and worked on a ranch for the summer. It was a great experience."

"What? Well, I'll be. I had no idea you were heading out that way. You never told me." She almost looked angry, peering from beneath the glasses that magnified the piercing blue of her wide-spaced eyes.

"Sorry, Grandma. I just didn't want to worry you. You had enough on your mind as it was."

"Suppose you're right," she said and after a pause added, "How did your father ever let you go off on your own? Figures he'd encourage such an adventure, hitchhiking to Alaska like he did at sixteen," she said disapprovingly.

"Actually, Grandma," Amelia laughed, "you'd be surprised at how disapproving he would have been! He kept me a prisoner in Honduras. I never had a minute to myself, let alone a chance for an adventure. So, I didn't tell him *where* I was going."

"So, he assumed you were here the whole time. That's what he gets for never calling me. We haven't even gotten an email from him telling us why he never made it to the funeral."

Amelia felt momentarily anxious, but her grandmother's next statement set her somewhat at ease.

"So like him really. I'd say I've gotten less than six letters from him in the last ten years. Not sure what I did to deserve a son like that, but that's my cross to bear."

"Better a son than a father!" Amelia laughed.

"Is he really that bad?" Her grandmother queried, suddenly quite serious.

"Maybe we can't fault him after what he's been through," came Amelia's evasive answer.

"Suppose you're right," her grandmother said, taking another bite of the hot dish, and this time really tasting it. "Not bad, not bad. What do you think, Amelia?"

"I haven't had a chance to try it, Grandma," Amelia chuckled, "what with the inquisition and all!"

"Okay, okay, I'll give you a chance to take a bite. So, Montana," she said barely pausing, "what's it like?"

Amelia took a moment to chew the mouthful she had just taken.

"Beautiful," she responded, swallowing at the same time. "I worked in the mountains. Very dry, but beautiful in its own way. It's amazing how many shades of earth and stone there are once you pay attention. Great hot dish, by the way, Grandma. I think the blue cheese gives it a kick."

"Wait until you see what I made for dessert. A variation of the apple torte recipe my friend Irma cut out of the *Better Homes and Gardens*."

"Any blue cheese in it?" kidded Amelia.

"Oh no. But it did call for some cardamom, which I thought was odd. We'll see."

The evening went by quickly as her grandmother continued her inquisition interspersed with her own memories and related commentaries. Amelia marveled at how sharp and alive she was. She made Amelia wonder what kind of woman she, herself, would be at eighty-seven. First, she had to make it there, and the way things were going, even thirty seemed like an unattainable goal.

The following morning, Amelia's grandmother was up and about by 6:00 a.m. Amelia, though used to an early schedule, decided to lie in bed, drifting in and out of sleep, reveling in the freedom to choose whether to sleep or to rise. She finally chose to rise, more to avoid the memories of Donovan than of her own free will, and went down to the kitchen to see her grandmother.

Her grandmother was busy at the stove but already dressed to venture out for the day.

"I'm making you some pancakes, dear, but then I have to rush off to a morning tea at the governor's mansion. The historical society I belong to is having its monthly fundraiser. Look what I'll be wearing."

She picked up a pillbox hat from the counter and placed it delicately on her head.

"That's gorgeous, Grandma!" Amelia exclaimed.

"I made it," her grandmother confessed. "And get this," she said approaching Amelia with her head lowered. "It's made out of garbage bags!"

"No way, Grandma!"

"Really. It is. Touch it," she insisted, lowering her head further.

Amelia ended up taking it from her grandmother's head and running her fingers over it. "You're amazing, Grandma. A true innovator in the kitchen and a mad hatter!"

"Well, here are your pancakes, dear. I'm off to the Governor's. Make yourself right at home."

Her grandmother was out in a flash, and Amelia hurried through her pancakes, drawn to the sitting room by the television she had rarely watched in over a decade. She spent the rest of the day watching soaps and game shows and digging through her grandmother's cupboards to snack on cookies, chips, and candy. She ended the afternoon with a sickening, yet mesmerizing, double dose of talk shows: reruns of Jerry Springer then Maury Povich. She realized how much American culture she had missed... "*Not*," like the teenage snot on Jerry Springer would say.

After an evening of reality shows and CSI, she went to bed drunk on fantastic dramas that blurred the line between the real and imagined and turned her own pain and longing into a distant memory. Or had it all been imagined?

Chapter 36

Amelia continued her binge throughout the next day, this time while her grandmother bustled around town for her hair appointment and then bridge with the gals. But on the third day, somewhere during reruns of *General Hospital*, her drunk wore off. She knew she could no longer escape what she needed to do.

"Grandma, are you going out again today?" she called from the den, setting down her third bowl of fruit loops.

"Yes, dear," her grandmother responded from the kitchen. "Later in the afternoon, I'm having dinner at the country club. But don't worry, dear, I'll cook you up something before I go. Do you like lasagna?"

"Please, Grandma, don't trouble yourself," Amelia replied, joining her grandmother in the kitchen. "I can cook too. But what I wanted to ask was if I could use your car today. There are a few places I need to go."

"Without a license, dear?" her grandmother asked disapprovingly.

"Don't worry. I've been driving since I was eleven. I'll be very careful, though, and I promise I'll get my license as soon as possible."

"Whatever you need, sweetheart," she acquiesced, scooping the keys out from her crocheted bag and depositing them in Amelia's hand.

Amelia parked the car and sat for a moment looking into the drizzle that spotted the windshield. How well she remembered fall in Minnesota. Although she was not afraid of getting wet or cold, she refused to move from her place behind the steering wheel. She sat there for an hour, the windows of her grandmother's Buick thick with steam. Finally, she opened the door.

The cold slap of drizzle upon her face awoke her from her stupor, and she began to meander through the rows of headstones that lead to theirs. She read the names and dates she passed as she unhurriedly and haphazardly made her way forward. She had been here twice before, once for their funeral and then a few months ago for her aunt's. Neither time had she really paid attention to where they lay. Today she would.

She could no longer escape the inevitability of her approach, for in front of her lay the family plot, the Kingston pillars standing high upon the hill, a symbol of the family's prominence in this community throughout the generations. She saw her great-grandmother and grandfather's markers side by side and the mound of tender grass that formed her aunt's grave. Two of her aunt's brothers lay next to her. One bore the marking "Jonathon Kingston, Oct. 7-Oct. 10, 1952." Amelia could hardly believe his lifetime of three days was worth the lifetime of pain for his parents. The other was for his younger brother who lived to be forty-five and died of a drug overdose, she remembered. Finally, she looked at her grandfather's grave: Jan. 8, 1915 – Nov. 12, 1975. He had died of heart failure before she was born. She saw the empty plot next to him and knew her grandmother would soon join him, where decomposing flesh meets the satin of one's eternal rest.

She stood transfixed, the Kingston family legacy of pain prostrate before her.

Not the entire legacy, she knew, for with the turn of her head she would see them as well. She had avoided them when she came to her aunt's funeral, but now she turned and mechanically walked forward. She saw their names on her second step. Her third brought her to her knees before them. And her grief brought her to her belly. She lay there sobbing, the drizzle cloaking her like the sheet of damp grass that covered them. They were together again, united in the cold, damp, disinterest of the natural world.

She willed herself into the earth where her mother held out her arms and her brother taunted her with silly faces. But she could not reach them, and they could not come to her.

"Oh God!" Amelia cried, arching her shoulders back and lifting her face upwards. "Why did you take them from me? Why? I hate you! Whoever you are! You unfeeling bastard!"

He paid back her insults with a steady drizzle, constant in its indifference. None of it made any difference to Him, whether they were living, breathing creatures or rotting, charred cadavers. They were nothing. And she was nothing without them.

"I loved them so much!" she sobbed. "Maybe you didn't, but I did. Why wasn't that enough to let them live?" She lowered her head to the ground. "You bastard!" she repeated, her mouth buried in the grass.

She kept her head embedded in the grass until she could not breathe, and even then, she stayed there, not wanting to need the next breath. She yearned to succumb to the earth that suffocated her, to let it take her in its grasp like it held her family. When she lifted herself to gasp for air, she sobbed for her weakness. Such a paradox to create a breathing creature who fights for survival within a system of inevitable, punitive death. As much as she wanted to, she could not defy this natural law.

She had no idea how long she had lain there, but when she tried to rise, she found that her legs were too cold and cramped to obey. She made it to her knees and knelt there rocking, deciding whether to topple or try again to stand.

"Let me help you," she heard someone say. Before she could turn her head to see the young man who spoke, he was squeezing her arm and helping her to her feet.

"You're shivering," he said. Amelia looked to her side to see a tall man in a black suit, his wet, reddish-blond hair smoothly plastered to his head.

"You've got mud on your face," he said, removing the white handkerchief from his breast pocket.

Suddenly Amelia laughed, lifting her face to look heavenward.

"Highly convenient, God!" she laughed.

Like the two other saviors she'd been sent, just another cosmic joke at her expense. Only this time she was not fooled.

"Thank you, but no," she told the handsome man, dismissing him and his handkerchief with an abrupt wave of her hand. "I'm better off with mud on my face."

With that she began her descent from the family plot. She called back over her shoulder, not to the perplexed young man returning to his nearby funeral party, though he did look back.

"See you later Mom, little brother!" and then she took a more direct path than on her arrival, returning to her grandmother's car.

Chapter 37

The following day, Amelia began her search for the truth in the likeliest of places, the internet, but since her grandmother refused to enter the era of technology, she made her way to the public library just down the block. Her love for the public library had begun at this particular library long before she ever heard of Marty Robbins. It had a new annex now and some modern metal sculptures in front, but she felt the same as she always had as she entered—alive.

After taking a moment to discover the few minute details that had not changed during the library's complete renovation, Amelia headed toward the computer area. It took a bit to convince one of the nearby patrons, a well-pierced teenage boy thumbing through a *Popular Mechanics* magazine, to borrow his library card number, but soon she was typing it in to access the internet. She pulled up the *Pioneer Press* website and began her search. After her visit to their graves the day before, she felt prepared for anything, and calmly with even a bit of anticipation, she fed the date into the search engine.

It was front-page news that day following the tragedy, and Amelia quickly focused in on the black and white image of the devastation. It was not as she remembered, obviously taken some time later when the smoke and dust had settled and the bodies had been removed. It showed heaps of dirt and ash and debris strewn about the lot, its center still smoldering. Staring into it on a computer monitor, Amelia felt detached, a witness to someone else's tragedy.

Two St. Paul residents were killed in a house explosion yesterday on the 1700 block of Bush Avenue. 41-year-old Tracy Kingston and her 5-year-old son Scott died instantly in the explosion. Emergency crews arrived at the scene just after 9:00 P.M. to find what remained of the home—a smoldering crater and mounds of ash and flaming debris. The remains of Tracy Kingston, her son Scott, and their family dog were found in the rubble.

"Although it will take some time to investigate the exact cause of the explosion, preliminary evidence suggests that the explosion was caused by a gas leak," the fire marshal reported.

Amelia plugged in the date for the following day. The next story contained much the same information with a few additional anecdotes from friends and neighbors and a brief biography of her mother and brother.

Tracy Kingston was a respected member of St. Paul's East Side community. She was a beloved third-grade teacher at Monroe Elementary and a District 5 city council member. In addition, she volunteered with Meals on Wheels and as a Heritage Theater board member. Born Tracy Milton, Tracy grew up in Madison, Wisconsin, receiving her teaching degree at the University of Madison and later marrying lifelong St. Paul resident Robert Kingston. Tracy and Robert were the parents of two children, Amelia Sue and Scott Milton.

Scott Milton Kingston, a well-liked kindergartner at Monroe Elementary was described by his teacher, Kelly Madison, as a "friendly, eager learner, who loved to be silly." He would have celebrated his 6th birthday on Saturday. Lois Halstrom, friend and colleague at Monroe Elementary, spoke sadly of the planned birthday event: "I believe she (Tracy) had invited some 25 kids, and there was going to be a clown. Now we're having a funeral instead."

Services for both Tracy and Scott Kingston will be held at the Sacred Heart Church, 320 East 7th Street. Expressions of sympathy and contributions can be made to: Friends of Tracy and Scott, c/o the Heritage Theater Company, 2100 White Bear Avenue, Maplewood, MN, 55109.

Even though Amelia knew she was reading about her mother and brother, she felt as detached as someone who had never known them. Nothing that she read seemed to capture who they really were. Her mother wasn't simply respected in her community, she was adored. The elderly she visited every Saturday on her Meals on Wheels rounds waited all week for her smiling face and kind words. Amelia had often gone with her mother and remembered most the sadness in their eyes when it was time to leave.

"But Mr. Larson will be starving to death if I don't get these pork chops to him ASAP. Don't worry. I'll try to come a little earlier next week so we can have some more time to chat." She used to jockey her schedule around so she could arrive early and stay late with someone new each week.

Amelia believed her mother had some political aspirations as well. She used to tell Amelia that politics needed another Paul Wellstone. She often wished aloud that she could one day have his strength and focus, that maybe then programs like Meals on Wheels would become obsolete.

Theater was her other love. Amelia suddenly remembered a conversation they had had on their way home from the Heritage production of *The Sound of Music*.

"It's almost too painful to watch," she said sorrowfully, "when all you can do is regret not being the one on stage. I don't want you to have those regrets, Amelia," she said, coaxing a loose strand of Amelia's hair back behind her ear. "You go for everything you want in life one hundred percent. Promise me?" Amelia had promised her earnestly, but how could she have known how difficult, or maybe impossible, it would be to keep that promise?

A couple words in Scott's biography did evoke some emotion. His teacher had been right; he loved to be silly. She remembered his repertoire of dances—each special dance reserved for just the right occasion. She remembered his "I'm right and Amelia's wrong" dance above all others. Combining his "happy dance" of Russian-like kicks with Conga-line arm movements, he would flaunt his superiority throughout the house. Amelia almost preferred to be wrong, just to see that goofball show.

She remembered, too, his cartoons. He wasn't a great child artist, but she loved the funny situations his Super Friends always got into, like Batman swallowing the Joker's laughing gas after eating the baked beans Jeeves had served him, the combination of gasses proving toxic not only to Batman but to the whole of Gotham City. Superheroes meet potty humor. Classic Scottie.

She continued to search under each subsequent date until she located what she was really looking for. The fire marshal had released the results of his investigation and determined that the explosion "was the result of a natural gas leak that we believe originated from the natural gas valve. When the Kingstons arrived home that evening, a spark, most likely caused by a flip of the light switch, appears to have ignited the gas, triggering the explosion."

Amelia was struck by the obvious negligence this suggested. Wouldn't the gas company have been at fault for the explosion? Couldn't they have sought damages that would have allowed them a lifestyle other than one of abject poverty in some third-world country? She was amazed she had never thought of that before.

She was even more amazed that her father, a newspaper journalist, would not have demanded a more thorough investigation. Why hadn't he filed a lawsuit? Why had he accepted this simple explanation for the deaths of his wife and son and not sought redress? Had he simply been too grieved to really care?

No wonder they wanted me to find the truth, Amelia thought. Their deaths had gone unchallenged, the negligent party unpunished. *And my pain*, she bemoaned, *unavenged*. She knew it was up to her to remedy the situation, to make the company accountable for its negligence. And how, she wondered, would she make her father accountable for his?

She hated him at that moment, so intensely that had he been immediately present she would have smashed his head against the computer monitor. Instead, she settled for the image of his bowed cowboy hat framed by airport security.

Chapter 38

Making her way from the computer area, she was suddenly stopped by her name being called. She turned to see an oversized librarian bursting from behind the information booth.

"Toby!" Amelia exclaimed, wrapping her arms as far around her favorite librarian as they could reach.

"I can't believe it's you, or at least what's left of you!" Toby cried, giving her the once over. "When did you get back?"

"Just…"

"Wait, wait. Let's do this right," Toby interrupted. "I'm going on break, Alice," she yelled behind her, perhaps unfamiliar with library etiquette. "Let's get some coffee," she commanded, dragging Amelia to the Dunn Brother's Café, another addition to the library.

Cappuccino was coffee Amelia could stomach, so she stumbled after Toby with little resistance.

"Okay, where were we?" Toby continued after ordering them both a double cappuccino and a chocolate-frosted brownie. "Oh yes. 'Just'…" she repeated, motioning with both hands for Amelia to continue.

Amelia laughed, nearly spraying the sip of cappuccino she was in the process of swallowing.

"I was going to say *just* a few days ago."

"And how much longer were you going to wait before coming to visit your Auntie Toby?"

"I had no idea you'd still be here," Amelia assured Toby, who wasn't really her aunt. "I thought you'd be at some think tank in Washington, D.C., by now!"

"Always the smart aleck," Toby admonished with a gentle pinch to Amelia's cheek. "Glad to see not much has changed. Guess not much has changed with me, either!" she said, spreading her arms out wide. "A few more diets under my belt. Tried that low-carb one for a few days. Found out brownies weren't on the menu and rushed to Byerly's to officially end it. Nothing like holding on to a bad diet in between binges and later bemoaning that it didn't work. I prefer admitting it isn't for me right up front rather than living with the guilt and remorse. Anyway, got me that promotion to manager of the 'oversize books' we always joked about. Really, I'm not kidding. I asked for it one day, and they wrote it up in my job description. Something about being around those big books makes me feel normal."

"You are normal, Auntie Toby," Amelia assured her with a pat of her hand.

"Well, looking at the contrast we make, one of us isn't. I guess if it's not me, then it must be you! Always thought it was freakish being skinny, but you've always been my favorite skinny person."

"That means a lot coming from someone who spends her days blaming skinny people for inventing chocolate and ice cream!" Amelia chuckled. Then turning serious for a moment whispered, "I really missed you, Toby."

"You too, sugar. And of course, your mom and Scottie too. Thought I'd never see any of you again. I'm glad I was wrong."

They smiled silently at one another for a moment until Toby shook her head in confusion and asked, "What's up with your father, anyway? He exiles you to some foreign country and a week later, the FBI shows up here demanding a printout of the materials he'd checked out. I didn't even know they could do that, but they told me a true librarian would have read Section 215 of the Patriot Act by then and been aware of the 'library clause.' They even gave me a website to look it up on. How kind. What was your father messing around with? Must have been pretty serious. Don't think the FBI was just checking to see if he'd read his 25 books."

Amelia could only gape at Toby, the images of her father at the airport and Bull's enormous face haloed by flames danced before her. Luckily, Toby was paying more attention to her brownie than to Amelia's face and continued with barely a pause.

"Hope all those Harry Potter books he checked out for Scottie didn't incriminate him too much! With all that 'devil-worship' stuff in them I'd be surprised if he's not in jail by now!" Toby laughed, unaware of the possible irony.

Amelia wasn't sure what to say. She could see her father being led away past terminal 24,23, 22—his head lowered, the two airport security guards towering above him on either side, each gripping an upper arm. There was nothing to say. She knew nothing about what had happened to him, if anything. But the FBI? What had her father been involved in?

Toby needed little feedback, as was her custom, and within minutes covered a half dozen other topics before becoming aware of the time. Emptying her last sip of cappuccino, she declared, "Break over. But I'm not letting you go until you promise you'll come back and see me soon. You promise?"

She gripped Amelia's hands in her large ones, unwilling to let them go until she agreed.

Chapter 39

Amelia awoke the next morning with obligation upon her brow in the form of sunlight that wormed its way through the gap in the pink brocade curtains. She turned her head away from it, but as she considered her other options—*lie here, indefinitely; watch reality TV, indefinitely; work on a crossword with Grandma, indefinitely*—she decided there were worse things to do than continue the journey she had begun.

As she ate the waffles her grandmother heaped before her with real maple syrup ("made by real Indians, or I guess Native Americans is the correct term these days") ladled generously atop, she listened to her grandmother's stories. Her tales of trips to the casino (where she got the maple syrup from "this beautiful woman with long black, braids, just like the picture books") and day-to-day happenings wove together the past and present so intricately, there was no reason to know which was which, or rather, when was when. Somehow within this comingling of tenses, Amelia made her way out the door with car keys in hand before realizing that this sunny day, in which she found herself, was the present.

As she made her way down the same streets she had negotiated a few days before, she felt again the trickery of time, but the change in weather and in her own state of animation assured her that she wasn't repeating the past. The sunshine and cool breeze welcomed her as she made her way through the maze of headstones towards the Kingston plot. By coincidence, she spotted some of the same headstones as the time before and decided one could make friends with the dead as well. At least they would always be there to welcome her upon each visit.

Unlike her last visit, she took little time in making her way up the hill and this time smiled as she saw their names etched before her.

"I'm back," she called to them, seating herself calmly between their headstones. She traced their names with her finger, feeling the subtle scratch of the fine edge upon her fingertips.

"Didn't expect to see me back so soon, did you? Don't be surprised if I make a habit of it. Little more convenient to visit now than before. I'm so happy to be back."

She could see their faces before her as if they sat leaning upon their headstones, ready for some bizarre graveside family picnic. Yet instead of being creepy, it was comforting to feel them there and have the power to imagine their faces so close to hers.

"I suppose you know I'm kind of sore with Dad, I guess. I see now why you wanted me to find the truth for you...and for Scottie. Someone needs to take responsibility for the accident. Don't you want that too? And Dad did nothing. I never realized how difficult it must have been to be married to him. I can kind of remember now some of the cruel times you went through. But I'm not here to slander him. I just hoped you could...I don't know what I hoped. Maybe I hoped you could help me forgive him for running away. For abandoning you. But I'm not going to abandon you ever again. I'm going to find out the truth. I'm not sure how, but I'm going to do it for you and Scottie. I miss you two."

She sat there for some time, staring into the etched names that held the wavy images of their faces. She needed answers, she knew, but for the moment she was content to sit, feeling the sun play upon her face and the damp grass work its juice into the fibers of her jeans. Then she let her mind drift to the newspaper entries she had read. She needed to find out who was responsible, but she had no idea what her next step should be. Suddenly, she smiled, as the image of an afro erupted over the already superimposed images of headstones and faces. "Of course," she mumbled, "Connie."

Her thoughts were interrupted as someone passed through her peripheral vision, his strawberry blond hair teasing the autumn sun as he made his way to the parking lot. A vague sense of recognition caused her to cock her head slightly to get a better look. His profile reminded her suddenly of her last visit and the handkerchief she had declined. *His* handkerchief. Seems he, too, had family picnics in the cemetery.

Her "picnic" finished, she stood up and with the front of her hand laid kisses upon each etched name. "I'll see you later, Mom, Scottie," and she left them to rest once again.

She saw his hair before she made it back through the winding trail of headstones. It was dancing in the sunlight above a tan face whose eyes squinted at her approaching figure.

"If I didn't know any better," he called, as she reached the road, "I'd say it was the sun itself that came to rest upon your shoulders. You're more radiant than the first time we met," he said grinning, apparently as aware of her hair as she of his.

"Ah yes, nothing like a good mud mask to bring out that inner glow," Amelia quipped, feeling both sheepish and a bit put off by his compliment, if that's what he intended it to be.

"Don't worry. I'm not going to hand you a hanky. Just thought I'd take the opportunity of this coincidence to introduce myself this time. I'm Jonathon Lundberg."

"AKA Prince Charming, ready to swoop up damsels in distress with his white hanky," replied Amelia, not yet ready to offer her hand.

"Okay, okay. If I had my handkerchief with me this time I'd surrender."

That won him a smile.

"Just not used to cemetery-style compliments, I guess," she confessed, offering her hand. "I'm Amelia Kingston."

"Nice to finally meet you," he said. "I was worried about you. I mean I didn't even know you, but I was worried. You were so distraught."

"Nice word, 'distraught.' Let me guess, you're a psychiatrist," she posed sarcastically.

"Close. A lawyer," he answered.

"That was going to be my next guess. And said with no apology, so either a pretentious one or one that actually serves. Which do you profess to be?"

"The latter, of course, though we lawyers are always presumed guilty before proven innocent." He paused for a moment running his fingers through his hair.

"At the risk of being forward..." he began.

"Oh, you already crossed that line," Amelia quipped.

"Well then, why stop now. How about you meet me for coffee tomorrow, and you can prosecute me further?"

"So, Attorney Lundberg, AKA Prince Charming, do you make a habit of picking up women in cemeteries?"

"When I get the chance, but pretty slim pickings on a normal day."

"And is this a normal day?" Amelia inquired, enjoying the light-hearted banter after the past few weeks of a heavy heart and troubled thoughts.

"Not even close. This is truly abnormal, and I'm hoping you'll make it even more abnormal with a 'yes.'"

"Now you found my weakness. Always one to applaud the abnormal. I have to say 'yes.'"

His crooked smile showed both his pleasure and his attempt to subdue it as he shook Amelia's hand again.

"12:00 tomorrow at Nel's Place on Selby?" he asked, not ready to drop her hand.

"You *do* do this often!" she laughed. "Yeah, noon sounds fine. But be ready to be thoroughly cross-examined."

"Looking forward to it," he said finally releasing her hand and walking back to his car.

Amelia watched through her rearview mirror as he drove away. Jonathon probably didn't realize he really was on trial, and his former charges under the aliases of Rigoberto and Donovan were sure to hurt his case. Life wasn't fair, not even to those on the other end. Somehow this realization gave Amelia great comfort.

Chapter 40

That afternoon, Amelia climbed the steep staircase she remembered so well. She felt the same exhilaration she always had as she took the steps up to her father's office. However, she realized she had always climbed back down disappointed. She hadn't been able to understand her feelings then, but she suddenly realized that each climb for her had been an attempt to reach him. The message she got each time, "Stay out of my way and I'll tolerate you," made each attempt a failure and each descent a disappointment. He had tolerated her, yes, but never noticed her. By the time they moved to Honduras, she had already internalized—though had not understood— this message and managed to be disappointed before she took even the first step of her climb home.

Today Amelia felt the exhilaration for another reason.

Back in Minnesota, she was here to find answers and was hopeful that a newspaper office was just the place to start. But the quiet that greeted her was just another reminder of how much of her life had been taken away. Where were the sounds of clicking keyboard keys, shuffling papers, and muffled voices aimed into telephone receivers that had always greeted her? Where was Connie's '60s Afro that always seemed to explode through the beveled glass from the opposite side of the door?

Once she had thought of Connie, she had immediately felt hope. Connie would know what to do. She always had. But instead of her blurred image through the window, Amelia was staring into a "For Rent" sign.

That evening, Amelia pondered her next step. Yes, this was a setback, but she wouldn't let it dishearten her. She realized more than ever she needed Connie's help. After looking through the phone book with no success and calling 411 with the same result, it occurred to her that her grandmother might know how to find her.

Looking up from *Vanity Fair's* interview with Jennifer Anniston, her grandmother nodded her head slowly.

"Of course, I remember Connie. She was so good to us after the funeral and even after your father took you to Honduras, she would stop by and see me. Seems like the newspaper went bankrupt after your father left. Connie couldn't keep up with it herself. But let me see, where would I have her information?"

She got up slowly from a too soft chair, the armrest giving her the leverage she needed to stand and move toward a desk cluttered with papers and letters.

"I'd guess her address will be on one of these cards I got when your Aunt Susan died. I know Connie sent me one..."

Chapter 41

Driving down Makubin Street, Amelia compared each house number she passed to the envelope she grasped in her hand: 1953...1955. She slowed down to a stop in front of a small, one-and-a-half-story, brick home, its ivy beginning to brown with the change of seasons. She knew it was probably too early, yet she wanted to make sure to catch Connie before she went to work.

It seemed forever before Amelia heard the jostling of the lock and chain, but in less time than it took Amelia to recognize Connie beneath her disheveled hair and housecoat, Connie had already snatched her up.

"Amelia!" she cried, squeezing her until her feet lifted slightly from the ground. "I can't believe it's you! You've grown so much!" she exclaimed, setting her down. "You're so beautiful! Look at you!" And with that she gave her another tight squeeze, this time shaking her back and forth.

"Well, you've gotten stronger, Connie," Amelia laughed as Connie released her from her rag-doll reception.

Connie laughed. "Oh, I'm just so happy and surprised to see you. Come in! Come in! You'll have to excuse the mess. I was up late last night working on an article and well, to be honest, I've never been much for housekeeping. But here, have a seat," she insisted, gathering up a load of newspapers and magazines from one chair and depositing them on top of a similar heap on another.

"How's your father?" she inquired, as she swiped up random papers and envelopes that lay scattered upon the table and snatched up the remaining coffee cups and glasses that were suddenly unearthed.

Amelia hesitated for a moment. "Well, I'm not quite sure how he is. But let's talk about that later. How's Ricky?"

Connie took a seat across from Amelia on the only other unoccupied chair, and they spent the next half hour talking about family, the lighter side of the past, and plans for the future until neither of them could deny the pink elephant any longer.

"How are you, Amelia, really?" Connie asked, concern written in the lines of her eyes and brow that had become noticeably deeper since they last saw each other.

"I'm getting better. It's been a long road, longer than you can probably imagine," she smiled, thinking of all the Honduran details Connie would never know. "But I'm making progress."

"I've thought about you and your dad so much these past years. Your father really knows how to choose the road less traveled. So, tell me why you're really here, even though I know you couldn't wait to just chew the fat with your dad's wannabe, Connie."

Amelia laughed at the old nickname. It always seemed a bit cruel in the past, but she had come to realize that her dad had chosen it from Connie's very own repertoire of self-ridicule, that once coined, made her recognize her low self-worth and rise above it. She doubted her father had planned such results.

"Well," Amelia finally said, "I did a little research on the explosion, and I was just surprised at how negligent the gas company seemed. It made me think that they should have been held responsible for the accident. Did you ever think that?"

Connie was caught off guard by the question at first, then responded, "Yeah, I suppose so. Didn't your father pursue a lawsuit or anything?"

"Not that I know of. In fact, I'm pretty sure he didn't. Do you think I should look into it?"

Connie began to nod her head slowly and then more vehemently as the idea took root.

"You're right. The company should have been held responsible at some level or other. I just assumed your father had settled out of court or something. I guess he didn't have time to follow up on it. But I agree with you," Connie continued with a few more deliberate nods. "You should look into it. Speaking of your father, is he back too? God, it's been such a long time."

"To be honest, I'm not one hundred percent sure where he is. I assume he's back in Honduras. I really haven't bothered to check in with him."

"Really…" Connie responded with measured curiosity.

"You know, Connie," Amelia began with a sigh, "sometimes I'm just so angry at him. How could he have just run away like that after the accident? He should have followed through and had the explosion thoroughly investigated. No one ever took responsibility for their deaths."

Amelia sighed, turning over her hands to remember their sparkles upon them.

"Funny he'd be more intent on finding out the truth about everything else in the world than about his own wife and son. I just can't stomach that he abandoned them."

"Maybe there's more to it than that, Amelia," Connie suggested, capturing Amelia's outstretched hands in her own. "Your father was a complex man."

"Is that PC for jerk?" Amelia rejoined. "He was a coward, so he took off and let the gas company off scot-free. My mom and brother deserved more than that. So, I guess it's up to me."

"And me," Connie added, patting her hand. "Angel, we're in this together. I'll see what I can figure out. You go home and get some rest. Looks like you could use some."

Chapter 42

Amelia didn't go home to rest, however. She had something more important to do. She risked a few moments of closed eyelids and neck rotations before returning her attention to the street she was navigating. She was determined to be fresh with denial and was banishing for the hundredth time any thought of her family when the Saab directly in front of Nel's generously gave up its parking spot. *How auspicious*, she thought, or rather hoped.

Jonathon was standing inside facing the door, paying little attention to the newspaper he held in his hand. He let out a crooked smile, as he saw her. She wondered how big his smile would get if he just let it be.

"Hello, Amelia. It's nice to see you again," he said, grabbing her hand and shaking it in both of his.

"Imagine us meeting again. So many coincidences," she kidded.

"What can I get you?" he asked pointing to the menu above the counter.

After ordering sandwiches and coffee, they found a seat by the window, the sun once more reveling in the tawny waves of Jonathon's hair. This time Jonathon seemed more intent on Amelia's eyes, as he stared into them for the first time. He flashed his crooked smile as he caught himself.

Without a blush he admitted, "You just catch me off guard, Amelia."

She, however, did blush and for once without a comeback, turned her head. The sandwiches arrived just in time to give her a legitimate excuse to look away.

"So, you know what I do," Jonathon began, "but what about you?"

She was surprised to discover she was completely unprepared for the question. She suddenly realized she had no inkling of her future career plans. Her life in Honduras had been day-to-day, and her life here was now a reality TV show of the investigative kind. The closest thing she had to creating a future for herself was putting an end to her past. How could she say all that?

"I didn't realize I asked the million-dollar question," Jonathon laughed. "Maybe you're a student?" he suggested.

"To be honest," she finally replied, "I've just recently got back to the States and haven't had much time to contemplate what I'm going to do."

"How old are you, anyway?" he asked a bit surprised at her answer.

"Twenty-one."

"You're younger than I thought," he replied even more surprised.

"It's that third-world lifestyle. Ages you beyond your years. I may as well be fifty! But at the same time, I've really just begun my life." She was staring off somewhere beyond the tips of his wispy hair, barely aware of her candor, when she suddenly felt one of his hands on hers.

"You have lived beyond your years," he responded softly. "Haven't you? Where were you?" he inquired earnestly.

His hand and words brought her eyes back to him and with it the realization of her vulnerability.

"You know," she said, using her sandwich as an excuse to withdraw her hand, "unless you have three hours off for lunch, we better save all that for another time. Suffice it to say, I've been in Honduras and recently escaped back here where I'm figuring out what to do next. Anyway," she added laughing, "you're supposed to be the one on trial here, remember?"

"Somehow I have a feeling your trial would be a lot more enlightening than mine," he mused, "but have it your way. I'm twenty-nine, a personal injury attorney at Lundberg and Son, and recently lost my mother to cancer."

"So, our mothers are neighbors," she replied. Then realizing her response sounded flippant quickly added, "I'm sorry for your loss."

"So am I, and for yours too. When did she pass?" he asked turning the tables once again.

"Over thirteen years ago, but I hadn't been back until last week." Amelia stopped there, aware she was heading back into dangerous territory. "What was your mother like?" she asked.

As she had hoped, he was more than eager to pick up the thread. Amelia actually enjoyed his eulogizing, seeing in his mother the things she had so loved in her own. The time passed quickly in this way, and Amelia was excited to see Jonathon check his watch before she ever had to answer another probing question. Except for one, but when he asked her if he could take her to dinner Friday night, she was quick to answer "yes." Amelia wasn't sure if the quickness of her response was due more to the fact that she had never been on a formal date or that she was interested in him. But when she found herself picturing him arriving for her, it was Donovan who stood at the door. She realized above all, she just wanted to forget.

Chapter 43

She hadn't planned on talking to Connie again that day, but the moment she walked through the door, her grandmother held out the phone.

"Connie's on the line," she smiled. "So good to talk to her after so many years. She's really a dear, that one."

"Thanks, Grandma," Amelia responded, grabbing the phone and stepping into the hallway for more privacy. "Hey Connie. Missed me already, huh?"

"Yeah, something like that," Connie snickered. "Actually, I'm calling 'cause I've got the obvious solution to our most recent dilemma."

"Oh yeah? What's that?"

"We hire an investigator."

"Oh yes, with the two thousand dollars I saved over the summer. Be realistic, Connie. I have no money and no job, and your freelancing doesn't actually rake in the dough."

"No really. It's quite simple. We hire a lawyer who requires a minimal retainer to represent you in a claim against the gas company. The law firm will pay for the investigation and will get paid a percentage of your settlement if you win."

"Is that how it works? It does sound easy," Amelia agreed. "Of course, there's the small thing about the retainer, and then the other small thing about finding a lawyer dumb enough to take a cold case." Then she smiled. Maybe dumb wasn't necessary when chivalry was still alive.

"Yes, I think we have a plan," Amelia concurred.

Chapter 44

Amelia decided to tell her grandmother about her plan to hire a lawyer. Her hope was that her grandmother would offer to loan her the retainer. She was unprepared for her grandmother's response.

"Why aren't you going to use the money your mother left you?" she asked.

"Excuse me?" Amelia said, unable to believe she had heard correctly.

"From her life insurance policy. Don't tell me you don't know anything about that!" She suddenly threw the hot pad she held in her hand upon the counter. Amelia had never seen her angry before. "I've made a lot of excuses for him in the past," she exclaimed, fists clenched, head lowered towards the counter, "but this is inexcusable." She lifted her face and looked over at Amelia. "As far as I'm concerned, your father is no longer a son of mine. Sit down. Let me tell you what he should have told you a long time ago."

They sat down at the table, her grandmother's pot roast and potatoes momentarily forgotten as they cooled on the stove.

"Your mother had a fifty-thousand-dollar life insurance policy divided equally between the three of you. Since your brother died as well, it was split between you and your father. A lawyer drew up accounts for both of you. Yours was available to you once you turned eighteen. I believe your father took his to Honduras."

Amelia couldn't believe what she was hearing. They had lived like peasants in Honduras. Sometimes worse than peasants. She had slaved for him until she was twenty-one, and here there had been a ticket to freedom awaiting her since she turned eighteen. Three years lost in that hellhole when she could have gone to college, or traveled abroad. Or gone to college abroad. The world would have been opened to her.

Instead she spent each day as much a beast of burden as her burro Destino had been. She was furious, but lacking a hot pad to throw, she sat there staring at the table, her fury fueling the nausea that began to bubble within.

"I have the lawyer's name here somewhere," her grandmother recalled, scrambling to her feet and making her way towards the den. "It'll take me a bit to find it. I've got a bit of a mess over here. Tomorrow you could go to see him and get this all straightened out. No wonder you were in no hurry to get your own place," she called back over her shoulder. "Here I thought you just liked my company when here you thought you hadn't a penny in the world. Don't feel you need to rush out of here, though," she added. "I have liked the company more than you can possibly know."

While her grandmother searched through the drawers and shoeboxes of papers on her desk, Amelia occupied her time with plans of revenge. She wouldn't waste one more second worrying about her father. She would collect her money and go to college anywhere in the world she wanted, and she would never lay eyes on him again.

It felt good, this fantasy, almost as good as the fantasies that woke her in the night yearning for Donovan. But like those fantasies, reality—and one's place in it—turned the sweet to bitter. She sat, still staring at the table, tasting the bitterness of knowing she needed to stay to pursue the truth that her father had not.

"Ah, ha!" she heard her grandmother cry from the den. "I can't believe I actually found it. Not the best filing system, but a shoebox marked 'tragedy' does the trick." She waddled out of the den, a business card extended from her hand. "This'll give you something to do tomorrow. But right now, let's get you fed. No sense coming into money on an empty stomach."

Amelia heeded her grandmother's wise advice and for the first time, as she savored the tender roast and potatoes, she became excited about the money. She had thought she had no future, yet here, in the midst of discovering her past, she had uncovered a wide-open future. She remembered those glimmers she had held in each palm and suddenly wondered what they actually meant about finding the truth. She had assumed they meant finding out more about the tragedy and about her father, but maybe it was as simple as finding this money. She truly wished that were the case, yet she knew she had gone too far to turn back now, despite the complications and her anger and bitterness. She would search on, twenty-five thousand dollars better equipped.

Chapter 45

She met with the lawyer the next day, and he confirmed everything her grandmother had said. In fact, the news was even somewhat better. In spite of the fact that he had collected his fees out of the original twenty-five thousand dollars, it had been invested and was now a portfolio worth thirty-five. He admitted to her that he had been surprised to see her eighteenth birthday come and go but decided she had simply been patient enough to wait until she really needed it. She didn't tell him the truth, but she did suggest that he must have been just as surprised that her father hadn't touched his account, either.

"No, he withdrew it all as soon as it was available, along with the home insurance claim I handled. I suggested he invest it, but he said he needed the cash. It's not my job to argue, so I got it for him."

Amelia could not fathom what he could have done with the money. She was sure none of it had made it to Honduras. That twenty-five thousand along with an insurance settlement would have left him with sufficient start-up funds in the U.S., let alone in a third-world country where the dollar would stretch ten or twentyfold.

She decided to concentrate for the time being on her money and told her lawyer that she was content with a few thousand dollars for now and would keep the rest of the portfolio intact. He said he would be delighted to help her, sending her away with a polite handshake, the details of her portfolio, and a five-thousand-dollar check.

As she left his office, she remembered suddenly the date she was to have that evening with Jonathon. She realized that a pair of ratty jeans would never be acceptable, but in the afterglow of dollar signs, she gave herself little time for concern. She simply went shopping.

Chapter 46

Several hours later, she was waiting at her grandmother's door in an outfit that cost her more than four months' wages in Honduras. She hadn't flinched as she paid—okay, she had, but it took her little trouble to justify it upon remembering the years stolen from her. She had painted her finger and toenails to match the pink of the negligee-style top that hung to her hips from beneath the black, loose-knit sweater that tied across her slender waist. Her shiny black pants began at the hem of her camisole and ended at her pink toenails that peeked from beneath the rhinestone circle of her peekaboo pumps. Catching a glimpse of herself in the darkened windowpane, she realized looking *that* good was worth four months' wages, regardless of where the money came from. She smiled feeling a twinge of excitement, knowing that Jonathon would be impressed. Her smile was short-lived as she realized Donovan would have been amazed.

She saw his headlights stop below the front steps before she had the chance to ruminate further. No need to have him up for introductions since her grandmother was already at a cocktail party, so Amelia made her way out the front door. Her grandmother would have been thrilled to meet him she knew, and for a moment, Amelia almost felt it was up to her to make her grandmother proud. After all, her own children had left her disappointed. No lawyers or doctors among them, not even by marriage, but here she was, her lawyer looking up at her as she descended the front steps, cutting another of her mental ramblings short.

"Wow," he exclaimed, giving her the once-over as politely as he could. "You look stunning."

Amelia couldn't tell what he looked like under the double-breasted wool jacket he wore but assumed he couldn't look much better than he already did. His coat and the northern breeze suddenly made her realize she should have spent another month's wages on a fall jacket. But as Jonathon took her arm and led her to the car, the warmth of his hand through the mesh of her sweater assured her she wouldn't be needing it, not for that evening at least.

La Belle Vie was a posh downtown Minneapolis restaurant and even after splurging on her outfit, she felt underdressed. Jonathon demonstrated his good breeding by pulling out her chair and gently pushing it back in once she was seated. Amelia tried to picture Donovan in this setting and realized with a smile how out of context he would be. That realization, however, brought home to her how out of context she was as well. Suddenly she felt like an imposter. Who did she think she was? So, she had a portfolio worth thirty-five thousand dollars—pocket change to these people—and an outfit worth two hundred, probably the price of the underwear the lady at the next table was wearing. How much more comfortable she had felt in the grungy shorts and T-shirt she was stuck in for three days on the reservation. How much more at home looking into Donovan's black eyes than into Jonathon's blue ones, which she now found staring at her.

He had removed his jacket, and Amelia was struck by how amazing he looked. He had forgone the tie, and instead the top two buttons lay open, revealing the beginnings of his prominent chest that pushed at the buttons of the blue and white striped shirt he wore beneath a blue pinstriped vest. Amelia remembered suddenly that she had been as overwhelmed by the whole of Donovan as she now was by Jonathon's looks alone, and as unaware as she had been of Donovan's good looks, she now was of whom Jonathon really was. The magazine cover was so flawless that Amelia wasn't sure it was worth opening at all. Not only in her opinion, she felt, but in Jonathon's as well.

She caught his crooked grin and knew she had been caught admiring him. In spite of her blushing, she managed to remain coy.

"I've never dated a GQ cover boy before," she grinned. "I'm a bit taken aback, not to mention by all this as well," she added, spreading her arms wide.

"I hope that means you like it," he replied, fighting the grin that threatened to spill across his whole face.

"It's perfect," she responded in all sincerity, "but coming from four months on the trail, not to mention the thirteen years spent in a shack in a third-world country, it's a bit overwhelming, to say the least."

He was about to respond when the waiter arrived to take their drink order. Jonathon ordered a bottle of wine.

"I hope you like wine," Jonathon said. "Pinot Grigio has a subtle sweetness, a hint of fruit and not too dry. I think you'll like it."

"That will be fine," she replied, remembering how she had enjoyed her first glass of wine with Pamela.

The waiter returned with their wine, and after he poured it, Jonathon swirled and tasted it and waited for Amelia's opinion.

She passed on the swirling and went straight to the sipping. "It's very nice," she decided. "I have the feeling I can trust your taste in about anything," she added smiling.

"Then let me recommend the salmon, if you like fish. It's delectable. If you prefer beef, their filet mignon is exquisite."

"The salmon it is then," she informed the waiter, appreciating the help with a menu she could barely follow. "I ate so much steak this summer that my heart might go at any second. Better to be safe with the salmon."

After he ordered the salmon as well, Jonathon returned the conversation to its beginning.

"Don't think that I've forgotten your intriguing conversational lead in," he admonished. "Just not sure which to ask about first, the trail or the shack. Heads shack, tails trail," he said flipping an imaginary coin.

"Tails, it is," Amelia quickly responded. She didn't feel quite ready to tackle the shack. She found it quite enjoyable, however, reminiscing about her summer at the ranch. They were both so thoroughly engaged that they had barely touched their salads by the time the main course of salmon arrived.

"What amazes me," Jonathon admitted between bites of salmon, "is how courageous you were to go out there in the first place, without any money and any idea that they'd even hire you. I've never done anything like that in my life."

"Actually, I'm more afraid right now in this restaurant than I was during the entire summer!" Amelia confessed, laughing.

"Now that I don't believe. You're a natural it would appear in any setting."

"Anyway, you're the courageous one. First, I can't imagine even completing a law degree, but then to have to represent someone in court, well that's brave."

"Not when you've been raised a lawyer, by a lawyer. I never knew anything else and never even considered that there was another choice. In many ways, I took the easiest route." It was the first moment of introspection she had seen in his eyes, and it made his already handsome face even more appealing. Or maybe it was that second glass of wine.

"I guess easy versus hard, courageous versus safe are all relative," she suggested.

Jonathon liked her suggestion so much that he placed his hand over hers, lightly caressing her fingers as he did so. It wasn't the supercharged electricity she had felt with Donovan, but Amelia couldn't deny the tingle that rushed up her arm and heightened the warmth in her already wine-warmed cheeks.

"Tell me about Central America. Honduras, did you say? I want to know all about you." He insisted, his blue eyes boring into hers.

Maybe it was the wine, or his hand, or his eyes, but suddenly Amelia wanted him to know her too. She began with a vague reference to the accident and filled him in on some of the desolation and isolation of her life in Honduras. He was even more shocked than before.

"I had no idea that people really live like that. I mean… I guess I did, seeing it on the news and all, but to really hear it from someone who's experienced it firsthand is amazing. How did you survive?"

"You just do, by taking one gulp of air in and letting another out, putting one foot forward and then the other after. Eventually you're someplace where you can look back and see you've made progress. I'm just glad to be looking way back."

"I'm glad you are too," he replied, rubbing her hand magically once again. "If I promise to be a good boy, could we go someplace more comfortable?" he asked.

"Do you mean your place?" Amelia asked, not yet sure of dating code.

"Well, yeah, but we could go to a café or something too, if you'd be more comfortable."

"I think a café would be great," she replied, relieved. She knew he was too charming and her wounds too fresh. Neither of them could be trusted.

Chapter 47

The tingles Jonathon had given her at the restaurant were only a preview to those she now felt as she sat next to him on the café's leather sofa. Their coffee lay untouched on the coffee table while his hands encircled hers. She had turned the conversation back to him and listened as he described a comfortable, albeit lonely, childhood as an only child. His mother had been unable to carry another baby to full-term, so Jonathon had lost several siblings to miscarriages. Jonathon's story made Amelia understand for the first time that despite her brother's death, she was lucky to have had him at all.

Moved by Jonathon's candor and the clarity it had given her, she responded with her own, and within minutes told him of the tragedy that had ripped her family away from her thirteen years ago. When she finished, she remembered the plan she and Connie had and decided to plunge ahead with it.

"I want to file a personal injury suit against the natural gas company, and I was wondering if your firm could take my case."

She could see immediately that she had made a mistake as she felt his hand and the thigh that had rested against hers move away.

"I'm sorry," she responded instinctively, reaching back for the hand he had withdrawn. "Please don't think this date has anything to do with my request. I just couldn't keep myself from asking. Just forget I ever asked." She wasn't entirely dishonest, for she really had planned to ask him, she just hadn't counted on the strength of their connection making the request so awkward.

"Don't apologize, Amelia," he replied, allowing his hand to be drawn back into hers. "I was surprised, that's all, and I can't deny that for a moment this date seemed like a convenient excuse for asking. But I believe you, and no offense taken."

Amelia didn't know what to say next. She wanted an answer to her question but at the same time wanted to recuperate the connection she had so suddenly lost.

"Listen, Amelia," Jonathon said, solving her dilemma for her. "Why don't you meet with my father and me tomorrow, and we can talk about it then. I can't really make a decision without him anyway. In the meantime, I want to say how sorry I am about what happened to your family, and I hope I can help you get the closure you're looking for."

She felt like an ass. If the sofa could swallow her, she'd feed herself to it in a second. She had a lot of making up to do.

"I'm so sorry to wreck this beautiful night," she apologized, removing her hands from his to cup them around his face. "Please forgive me," she added lifting her face up to touch her lips to his.

His response was immediate and forgiving, and the warmth of his lips as they welcomed hers weakened her knees as she uncrossed them to invite his hand upon her thigh. Amelia was both thankful and regretful of the public arena.

As for Jonathon, who broke their kiss to huskily scold, "It's time to get you home now," she was pretty sure he felt only the latter.

Chapter 48

She awoke the next morning with the memory of the dueling fantasies that had put her to sleep: in this corner, the exotic and raw Indian brave with his death-defying courage and carnal instinct; and in this corner, the exquisitely manicured attorney-at-law with his charming allure and social grace! It was an unfair fight, for as they carried her off to sleep, Jonathon all but disappeared, leaving Donovan's face, smell, and body entangled with hers. But this morning, her stomach was in no mood to abide her fantasies. And as she heaved her dinner into the toilet, she felt the irony of a kingly dinner being rejected by a peasant's stomach. Maybe next time she'd have the filet mignon.

Despite the fact that it was Saturday, Jonathon and his father would be at the office as was their custom. Jonathon assured her that they would be delighted to hear about her case and asked her to be there at 10:00 a.m. It was already 9:00 when Amelia realized she had nothing appropriate to wear, so she changed for the meeting in the Target dressing room, displaying the tags in her hand for the cashier to scan on her way out of the store. Though she made it to the building by 10:00 a.m., it was five minutes later by the time she got to their suite.

"Please excuse my lateness," she apologized, offering her hand to Jonathon and his father as she entered their office, "I'm still on Honduran time."

"No need to apologize, young lady. We're here to serve you on any time," Jonathon's father assured her, introducing himself as Jonathon Senior. He wasn't as startlingly good looking as Jonathon, but what he lacked there he made up for in charisma and confidence.

"So, let's get down to business," Jonathon Sr. said, after Amelia politely declined the coffee he offered. "Johnny says you'd like us to take a case for you. Why not tell us all about it."

It took a bit of weaving and backtracking to tell the tangled story, but when she finally finished, they were satisfied they had heard enough.

"That's unbelievably tragic," Jonathon Sr. consoled. "I am so deeply sorry for your loss. As you may know, my son and I have suffered a loss, ourselves, recently so I can assure you I can understand how you must feel. Here's what we can do for you. We'd need a three-thousand-dollar retainer to get started. Because you just recently discovered the company negligence, the 'discovery rule' should supersede the statute of limitations. However, until we get a preliminary look at the evidence, I can't commit to taking your case. I'll tell you what we'll do. We'll take a look at the evidence, and if we decide we don't have a case, we'll refund you any of the retainer that wasn't used to cover our expenses."

If Jonathon hadn't been sitting next to him, Amelia would have felt sure she was being swindled by some charming, smooth-talking, charismatic salesman passing himself off as a lawyer. But when she looked over at Jonathon, he assured her with his smile that she was among friends.

"That sounds just fine," she consented.

"Johnny, get her the paperwork for the retainer. We'll need all that filled out," he explained as Jonathon handed her a folder, "and the retainer before we can get started."

"I'll have it to you on Monday," she promised.

Chapter 49

Monday took its time arriving, but at least that gave Amelia some time to catch up with her grandmother.

"What have you been up to, dear?" her grandmother asked. "Besides not getting your driver's license," she added admonishingly.

Amelia winced sheepishly.

"I know. I know. I didn't use one in Honduras, so I just keep forgetting that I need one here. I'll take my permit test next week. Promise."

Then she filled her grandmother in on her encounter with Toby and her visits with Connie, without the details of course. To make up for procrastinating on getting her driver's license, she capped off her account by sharing her date with Jonathon.

"We had a really great time. He's a lawyer." She knew that would get her grandmother's attention.

"How grand! I always told my daughters to marry a lawyer or a doctor, or even an engineer. 'Deadbeat' was never anywhere on the list but somehow, they each found one. Look where that got them. Not that I can really blame Susan's death on that Deadbeat Dennis, but might as well, since he made her life a living hell in every other respect. I think about that now, and it actually gives me comfort to know she's away from him. Good-for-nothing. So, a lawyer," she repeated back on track. "How nice. You have a good time with him, dear, and don't let him get away!"

"I was thinking about getting to know him first, Grandma. You know, see what kind of person he is before hauling him to the altar."

"Well, if you ask me, anyone who has enough intelligence and motivation to make it through law school and pass the bar is a good enough person to marry. You'll always be well provided for and respected in your community."

"Maybe, Grandma. But women are a bit pickier these days. We expect passion, love, and mutual understanding."

"Maybe so, but when all that fluff blows off in the wind, the providing part is the one thing you can rely on. That's the backbone of a lasting relationship."

"You win, Grandma!" Amelia laughed, picturing passion, mutual respect and love all fluttering off on the breeze like so many feathers from a ruptured pillow. Suddenly remembering another feather pillow, she realized maybe her grandmother was right.

Chapter 50

As Amelia rode the elevator to the offices of Lundberg and Son, she began to contemplate what this lawsuit would mean for her. She already had some start-up capital, so although the money would be nice, it really didn't matter much. Of course, she hoped that she would feel some closure knowing that someone had paid for the accident in the moral sense, and that it hadn't just gotten swept under the rug, or into a landfill, in the literal sense. More than anything, however, she hoped to fulfill her promise to her mother and brother, and that the act of fulfilling it would allow her to move forward with her life. When the elevator door opened to reveal Jonathon before her, she realized another benefit: she would have plenty of time to get to know *him* better.

"I...I've got the paperwork and the retainer for you," Amelia stammered, breaking the giddy pause as they grinned at each other. Jonathon took the folder she handed him without breaking her gaze.

"Follow me into my office," he said motioning her forward, "I've got something to share with you, as well."

"First," he said, closing the door and drawing her to him, "I need an appropriate hello."

It took little for her to recall the sweetness of their shared kisses, and even without the wine, she felt her face, and other areas of her body, flush.

"Much better," he said, pulling out her chair and motioning for her to be seated.

"Are you always so welcoming with your clients, Attorney Lundberg?" Amelia chided as Jonathon took his seat across the desk from her.

"Of course," he confessed. "It's what distinguishes us from the competition."

Amelia felt like pouncing across the desk to lap away his lopsided grin with playful kisses, and may have succeeded in doing just that had Jonathon not resumed the conversation so quickly and so professionally.

"Well, Amelia, I had a chance to look into some of the evidence from the explosion. I know I was supposed to wait," he said, responding to her expression of surprise, "but I was just too impatient. I looked up the report and was discouraged to see that it pointed to a loose valve and not a faulty one. I'm sure your family hadn't messed with the valve, but we'll need another witness to support that. Would your father be able to testify?"

Amelia looked at him. Why hadn't it occurred to her that she might need her father for this? He was the reason she was here in the first place, having shirked his duty so many years ago. And now she was going to need him?

"Is that necessary?" she finally asked, before adding, "I'd like to leave him out of it if at all possible."

"Well, this is going to be an uphill battle, Amelia. We can use all the help we can get. I guess we can go ahead without him if we have to, but I really don't recommend it. His testimony would definitely help your suit."

Amelia sighed.

"The truth is that he's not here...not in Minnesota," she responded.

"Oh. He's in Honduras, then? Yes, that makes it trickier, doesn't it?" Jonathon mused.

Amelia didn't bother to correct him, or rather, didn't know whether or not he needed correcting, so she kept mute as he considered their options.

"We could depose him," he said. "We could set up a deposition with an attorney in Honduras, and they could forward it to us. It's a little complex, legally, doing this across borders, but I think we can work through the legal complexities. Could you get your father to set it up?"

Amelia knew that even if her father were at all inclined to pursue a lawsuit (which she doubted since he never had), and even if there weren't a question about whether or not he actually was in Honduras (which she hoped was the case but had no verification of), that it would still take painstaking effort and patience to coordinate a deposition with the

Honduran legal system. But if that was what was needed to make this work, she would make it happen.

"I'll call and get things rolling," she finally assented with more confidence than she felt.

"Excellent! While you move ahead with that, I'll look deeper into your case. You free for lunch?"

"Absolutely!" she exclaimed. "But this time it's my choice. You should ditch the suitcoat and tie," she advised. "You won't need it where we're going."

"Now you have me worried," he kidded, proceeding to do what she had requested, and as he removed his suitcoat and undid the few buttons that secured his tie, Amelia couldn't help but wish he would continue down the row, releasing one button at a time until they all parted to reveal the breathtaking view she knew they concealed. When she looked up from his buttons, she saw that he was watching her. As a blush rose to her cheeks, she noticed a similar color climb to his. *His*, she realized was rooted in a different cause. She marveled at how such subtle differences in hue could communicate so much between a man and a woman.

Chapter 51

That evening, after a hot bath and while her grandmother chatted over drinks at her country club, Amelia dialed the telephone. She had put off contacting her father ever since she returned from her lunch with Jonathon. Instead, she had daydreamed about Jonathon, going over the details of their date, relishing the memory of the fun they had had.

She had taken him to El Burrito Mercado in the West Side neighborhood of St. Paul. Its yellow stucco façade set within a neighborhood that hosted brightly painted murals celebrating Latina culture was a welcome beacon to anyone tired of America's take on Latino fare. Inside, as its façade promised, colorful Mexican *artesania* and décor bedecked its walls and invited patrons towards grocery aisles and a deli-style restaurant. *Banda* music pulsed through the air, and patrons— nearly equal parts Latinos and non-Latinos—flooded the aisles shopping for food, lined the restaurant counter ordering or awaiting their orders, or sat within the seating corral partaking of a variety of authentic Latina *cocina*, cuisine.

Amelia's family had often gone there in the past both to get Mexican groceries and to eat together. It made sense that her father would want to run away to Latin America to recapture some of the flavor they had all enjoyed. He probably hadn't figured on Honduran food being a distant cousin twice removed of other more flavorful Latina cuisine. It was another irony Amelia had endured, longing for the Latina cuisine of her Minnesota home as she resided in an actual Latin American country. Loni had tried her hand at a few Mexican dishes along the trail, but this would be the first time in thirteen years that Amelia would again indulge in the rich textures, colors, and spices of the authentic *cocina* of Mexico.

Amelia was not disappointed as she savored her *tacos de carnitas*, pulled-pork tacos. They were every bit as delicious as she remembered them. Though somewhat poignant, remembering her family here sharing similar moments together, she couldn't help but delight in the convivial atmosphere and in her present company.

There were not only memories here, she realized, but new things for her to learn as well, for example, that a face could flush yet another hue of red for a very different reason. While Jonathon learned this the hard way, biting into his *chile relleno*, Amelia learned it vicariously, as an entertained observer. Laughing, she had handed him his *agua de horchata*, rice water, which he proceeded to down in two or three gulps.

"They're not even hot!" Amelia had insisted through her laughter.

"The hell they're noth," he had protested, pronouncing 'not' with a 'th' as he held an ice cube to his tongue.

"Miscalculation, then," Amelia apologized. "Here, let me get you something more 'Swedish,'" she had offered and went up to the counter to order something different before he could protest.

"These aren't Swedish meatballs," he had surmised, as she handed him the tortilla soup.

"Appears that the *chiles* didn't wipe out your power of deduction," she had quipped. "But this is mild. I promise."

He had looked at her and then back at the soup.

"Fool me twice, shame on me," he had announced, scooping up a spoonful and emptying it into his mouth.

"Mmmmm," he had admitted. "*This* I can eat."

All too soon it had ended. But she knew that like so many other things, good and bad, this, too, wasn't really over. They would relive it in their shared conversations and memories, with fondness, or, she had to concede, regret. There was no way to know which direction it would lead.

What she did know at this moment, as she held the phone in her hand, was that she felt no fondness for the memories that she now faced, nor for the task that lay before her. But like so many times before, she just took the step.

A female voice answered on the other end, "*Buenos tardes, Radio Libertad Centroamericano.*" Good afternoon, Central American Liberty Radio.

"*Buenos tardes, señora*. My name is Amelia Kingston, and I would like to contact my father Robert Kingston. Do you know where I can find him?"

Amelia listened to the woman on the other line, each moment her face growing paler, until she could barely hear the words over the pounding in her eardrums.

"*Gracias, señora*," Amelia said as she finally set the phone down. She gazed out the window, its darkness reflecting a haphazard collection of trinkets, crafts, and pictures framing her in a picture of her own, a ghostly face peering into the blackness beyond.

Chapter 52

The Minnesota landscape was gradually falling from view, the auburn and golden hues of fall muting into blotches of color bordering bisque squares of harvested fields. As the vaporous clouds outside her airplane window slowly engulfed the panorama below, Amelia felt her lungs constrict with each inch obscured by clouds, until the blanket of white stopped her breathing all together.

She was leaving behind her true home once again, and though this time her feet could reach the airplane floor, she felt as if she were eight again. The same fear and despair that gripped her then, gripped her now. But this time, her father was not beside her. Rather, a middle-aged hefty man who was already asleep with a soft, lazy snore. This time, she was not being taken against her will. *She* had made the choice—sure the only real choice she had—but a choice all the same. And *this* time, she would come back. She gripped the return ticket in her hand more tightly than ever to ensure that it was real. Finally assured that it was, she took a breath.

She'd be in Honduras in six hours. Her body was already leaden with dread. How heavy would she feel by the time she touched down in that godforsaken place? She imagined being unable to lift her feet as if the mafia had cemented them beneath her. She found the image reassuring. She'd be stuck on the plane and would have to use her return ticket without ever touching Honduran soil. If only the Godfather were alive and well.

The first time she had flown to Honduras, her father had filled her head with lush visions of banana and pineapple plantations, palm trees, and ferns taller than trees. A tropical paradise. He spoke to her of white sandy beaches and of the ocean expanding in either direction as far as the eye could see—then even further than the imagination could go. The tropical birds with their trilled melodies stopped you in your tracks, overcoming you with their beauty, and their plumage made you blush, sure that anything so breathtaking must be indecent.

It had taken some of the fear away then, but this time Amelia knew better. She knew that when the plane landed, she'd be stepping onto a rutted tarmac, the dust from nearby gravel streets combining with the intense heat and humidity to violently assail your eyes, nose, and lungs. She knew that as soon as she stepped out of the airport's glass doors, she'd be greeted by the outstretched hands of decrepit old women holding bloated babies with snot-filled faces and by the raised arms of old men's torsos that scooted along legless on makeshift, four-wheeled dollies.

She knew this because it was so, and it had become more and more so during the thirteen years she had lived there. Torn apart by a military *coup d'état*, the Honduran poor and unemployed had grown in leaps and bounds. So too had the crime, rising to become the "murder capital" of the world. Many of these murders were politically motivated, but an equal number were the handiwork of youth gangs and drug cartels that had sprouted up all over Honduras as the economy was ravaged by nature and foreign interests. She had lived there long enough to see the country rot from the inside out and from the "outside" in.

Landing in San Pedro Sula, Honduras, thirteen years ago, she had been struck first by the heat and dirt and then by the abject poverty as they walked from the airport to the taxi. She remembered the dirty children in raggedy clothing swarming them begging for *lempiras*, Honduran currency. She had seen a pack of mangy dogs trot down the street, skin against bones, hairless patches from snouts to tails. She had looked past all of that, yearning for a bearable first impression.

"Daddy, where are the birds?" she had asked looking up at her father hopefully. "I want to hear them sing."

Her father had answered, "Out there, Amelia. Outside the city. We'll see them soon."

It wasn't to be, however, at least not for the first three years, for they never left the city limits of San Pedro Sula. Amelia clung to images of the ocean, the vegetation, and the birds her father had painted for her, but even when they moved to the mountains, only the image of the vegetation became a reality.

They had lived in a filthy hotel for the first three months as her father looked for a job. He finally found one teaching English at a high school. It wasn't enough money to live a life void of poverty, but it did allow them to move into a cleaner home.

Amelia was enrolled in the local elementary school. She knew no Spanish, yet gradually, over the course of that first year, she became fluent enough to keep up in school and make a number of friends. She had suffered, but wrapped in a cocoon of numbness since the tragedy, her life those first few years were but a series of pinpricks, fate's Voodoo doll.

"Something to drink?" The flight attendant and her beverage cart slowly came into focus as Amelia zoomed out from her past and into her present. The hefty man stopped his soft wheeze of sleep just long enough to order a Coke.

"Sprite," Amelia answered. The crunch of the metal scoop on ice was familiar. Don Ronaldo vended icies up and down the street near their home. Hunkered over his cart, he'd push it from dusk to dawn crying, "*¡Hielo! ¡Hielo!*" Icies! Icies! Kids would rush up to him and drop lempiras into his gnarled, arthritic hand, salivating as he scooped the ice and pumped the cherry syrup over the top. Her father had never once bought her one. Instead every once in a while, a friend would. She remembered how the ice melted on her hot tongue, leaving the cherry sweetness behind to be savored before the next bite.

"Huh?" Amelia found herself saying.

"Your Sprite, dear," the flight attendant answered with some annoyance.

Yes, there is a thin line between the past and the present. How I long to dig a ravine! thought Amelia.

Chapter 53

Amelia knew that digging a ravine would be impossible when she spent so much time crossing back and forth. She comforted herself by promising that this would be the last trip she would ever take to Honduras. She would wrap up this chapter and never open it again. She sighed. She remembered promising herself that before, yet here she was just two hours away from touchdown.

She had considered not going. But when it came right down to it, she felt more than just obligation. It wasn't love, probably not even caring, but perhaps pity? Yes, that's what it was. Pity.

And retribution. *That* she couldn't deny. From the moment she met her stepmother, Amelia had been her mark, from mocking her Spanish to scoffing her tortilla making. Amelia fought back in her own subtle way, purposely speaking Spanish at home with a deep American accent and forming tortillas that were so lumpy and uneven that finally her stepmother had removed her from that duty. These were victories to be savored, especially seeing the mixture of indignation and resignation on her stepmother's face. But these victories were few and far between, and the victories on the other side were brutal with devastating consequences.

After Rigoberto, Amelia's life had become unbearable. Not only was she dealing with the shame of her naïveté in knowing what Rigoberto had been doing and being too shocked to try to stop it, but also, she had to deal with her stepmother's brutal reprisals—from standing naked while her stepmother scrubbed her down from head to toe with scalding water to spending a mandatory hour each day after school kneeling on the stone floor of the Catholic church praying for forgiveness. It only took Amelia a couple of days to realize there was something more urgent to pray for: escape. One hour each day, her knees against the damp stone suddenly served a purpose. *Her* purpose.

After two weeks of this ritual, she realized her prayers were being heard.

"Amelia," Sister Rebeca called as Amelia made her way to her usual pew. "Prayer is not the only way to redemption," she counseled. "Good deeds are as well. I can't help but feel your time would be better served by serving others. I imagine it's pretty tiring all this praying day in and day out. Are you interested in an alternative?"

Amelia was more than happy to hear of any option available that did not involve her boney knees on cold stone, so she eagerly nodded her head.

"You speak English, correct?" the Sister asked. "How would you like to offer an English class every day to the people in the community? I will make sure you have students, a place to hold the class, as well as a blackboard and some paper and pencils. You come each day and teach them what you know. You can even put out a box for donations, if you want. If someone has an extra *lempira* or two, that can help pay for your time. What do you say?"

Amelia had nothing to say. Instead a steady stream of tears began to roll down her face, increasing in volume with each nod of her head until Sister Rebeca gathered her up in a warm embrace.

"Very well then. That's settled. I'll see you here tomorrow to get started."

True to her word, Sister Rebeca had a group of twenty students the next day, ranging in ages from five to Don Jesus, who at seventy-nine had taken time off from working in the coffee fields to recuperate from an injured leg.

They met in a small room off to the side of the sanctuary. The room was stuffy, but between the stone walls that kept out most of the heat and the open window that let in a small breeze, it was tolerable for an hour-long class. There was also a small blackboard propped up on a chair against the wall. It was obvious to Amelia from the cobwebs affixed to its corners that it hadn't been used in some time. Finally, there was a stack of paper and a box of pencils sitting on the table in the middle of the room.

The table was small and considering there were only four chairs, it was soon pushed to the side of the room, the four chairs stacked on top. Twenty students sat cross-legged around the room, except for Don Jesus whose bad leg jutted out in front of him, dangerously close to the squirming five-year-old. Amelia stood in the remaining two-foot-square area by the blackboard, ready to start class.

The class was fun, most of all for Amelia, who for the first time felt as if she were an important part of the community. In this tiny, stuffy room, she was given the respect she had never felt since her arrival. She wasn't sure if her students were really learning English—sure, they now knew the alphabet, greetings, and how to introduce themselves—but she was unconvinced that any of them would ever be able to hold a true conversation. She did know, however, that they were making connections on a human level that had nothing to do with culture or hair and skin color. Most of all, she knew she was making them laugh and if their laughter was in English, then it was safe to say that the classroom was filled with English from start to finish.

There was another unexpected benefit as well, for although her students were poor, even poorer than her own family, they had managed to put in a few *lempiras* here and there. Amelia had been uncomfortable with putting out a donations box, but after a week of class, a box appeared on the table under the stacked chairs labeled "Gracias Maestra Amelia!" She never saw them put money in, but by the end of each week, she would have 50 to 100 *lempiras*, the equivalent of five to ten U.S. dollars.

By the end of her first month teaching, she had thirty dollars. That's when she realized someone had been listening to her prayers. Afraid to go directly to a travel agent in case word would get out, she used the internet at the library in San Pedro Sula to price one-way tickets to Minneapolis, Minnesota. Just over $600 was the answer. Amelia had been hoping for half that amount, but she realized in two more years she would be graduating, so the timing would be perfect.

She wasn't overly creative with where she kept her savings, just in a small cloth coffee bag behind her makeshift nightstand. Whenever she was sure she was alone in the house, she would take it out and count how close she was to her goal. Two years was a long time, but between her teaching, her academic success at school, and her music, finally one day she held $600 worth of *lempiras* in her hands.

Until that moment, she hadn't thought about how to tell her family that she was leaving or even if she would tell them. Finally, as they were finishing up dinner one night, she decided that her father should know.

After all, she was an adult and would be graduating from school at the end of the month.

He was silent at first, a whole minute or two, but his silence appeared anything but ominous, rather a thorough evaluation of the information. Finally, he said, "I don't see a problem with that," and stood up to leave. Just as he was at the door, he turned around. "I'm assuming you'll take care of the ticket yourself?" Amelia nodded her assent.

The next day after her English class, she went to retrieve her money. She had an appointment with a travel agent that evening. Her hands were shaking as she inserted them behind her nightstand. She wiggled her fingers around, rooting for the cloth bag. There was nothing. Frantically, she pulled the nightstand away from the wall and looked behind. Nothing.

"Money made in this household stays in this household," came her stepmother's cold yet triumphant voice behind her. "Even if it comes from whoring," she added as she walked away.

Yes, Amelia sighed, her mind returning to the present, *retribution is sweet*. But that alone wouldn't have made her return. That also took pity. So here she was.

Amelia hadn't told her grandmother about her father—just that his family was in trouble. Her grandmother insisted on paying for the trip in spite of Amelia's new wealth.

"You're going to need that for college," she declared. "All of it, with the cost of education being what it is. And anyway, they're my family too, even though I've never met them. Those of us who are blessed with good health and good fortune need to look out for those who are not."

Good health, yes. Good fortune? Well, that was up for debate, but Amelia let it slide, thanking her grandmother and promising her she would keep her updated on the situation.

Chapter 54

When Amelia stepped off the plane onto the Honduran tarmac, the airport, the runway, and the surrounding city looked the same as if she were still that eight-year-old girl. Dust and humidity consorted to engulf the entire view in a gray haze. Had her eyeballs had windshield wipers, she would have put them on full blast. Even the blades of grass reclaiming the tarmac appeared to be the same, stubbornly clinging to patches of earth to live out hardy, long lives.

Yet, everything was different. Though the pack of dogs that jogged past and the beggars' outstretched hands were replicas of those thirteen years past, Amelia no longer saw them as that little girl. There was none of the shock or fear she had felt, nor was there the optimism, only a heavy shroud of oppression that fell upon her like the earth upon her mother's and brother's graves. It was the return ticket in her pocket that gave her the strength to put one foot in front of the other until she stood at the door of the taxi.

"To Catarina Rivas Hospital," she told the taxi driver, and soon they were rolling down the uneven streets she had once traversed. She felt no nostalgia as they passed the shops she had frequented, all touting painted promotions upon their facades: *"¡Abarrotes!"* *"¡Pasteles!"* *"¡Helados!"* Groceries! Cakes! Ice cream! in bright red, blue, and yellow. Such a deep contrast to the roused dust of the street and the dread in Amelia's heart.

She wondered what the scene would be like when she got to the hospital. So little had been said on the phone, yet the urgency could not be denied. What had happened? And how did it fit into the truth that she was trying to discover?

Soon the four-story concrete structure came into view, its gray, water-stained exterior blending into the haze of the darkening sky. Only the red metal awnings beneath the windows and a few shrubs and palm trees brought color to the scene. The outside of the entrance had been painted white at one time, but most of the paint had peeled off, leaving it as gray as the main structure, yet pocked by flaking skin.

As Amelia entered the hospital, fluorescent lighting revealed yellowed walls and water-stained ceiling tiles as well as a long line of weary people at the check-in counter. Amelia joined the line, watching the clock as it neared the end of visiting hours. She felt both anxious and hopeful that she would be too late. In the end, she was checked in and on her way to their room with ten minutes to spare.

She knew her stepmother was in a coma, but she didn't expect her to look so lifeless, lying on the hospital bed covered by clean but threadbare linens, hooked up to breathing tubes and IVs. Amelia hadn't been sure what she would feel when she saw her. She was surprised that she felt nothing. Not sadness, not pity, not satisfaction—nothing. She was sure that she would have felt more looking at a stranger than at this woman she had lived with for ten of the past thirteen years.

Her stepbrother lay in the adjacent bed tethered to IV tubes and other apparatus that Amelia could not discern. Although he too was also in a coma, his was induced. His face was bruised and swollen, making him nearly unrecognizable. Amelia winced at the sight. It was obviously a brutal attack. Yet again, the feelings she imagined she should have never came. She did not know this boy and never had wanted to, nor had he wanted to know her.

It was easy to turn and walk away, yet she still had questions she needed answered. Hailing an approaching nurse, she asked about their condition.

Her stepmother had been in a coma for three days due to a blow to the head but was expected to recover. Amelia's stepbrother was in critical condition as well. He had undergone surgery to repair a ruptured spleen but was recovering well. It was unclear when either of them would be able to talk about what had happened. The nurse herself knew very little about the attack, only that they had been attacked in their home and transported by ambulance to San Pedro Sula.

As Amelia left the hospital, she thought back to the phone call. There had been very little mention of her father, leaving it unclear as to where he was at the time of the attack. She was hoping her stepmother would be able to answer that when she came to. *If* she came to.

Numerous scenarios ping-ponged through Amelia's brain as she headed toward the hotel the taxi driver touted as "clean." Between her preoccupation and exhaustion from traveling, once in her hotel room, she had little time to evaluate the driver's recommendation. Without removing her clothing, she clambered into bed and fell asleep.

Chapter 55

A call to the hospital in the morning confirmed that neither her mother's nor her brother's conditions had improved. Before hanging up, Amelia secured a contact for ongoing updates on their conditions; nothing like the smell of a potential remitter to promote steady communication. There would be no reason to visit them today since there was no way they would answer any of her questions.

Instead, she sat waiting for answers in a hot and stuffy police station. Every twenty seconds or so the oscillating fan in the corner gave her reprieve from the sticky, stale air and the odor of sweat from the elderly man sitting next to her. Dirt, or maybe it was mold, dappled the white-washed walls that provided a backdrop to the hundreds of flyers decrying the violence of the times.

Defiant faces of young Honduran men and women peered from beneath "Wanted" headings, proud of their alleged crimes of murder, assault, rape, kidnapping, armed robbery, drug trafficking, murder, murder, and murder.

Only three years previously, Honduras had become the murder capital of the world, according to the *New York Times*, with eighty-nine murders per every 100,000 people per year, above any country in the Middle East or Africa. And San Pedro Sula, Honduras's most dangerous city, earned distinction as the *world's* most dangerous city.

So here she was, sitting in a police station in the world's most dangerous city, looking into the sneering faces of the world's most ruthless gang and drug cartel members. The fact that their faces were confined to two-dimensional space did little to comfort Amelia's growing concern, for no longer could she deny that these thugs were out there, attacking, kidnapping, and murdering others—like her stepmother, her stepbrother...and her father? Where was he?

A half hour later, Amelia sat at the disheveled desk of one of the police detectives. He was hunched over his computer, typing in the information she gave him with thick, tobacco-stained fingers.

"Ah yes," he said straightening up in his chair. "I remember now. A young man and his mother were brutally attacked outside the city. It says here the woman was bludgeoned with what appears to have been the back of a revolver, and the boy was beaten with a blunt object and apparently kicked repeatedly. The motive is unclear. There doesn't appear to have been anything stolen, but the house was tossed. Without our victims' verification of that, we have no reason to believe it was a robbery. It doesn't appear to have been drug-related either, as the family was well-known and had a good reputation in their community. At this point it appears to be a random act of violence."

The detective's account seemed to Amelia like any other account of violence she had heard over the past thirteen years. They were just as much strangers to her, and though horrific, she had no connection to their horror. She did, however, have one burning question, and as much as she'd like to deny it, an emotional stake in its answer.

"And my father?" She asked. "Was he there during the attack? Does anyone know where he is?"

The detective looked back at his computer screen and slowly shook his head. "There's nothing in the report that indicates he was there. Witnesses are still being interviewed, so maybe we'll have more information about that soon. But for right now, we have no information on your father at all."

Although Amelia was relieved, she was also burdened by the knowledge that she would have to seek out her own answers. That meant she would have to return to the house and community she had so gratefully left behind.

Chapter 56

As Amelia walked to the bus station, she heard the cry of "*¡Hielo!¡Hielo!*" It was not Don Ronaldo's voice, but suddenly she felt the nostalgia that had so obviously been absent since her arrival. A handful of children raced down the street, unrestrained smiles stretching across dark, dirt-smudged faces, small fists clenching small treasures soon to be converted into a much greater treasure. Perhaps for the first time ever, Amelia sensed the beauty in the simplicity of the cry of "*Hielo*," of little girls and boys giddy for cold sweetness on their tongues, for brightly colored skirts ill-matched to equally brightly colored blouses, and Orioles and Red Sox T-shirts sported by little bodies who no more knew those teams than what lay beyond their city block. She found herself walking in the opposite direction of the bus station, past nearly forgotten shops and homes and apartments of long-lost friends, until she stood before their first Honduran home.

A woman was tending to the potted plants beneath the window, pulling a few vine-like weeds from beneath the lush leaves of the hyacinths that blossomed there. She did not notice Amelia, for if she had, she would have looked at her with the same surprise and curiosity every other person did as she passed. How could they know this had once been her home too? The woman emptied a small plastic container of water into each of the pots. It was obvious to Amelia that this woman knew how to take care of this home far better than her father had. The home had been recently whitewashed and the window trim painted a bright yellow. The house came nearly up to the sidewalk with thin interspersed patches of dirt and grass separating it from the passersby. Not quite a yard, but obviously groomed, with the appearance of having been swept not many hours before. She was humming, Amelia realized. Honduras was not just the home of beggars, starving children, murderous gangs and mangy mutts. People *lived* here. She had never appreciated that before this moment, as the strains of the familiar folk tune affirmed this truth. This was their *home*...this was *their* home. Another truth she could not deny.

Nostalgia made way to haste, and soon Amelia was standing aboard a bus to her former mountainside home. She had thought of splurging on a second-class bus but would have had to wait another two hours. This third-class bus was what she was used to anyway, crowded with passengers of all ages, three to each torn vinyl seat, their purchases from San Pedro Sula stacked upon the metal baggage rack above their seats, set between their feet as they sat or stood, or clutched to their sides and bellies as space permitted. There were no chickens, Amelia realized. Most often there were, restrained by bands around their feet and tucked carefully under an arm or within a loosely woven produce bag.

Amelia stood holding the bar of the baggage rack above her, keeping her knees loose to absorb the bumps of the road and the jolts of the bus as it stopped and started to let off and take on passengers. A constant stream of people walked along the roadside, heading into town or out of town, to the fields or from the fields, toward home or away from home. Large, woven reed baskets were carried upon the shoulders and heads of women half the size of the burdens they bore. Children too old to be wrapped against their mothers in blankets dawdled behind or scurried ahead. Horses and Brahma cows stood staked to the roadside, munching on the tender grasses found there. A foal stood in the ditch, nuzzling its mother who lay on the grass, her belly distended...in death, Amelia realized as the pair disappeared from view. The foal would drink from his dead mother's teats until they dried up and then be led away. His mother's carcass would remain as carrion for the vultures that already hovered above. Life here hid nothing. Everything that existed, existed within the perimeter of each 24 x 24-inch bus window. Was there beauty in that simplicity too? If there were, Amelia could not see it.

It was with this image of the foal nudging his dead mother's teats that Amelia descended from the bus onto her old stomping grounds. Don Filipe's shop, *Tienda Don Filipe*, stood to the right of the trail that ascended the small mountain to her former community. It was a convenience store of sorts: any number of sweets and goodies could be purchased there, as well as the staples of rice, seed corn, and dried beans. Children and teenagers were gathered at the open doorway, peering into the shop at the thirty-two-inch TV hanging in the corner. Amelia guessed it was a soccer game being broadcast, or perhaps *una telenovela*, a Latin soap opera, that usually commanded as large an audience as this current one.

She began her ascent, this time superimposing her trek up the Bighorn Mountains over this Honduran Mountain as she had this setting upon that one just a few months before. She smiled. It was like seeing herself in a mirror seeing herself, remembering herself remembering herself.

Her trip up the mountain wasn't so much different this time than it had been all those other times in her life. She passed the church, but this time she did not need to enter. She debated a moment on whether or not to visit Hermana Rebeca, but realized even this memory, though one of her best, was sandwiched between events that made bile rise in her stomach. She would not visit Hermana Rebeca ever again, just as she would not visit this mountain ever again, once her business here was done. She passed the Widow Doña Beatriz's house, the three youngest of her nine boys chasing each other around the yard with scrawny sticks, machine-gun fire exploding from their lips. Small dogs darted out from dirt-floor huts to yip, nip, and whine at her until she reached her home. Their dog did not come out to greet her. She wondered if it had been killed in the attack or if someone was taking care of it. She didn't much care either way.

As she stepped into the house, she smelled the musty odor of trapped humidity even before her first footfall landed on the shattered remains of a ceramic pitcher. The mismatched collection of plastic and ceramic cups, pots and pans, forks and spoons sprawled in a midnight orgy upon the dirt, kitchen floor. Carefully moving a few paces to the right, she found herself next to the overturned dining room table. She saw blood on the dirt near one of its legs and imagined it was her stepbrother's. As there were no walls to separate the rooms of the house, only the beams interrupted Amelia's view as she slowly turned to take in the slashed mattresses and bedding and mounds of scattered clothing. Violence had reined here, unmitigated violence—and fun. She could almost hear the laughter as her stepmother's undergarments were tossed back and forth until they landed by her unconscious body on the dining room floor.

Suddenly Amelia felt her stomach begin to churn. Tripping over strewn chairs, books, and memorabilia, she made it out of the house just in time to vomit alongside the rain barrel.

As she rinsed out her mouth with a handful of rainwater, she caught a glimpse of red. It was a T-shirt worn by Oscar, one of the neighbor boys, as he tended to the goats in the nearby pen. Amelia had forgotten all about their goats and what might be happening to them. It was relieving to see the neighbors were keeping them milked and alive.

She and Oscar had always been friends. He was two years younger than her and in spite of the fact that he had never gone to school, he was a smart kid with the goal of owning his own farm one day. He had the work ethic for it, but for every hardworking young man in Honduras, there were a negative number of opportunities. He would be forced to earn the average two dollars a week to barely support himself and his family, once he had a family of his own.

In spite of what she had just experienced, Amelia felt delighted to see him and hurried over to the goat pen, a loose definition for the sticks and misshapen branches that formed a parody of a parallelogram. Oscar was crouched alongside one of the goats, squeezing squirts of milk from her teats into a plastic pail. He was so focused on his work that he nearly tipped the bucket and himself when Amelia greeted him from behind.

"Shit!" he yelled in his rural brand of Honduran Spanish, both annoyed and delighted. "You scared the crap out of me. Whatcha doin' here? Where've you been? How are you anyway?" He rattled off, grabbing the milk bucket, coming to a stand, and embracing her all at the same time.

Amelia laughed. "Whoa! One question at a time! And put down that bucket before you spill it!"

Setting down the bucket, Oscar took a step back and surveyed her for a moment. "You look more or less the same," he finally said approvingly. "A few months in the U.S. hasn't corrupted you overly much," he added with a grin. Then suddenly somber, he nodded toward the house. "Who knows what would have happened to you had you been here."

Amelia had been thinking the same thing. She had seen the clothes she had left behind strewn around the house. It wasn't hard to imagine herself in a hospital bed or even dead. "Why did this happen, Oscar?" she asked. It wasn't a rhetorical question. People in this area knew more than they let on when the police were asking the questions.

"Amelia, you've always been a bit oblivious to what went on around here. Not sure where your head was but safe to say it wasn't here. Don't you know what your dad was involved in?"

A vision of Toby rattling on about the FBI flashed into her mind.

"Involved in?" she managed to sputter.

"Yeah," Oscar grunted, casually leaning his shoulders against the misshapen walls of the pen. Amelia, too invested in his answer to contemplate whether or not the wall would support him, waited intently. "After Celayas was ousted by the *coup d'état*, your father became very active in the resistance movement. As a reporter, he was in a dangerous position. Did you know that twenty reporters have been murdered in the last two years? Once Celayas was returned to power, we thought the political killings would stop. That hasn't been the case 'cause although Celayas is back, he no longer holds the real power. Foreign interests do."

"How…how do you know all this?" Amelia stuttered, looking at the eighteen-year-old unschooled boy standing in front of her with uncut hair and dirt-stained, tattered jeans.

"Didn't you ever listen to the conversations our fathers had with the groups of men they hosted? Weren't you ever curious to know what they were talking about? I was there for every conversation. Amelia, this is my home. It will always be my home. It doesn't matter how many murders there are, how many foreign countries buy up our land and exploit our resources and labor, or how many gangs and drug cartels sprout up out of this devastated economy. This is the only home I'll ever have and I have a stake in it."

It wasn't just a statement of fact, it was a critique and Amelia knew it was justified. She had never lived here, had never made this place her home. When she was not dreaming about her past life in Minnesota, she was plotting her return there. She had never once accepted that she would stay. It had merely been a prison sentence that her real life was waiting for her to serve.

"Oscar, do you know where my father is?"

"He's not with you in the States?" he replied with surprise. "We haven't seen him since you both left. Assumed he'd decided to ditch us. It's been a sore spot with us," he admitted.

"No, he's not with me," Amelia replied. "He was detained at the airport in Houston. I'd assumed he came back here after he was released. Are you sure he hasn't?"

"No. He hasn't been back. Guess you aren't the only one looking for him," he added, his eyes glancing warily at the house.

"Guess not," she admitted. "It's been good to see you, Oscar. Thanks for taking care of the goats."

"Just exploiting an opportunity like all the rest of humanity," he joked with little humor. "Goat's milk serves no one in the udder. Didn't think your family would mind."

"No one to mind," Amelia responded dryly. *And they're not my family anyway*, she thought as she slowly walked away without a last glance. Forever.

Chapter 57

She didn't feel as relieved as she thought she would as the airplane lifted from the runway. She would not miss Honduras, and the memory of her comatose stepmother and her unresponsive stepbrother would not haunt her. Not for long anyway. Yet, she felt as heavy lifting off as when she had landed. When the medical professionals at the hospital could offer her no reassurance that her stepmother and stepbrother would ever be able to answer her questions, she decided what she had learned from Oscar was all she was going to—from here anyway. She scowled out the window at the ragged rooftop line of the city. That life would go on without her, no matter how many thousands of miles she was away. No one would miss her as she missed no one. All wasted years. No, stolen years.

The rooftops and tropical forests faded beneath her scowl, but a looming image in her mind grew more prominent as the plane ascended. She wanted to smash that image with her forehead: his face, responsible for thirteen stolen years and two bodies languishing in hospital beds. When would his reckoning come? And would she be there to revel in it?

That's how she wanted to feel, yet her anger was mixed with questions. Where was he? What had happened to him? Had he left her forever? Like they had? More than retribution, she wanted answers. How would she find the answers? Then she remembered Connie's words, "Angel, we're in this together." And with a modicum of peace, she closed her eyes.

Chapter 58

Connie brought Amelia a cup of coffee once she was seated, even after Amelia insisted she rarely drank it, at least not American coffee. She had been spoiled on freshly ground Honduran coffee, fresh roasted with raw sugar over an open flame, filtered through a nylon stocking, and mixed with goat's milk. It had replaced the treats Amelia was never allowed—that they could never afford. Out of politeness, though, Amelia sipped the coffee, immediately wishing she hadn't. Black American coffee. Were the Quakers responsible for taking even the color out of coffee?

Connie didn't seem to know the coffee experience she was missing as she took several gulps from her own cup; either that or she was too tired to notice, having been roused from bed at 4:00 in the morning by Amelia's frantic knocking.

After a few more hearty gulps, she settled back in her chair and studied Amelia.

"So, what was so urgent you couldn't wait for a decent hour to see me?" she accused, somewhat in jest but more grumpily than she probably intended.

"Connie, my father's missing," Amelia blurted without preamble. "The airport security guards in Houston led him away on our way here for my aunt's funeral. I didn't think he'd actually been detained, so I just left him there and boarded the plane. No one in Honduras or Minnesota has heard from him in four months."

Connie looked at her for a moment in silence.

"And...you didn't think to tell me this earlier?" she admonished. "And I don't mean at 3:00 a.m. but maybe last month?"

"I didn't know. I mean I didn't know for sure. I called Honduras last week and found out there had been an incident. I mean something bad had happened. I flew there to see what was going on. And he wasn't there, anywhere."

Amelia spent the next ten minutes explaining her recent trip and what she had learned.

"And I came here as soon as I got back. I just didn't know what else to do."

"Well, you did the right thing, Angel," Connie consoled, "even if it is at 4:00 a.m.," she winked. "But to be honest, and this is going to surprise you, I'm *not* surprised."

"You're not?" exclaimed Amelia, indeed surprised.

"Not after what happened after ya'll went away and what he's been up to since. Let me get you a refill on your coffee first. This won't be easy to hear." Amelia was too distraught to point out that her coffee cup was already filled to the brim, so she watched as Connie dumped and refilled it with another round of its distasteful blend.

"The year after 9/11," Connie began, "marked a turning point for your father. He became obsessed with every aspect of that terrorist action and the War on Terror in general. I know you were only a few years old at that time, but did you read any of his articles later on?"

Amelia shook her head.

"Your father became convinced 9/11 was a government conspiracy."

"A government conspiracy?" Amelia responded incredulously. "I have to admit that sounds pretty out there."

"Yeah, a lot of people felt that way. He claimed, however, to have credible sources who assured him that the Administration's blatant disregard of pre-9/11 intelligence was intentional and that the events of the day didn't add up. First, on the morning of the attack, five different government agencies were involved in 'war games' that both weakened our domestic protection and confused our security forces. Then there was the way the Twin Towers collapsed, like a controlled demolition, which even mainstream news anchors reported. Building 7 which housed the CIA and Secret Service among other high-level agencies, was destroyed, which according to his anonymous source contained information that made these agencies complicit in the attacks. Finally, Even Flight 93 that supposedly crashed down in Pennsylvania seemed to leave questions unanswered. Even our Defense Secretary, himself, referred to the plane as 'shot down…over Pennsylvania.'"

Connie paused to sip her coffee. Amelia noticed again the deep lines that had wound their way around the corners of her mouth, further emphasizing the fullness of her lips that glistened as she passed her tongue across them. A couple of gulps later, Connie continued.

"Now, pretty much anytime a significant news event occurs, there are unanswered questions and conspiracy theories that sprout up to answer them. 9/11 was no different. More than likely, your father's conspiracy theory was no better or worse than any that preceded it. However, your father truly believed the government was responsible for 9/11, using it to justify initiating U.S. military actions in the Middle East, which obviously came to pass.

"But," she continued, tangling her fingers into her wild locks as she shook her head, "your father never could convince me of a government conspiracy that would go so far as to kill so many Americans. I didn't much care what evidence he thought he had."

Amelia had to agree. No matter how elaborate her father's conspiracy theory had become, it was more plausibly a paranoid rant than a mass-murder plot by a government she was so happy to once again call her own.

"He took this same skeptical line with every step the government took in the War on Terror," Connie continued. "He knew long before it came out in the mainstream media that the WMDs, weapons of mass destruction, were the 'fake news' of the time. And he didn't report it like the mainstream media did as an 'Oops, we made a bitty mistake,' but as a 'ploy' to increase our military response to the Muslim threat and, most importantly, to line the pockets of the defense contractors for many years to come. This wasn't a hard sell for a lot of our readers since our vice president had been the CEO of a defense contractor that incidentally, or I mean not so incidentally, had its defense contracts increased tenfold in two years. Follow the money, they say."

I've heard that before, Amelia thought as Bull's giant head came into view. *Seems to work in more than one context though*, she mused.

"And then there was his reporting on the Iraq war itself, how he believed the Administration misrepresented or fabricated intelligence about ties between Saddam Hussein and Al Qaeda and ignored or was indifferent to the fact that Al Qaeda used the vacancy of power to build a stronghold in Iraq. And then there was Abu Ghraib, Al Qaeda's retaliation, and the London bombing…" Connie paused. "But that's another chapter. Let's eat something before we go around that bend in the road."

Chapter 59

Amelia contemplated the overload of political information over bites of a stale powdered sugar donut. "Okay," she finally said, after dusting her mouth off with the back of her hand, "that is all very interesting, but what exactly does it have to do with the fact that my father's missing?"

"I'm getting there," Connie assured her, grinning for a second before replacing the grin with a knitted brow and pursed lips. "But first you need to understand the background. Abu Ghraib was the next story your dad latched onto. Your father was like any other reporter when the news of the abuse and torture of Iraqi inmates at the Abu Ghraib prison broke. He was determined to showcase the criminality of the situation and the US government's role in it.

"And then came the retaliation. The Islamic website of the group Muntada al-Ansar posted the video of the decapitation of Nick Berg. In the gruesome video, Al Qaeda not only claimed responsibility for the act but also touted it as retaliation for the events at Abu Ghraib. The media tide turned. No one was interested any longer in the abuse of Iraqi inmates. Except for your dad."

Connie reached for another donut, took a few bites, and then continued with a thoughtful look in her eyes.

"He would follow a story until it gave him what he needed or it died a slow, agonizing death. Abu Ghraib was that slow, agonizing death. All other newspapers had moved on. The American public had moved on, but your dad kept slogging through it. Readers jumped ship, sales went down. It was one big journalistic slump.

"And then," Connie continued, raising her eyebrows dramatically, "it all changed. As bombs went off in the subways of London, your dad renewed his journalistic vigor. Before other journalists knew what was happening, he was publishing scoops on the 2005 London suicide bombings that killed 52 people. Our readership picked up, including a sizeable online British readership as your dad had more information than the British media seemed to have. While other papers pondered the possibility of Al Qaeda involvement, your father asserted that Al Qaeda had indeed masterminded the attack according to 'an anonymous source close to the bombers.' His assertion turned out to be true several years later, but by then, as you know, he was far away and out of the newspaper-making business." Connie leaned back looking up at the ceiling, reluctant to continue.

"And then? What happened next?" Amelia insisted.

Connie lowered her eyes to meet Amelia's.

"The explosion, Angel. That's what happened next."

They both sat silently for several moments looking into each other's eyes, until Amelia broke her gaze to fumble with her fingers.

"And they're connected somehow?" she finally asked, restoring her gaze.

"Not the explosion, Angel, but what I can say is that your father's reporting finally did win him some attention at the federal level. Within weeks after the funeral, you were on a plane to Honduras. Did you ever wonder why you left so quickly?"

"I just figured my father was running away from the tragedy," Amelia conceded, beginning to formulate what Connie was going to disclose next.

"He was running away, but not necessarily from the tragedy. Two days after you left, the FBI came through his office and tore it apart. They took every box your father ever touched as well as the computers. That's the major reason we went bankrupt."

"Seriously?" Amelia exclaimed, shaking her head as if to displace this fact as well as the other Toby had revealed.

"I demanded to know under what authority they were confiscating all our things—without a warrant, mind you—when they informed me that the Patriot Act gave them every right to confiscate anything that belonged to a person suspected of 'terrorist ties or activities'."

"Terrorist ties? His source. That's what they were after, weren't they?" Amelia interjected.

"Yeah. That's exactly what they wanted. They even brought me in for questioning. They didn't learn much from me since I had no idea about any of it, but I did learn more from them. They insisted that your father had been in contact with several well-established members of the Al Qaeda network. They said the documents they confiscated would give them the proof they needed to convict your father and prove my collaboration. I said they were crazy. They told me the next time they saw me, I'd be behind bars for conspiring with a terrorist. It's been over thirteen years, haven't seen them since. Must not have been too much in those boxes."

Amelia nodded. She could see how even legitimate journalist activities in such a sensitive, volatile context could be perceived as terrorist collaboration. Suddenly she saw Bull's face, larger than life from across the flames.

"So, they put him on a 'no fly' list?" she ventured.

"That's a very probable scenario," Connie replied.

"But why after thirteen years would they detain him?"

"Well, that's where it gets even more complicated. Your father may have been physically out of FBI reach for the past thirteen years, but he's been anything but inactive. You know that he worked for the Central American Liberty Radio, right?"

"Yes, *Radio Libertad Centroamericano*," Amelia answered.

"Your father has spent the past thirteen years broadcasting information about the U.S. government that would be considered anything but favorable. Whether true or not—I don't have any of my own research to verify or discredit it—the U.S. would consider this inflammatory and sympathetic to terrorist organizations around the world. Taken together, his past associations and current activities could be viewed very suspiciously by the U.S. government."

They sat in silence for a moment, Connie taking a few gulps of her now cold, tasteless coffee while Amelia merely stared into hers. It was Amelia who finally broke the silence.

"What would they do with him next?"

"Now *that* I'm not sure about," Connie admitted, grimacing from the aftertaste of her beverage. "He most likely would have been charged in Houston, since he was detained there, *if* he was detained there. We can start by doing an inmate search of the U.S. Detention Centers and see where that leads."

"I can do that this morning at the library," Amelia offered.

"Make sure you have his personal information: full name, birthdate, social security number, and the exact date he was detained," Connie advised.

"Oh Connie," Amelia said, struck for the first time by her culpability, "had I known how complicated all this was, I would never have taken off to Montana. I would have tried to find him." She had used her anger and resentment to not only blind her to her father's possible plight, but also to revel in its very possibility. Now he had most likely spent four months incarcerated while she rode trails—*amongst other things*, her memory added bitterly.

"I can't believe I just let them haul him away. I didn't even ask where they were taking him. To be honest, I didn't even care. What kind of person am I?"

"One whose family dies and then is whisked away to a foreign country and neglected," Connie replied, leaning forward to touch her hand. "I know you, Amelia. Had you really known the stakes four months ago, you would have risen to the occasion."

She was right. Anything other than a mistake would have been absurd. Still was.

"Oh!" Amelia exclaimed suddenly aware of the passage of time. "I have to get the car back to my grandma for morning mass. Can I stop by tomorrow?"

"Promise you will! And don't worry, Amelia. We'll find him," Connie assured her with a tight handgrip that threatened to never let go.

What really worried Amelia, however, was how little she was worried about him. It was her *guilt*, she realized, that worried her most. Yet that, she finally decided, was a better motive for finding him than none at all.

Chapter 60

"My father's...missing," she finally blurted out, looking down at her hands folded upon the desk.

"Excuse me?" Jonathon sputtered, bewildered.

"He's missing," she repeated softly looking up at him, her defeated morale evident even in the slump of her shoulders. "I don't know where he is."

It was Monday morning and rather than put off till tomorrow what she could do today, she had decided to let Jonathon know that her father would not be participating in the lawsuit. He was surprised to see her and a little irritated that she hadn't returned his call from the previous week, but he had hugged her, offered her coffee, and seated her across the desk from him all with a warm smile.

Amelia had barely made it through the niceties before blurting out the truth, and, as she had expected, she had shocked him with the information. She knew he would only become more shocked as she shared with him the other details of the story, but she also knew she owed him that much.

"He's not in Honduras?" he implored.

"No. I had to fly out to Honduras last week. That's why I didn't return your call."

"Wait a second," he interrupted, stalling her with his hand. "You flew to Honduras? I didn't mean for you to fly there to arrange the deposition. I thought you were just going to call."

"I called," she confirmed, "but I learned that my stepmother and stepbrother had been attacked. So, I went down to find out what I could."

"Attacked? Amelia," he said with concern and shock, "I'm so sorry. That's awful! I don't know what to say." He reached over to capture her hand as it toyed with the edge of his desk calendar. "Did you find out what happened?" Similar to her recitation to Connie, Amelia recounted the situation in Honduras and ended by explaining that no one had seen her father.

"When's the last time he was seen?" Jonathon finally asked after sitting in shocked silence through her account of events.

"He was detained by airport security at the Houston airport a few months ago when we, he and I, were flying to Minneapolis for his sister's funeral. I haven't seen him since. I thought they were just going to question him, but there must have been more to it than that because no one's seen him since.

"Well, if he was detained, there would be a record of it," Jonathon offered, his legal brain kicking in.

"Except," Amelia interrupted, "there isn't. I stopped at the library this morning to check the Bureau of Federal Prison's database, but nothing showed up. A friend of mine believes he may have been detained by the Homeland Security Department or the FBI because of his connections as a journalist. We haven't really figured out what to do next," she ended.

"Wow. What you won't surprise me with, Amelia," Jonathon admitted shaking his head in disbelief. "Let me think here for a minute," he continued, running his fingers through his wispy locks as he looked up at the ceiling before looking back at her. "You think your father was detained by the FBI or Homeland Security. What makes you think that?"

"It's just that he was detained at the Houston airport, and then I learned about these no-fly lists, his involvement with possible terrorists, his anti-US radio station, and that the FBI had been looking into him after we left thirteen years ago. And well, it just looks like he's mixed up in something."

Jonathon gaped at her. "I have to admit, Amelia, it's not every day someone tells me their father is a suspected terrorist. I just don't know what to do with that information."

"Oh gosh, no. I'm not saying *he's* suspected of being a terrorist," Amelia replied with alarm. "He's a *journalist*. And all we can figure is he must have had some journalistic connections with a suspected terrorist or something. He's not a terrorist, for gosh sakes no."

"Okay, okay," Jonathon soothed, moving from his chair to sit on the edge of the desk in front of her. "I misunderstood, okay?" He slowly reached out his hand to capture a lock of her hair, gently running it between his middle and index fingers. He almost seemed to have forgotten why she was there and what had brought him to her side of the desk. Then clearing his throat, he moved his eyes from the lock of hair he let fall from his fingers and returned them to look upon her face.

"You've got me undone," he said in a throaty whisper. "Even if your father were a terrorist," he put his hand up quickly before Amelia could retort, "which he is not, I'll do whatever I can to help you. You know that, don't you?"

Amelia didn't know anything for sure, only that she wanted him to play again with her hair and to move those worried lips of his to hers so she could bring them relief. He was sincere in his pledge to help, she felt sure, and that both touched and terrified her.

"I know," she finally said, looking into his eyes. "You don't know how much that means to me."

"Okay," he replied, rising from the desk and reassuming his lawyer persona. "Let's think this through. Did you check the state pens? They usually don't hold people for federal crimes in those, but who knows? It may be worth a shot," he suggested. "Or we could also just call the FBI and ask them," he continued.

"I suppose we could," Amelia replied, embarrassed she had not thought to do just that.

"Why don't we call now, while you're here? To be honest, with a thirteen-year-old personal injury suit, you're going to need your father's testimony to get anywhere."

Jonathon made the phone call, and after being jockeyed around from department to department was finally talking to someone who seemed to be the person who could help. He explained in as much detail as Amelia had given him the situation and consulted the notes Amelia provided him, ones she had used earlier that morning, to furnish her father's full name, birth date, social security number, and date of arrest.

"Really," he said, finally looking earnestly over at Amelia. "So, you can only say that you have no record of him being charged but not whether he's being held." Amelia held his eyes with hers and eagerly watched them register each kernel of new knowledge he gleaned. "If you can't divulge any information regarding him, can I assume that sealing orders apply in this case? Or should we file a missing person's report? … In cases involving suspected terrorists? You mean to tell me that if he were being held for some case involving the suspicion of terrorism, his family may not be privy to any information whatsoever pertaining to his case? I see," he nodded, eyes still locked with hers. "Okay, then. Thank you very much for your time, Agent Lawrence, did you say? Thanks, again." He hung up the phone still looking at her. She couldn't move her mouth, let alone say a word, but her eyes that bore into his asked all the questions her mouth could not.

Finally, he spoke. "Basically, they can't tell us anything, but given that conversation, I'd say it was pretty likely his case has been sealed. That means he's probably in custody somewhere, but we can't get any information at all regarding him. Of course, it's possible he's simply missing, though the agent wasn't in a hurry to encourage my filing a missing person's report." He closed his eyes and took a deep breath before continuing.

"This sounds a bit more than some journalism work," he finally admitted. "Amelia, how much did you really know about your father? The FBI doesn't mess around sealing orders for a two-bit journalist here or there. Can you really be sure that he's not involved with terrorists?"

Amelia's face fell, tears forming at the corners of her eyes. "What happened to innocent until proven guilty?" she demanded resentfully. "You don't know anything about my father, yet you're already picturing him piloting an airplane that smashes into the American flag. My father's a journalist. He's only guilty of trying to find the truth. I guess that makes me guilty too."

Her face was hot and flushed. Had she been less agitated, she may have questioned why she would defend her father at all. But she didn't have time to deliberate her reaction as Jonathon's hand reached across to grasp the clenched one she had just set upon the desk.

"You're right, Amelia," he acquiesced. "I'm jumping to conclusions. It's easy to do that when you've had friends or family die in 9/11. I had both an uncle and a friend of my father's die in the attack. It's hard for me to keep an open mind. Do you accept my apology?"

She wasn't ready to nod just yet. She could only think that Donovan would have responded differently. Wouldn't he have thought of Leonard Peltier and understood instinctively the righteous rush to judge those who stood up to the government? Jonathon could never have that perspective. Yet, she admitted, he did have his own, equally rooted in history and personal experience.

"Okay," she conceded. "I can't expect you to understand someone as complicated as my father when I can't understand him myself. And I guess I didn't give you much time to contemplate the situation. Anyway," she sighed heavily, "what can we do next?"

Jonathon almost recovered his smile, but now it was hedged with misgiving and perhaps mistrust.

"I'm at a loss, really," he admitted. "I'll consult with some colleagues to see if they have any suggestions on how we can find him. I guess we can go ahead without him if we have to, but I have to say that his testimony would definitely help your suit."

There was nothing else to say, and as Amelia departed, she had only her father to thank for one more unfortunate situation. Why did he have to be her father? She let herself luxuriously imagine for the moment that Jonathon Lundberg Sr. was her father. He would have bought her a horse they'd stable in the suburbs and have gone to each of her riding competitions. She would have had voice and guitar lessons with the best instructors money could buy, and she would have entertained his clientele at the annual Christmas parties held at their mansion. And, she realized with a shudder, have had an incestuous affair with her brother. Maybe there really was a reason things were as they were.

Chapter 61

Although she hadn't slept more than a handful of the last forty-eight hours, Amelia was alert on adrenaline and eager to know what Connie had found out. She had called Connie after her meeting with Jonathon and described his conversation with the FBI. Connie had simply said, "You've got to come over, girl, I think I may know what's going on. See you in ten?" Now here was Connie greeting her at the door with a cup of black American coffee which, from the sip Amelia took out of politeness, may as well have been reheated from the cup she had barely touched the day before.

"So," Connie said, shuffling Amelia over to her cluttered kitchen table, "interesting information your lawyer friend uncovered. Set off the little warning bells in my head."

"How so?" Amelia queried, perplexed.

"I actually have a bit of experience in this area. Journalistic experience, not lived experience," she qualified. "I've written several stories about the misuse of something called the material witness statute, and I think that offers a possible scenario for your father's situation."

"Material witness statute?"

"Right on cue," Connie smiled, targeting Amelia with a quick finger point. "The material witness statute allows law enforcement to detain a person without charges until they give testimony in front of a grand jury or in a criminal trial. To get a warrant, a prosecutor must convince a judge that the person in question is privy to important or 'material' information concerning a crime and poses a flight risk. In your father's case, I think the FBI would be able to convince a judge on both counts. First, your dad publicly claimed to have a source 'close to the London bombers' and second, he left the country for thirteen years and just recently returned. Given the continued threat of terrorism and the fact that his informant claims ties to suicide bombers, and in turn their ties to Al Qaeda, I think a judge would be pretty convinced by this argument."

Amelia nodded. Although she hadn't heard of a material witness before, with this explanation it did seem like a plausible explanation for her father's detainment.

"I'm surprised to hear that someone can be held for information they know instead of a crime they committed, but if that's true, it makes sense in my dad's case. Wouldn't he get a lawyer though? And wouldn't we know about it?"

"Yes, he would get court-appointed counsel, but if they decided to seal the proceedings, then we really wouldn't know about it."

"How does that work?"

"Grand jury testimony is always closed, but the warrant and other proceedings are generally open. However, the judge could decide to seal the warrant and its subsequent proceedings if he believed knowledge of them posed a danger to the witness or to law enforcement's ability to make a case. In such a scenario, only the prosecutor, your father, his court-appointed lawyer, select law enforcement officials, and the judge would know about his detainment. However, the warrant should be on the docket, which is public, but we can only locate it if they include his name."

"Can we check?" Amelia interrupted.

"Already did before you got here. So that either means I'm wrong, and he's not being held as a material witness, or it simply means that the docket doesn't include his name."

"Okay, okay," Amelia sighed, shaking her head in frustration. "So, let's say you're right and he is being held somewhere as a material witness. How do we find him?"

Connie wearily shook her head. "Well, unless his counsel or another privy party breaks the sealing orders, there's nothing we can do."

Nothing we can do, Amelia thought as she drove away. *How can that be?* The pieces of the scattered puzzle whirred about her brain, and before she realized it, she found herself parked at the cemetery, the Kingston plot looking down upon her. She sat there, staring at the steering wheel, plotting the information she knew and the information she needed upon its axis. In the center stood the truth; they had wanted her to find the truth. One prong of the steering wheel led to her father, and another, the investigation into the explosion.

For now, the investigation was most likely a dead end without her father. All roads led to him. Except, as of yet, there was no road to follow.

Neither Connie nor Jonathon had discovered any information about him. He was a ghost in a machine. But didn't his name have to be somewhere? With all those temperature-controlled warehouses of wall-to-wall digital data, some database somewhere held his name. But whose? Then a giant head exploded through the waves of confusion in her brain. She knew whose. Bull's.

Chapter 62

After waving hurriedly through the car window up at her family upon the hill, Amelia raced home to her grandmother's. Before she had even caught her breath, she was dialing the number and listening to the phone ringing at the other end. When Pamela answered, Amelia found herself smiling, imagining the pleasure Pamela would feel at the sound of her voice.

"Pamela, it's Amelia." It didn't take much imagination, as Pamela's response echoed into her eardrum, forcing Amelia to jerk back the receiver.

"Yes, Pamela. Missing you already! How's everything going now that things are back to normal?" Amelia listened while Pamela told her how boring it was and how difficult to get back to Jack and Russ as her only companions. Finally, Amelia found the opportunity to ask for Russ. But before Russ could make it to the phone, Pamela was back breathlessly in her ear.

"Amelia, I almost forgot. Somebody called for you. Donovan something or other. Said it was urgent and asked if I had a number for you. I told him I couldn't give out your number, so he gave me his. Do you have a pen handy?"

In spite of herself, Amelia squeezed the pen she already held in her hand, unable to stop it from shaking. She knew she already had his number, but she couldn't help but jot it down again anyway. She barely heard Pamela's departing remarks and was little aware of her own when Russ's voice crying her name jarred her back.

"Same to you Russ! How are things going?" Like Pamela, Russ had a few complaints about the change of pace but was excited to share a bit of good news.

"Remember, Jason?" he nearly whispered into the receiver. "He called me the other day and invited me out to his cabin on Lake Tahoe! I'll be going next month. Not only good-looking, but as it turns out, rich!"

"And has the hots for you—a deadly combination," Amelia giggled.

"Definitely a combination I'm willing to handle," he replied.

Amelia took advantage of the pause in conversation to get to the point of her call.

"Russ, I'm calling to get some information from you. I know this is going to surprise you, but I was wondering if you could get me the phone number for Bull, I mean Mr. Goldfield."

"Who? Are you crazy?" he cried, unable to hide his consternation.

"Yeah, I know. The last thing you'd expect, but I need some information about the Terrorist Screening Center, and I thought he might be able to help me out."

"Not unless it involves interrogating you, he won't," came Russ's immediate response.

"You're probably right, but since he loves to feel important, I thought he might even appreciate my being beholden to him."

"You might be onto something there, Amelia. Tell you what. Let me look for his number, and I'll give you a call back tonight or tomorrow."

"That would be great, Russ. I appreciate it. It was great to hear your voice, and have fun at Lake Tahoe! Make sure to ask your rich *friend* if he has any rich straight friends for me!"

"I'll do. Take care, Amelia."

Chapter 63

As they hung up, Amelia caught sight of the number scrawled on the notepad, and her warm thoughts for Russ were suddenly replaced by an urgent longing that welled up inside her. It would be so easy for her to dial him, hear his deep voice on the other end, feel his breath in her ear. Her whole body spoke her need for him, and in spite of the tingles that traveled through her bloodstream and collected at the base of her pelvis, she remembered the last time she had called. The voice that answered hadn't been deep. With a shudder, she tossed the paper in the garbage, simultaneously realizing she wasn't breathing. She inhaled sharply. Instantly nauseous, she barely made it to the bathroom in time. *How far you can reach me*, she thought, and watched her lunch disappear down the toilet.

Throughout the course of the evening, Amelia fished out that paper and threw it back nearly a dozen times. Finally, when Russ called her back with Bull's number, she added his number to the paper, in the name of economy, of course.

This new number set her heart pumping as well, for obviously a different reason. What would she ask him? What would he know? What would he actually tell her, whether he knew something or not? She knew the questions were pointless and in spite of her unsettled stomach dialed the number.

She was about to hang up when Bull picked up. He was just beginning to bellow "Hello" into the phone for the second time when Amelia finally found her voice.

"Hello, Mr. Goldfield? This is Amelia Kingston. I was one of the guides on the cattle drive you went on this past spring. Not sure you remember me."

"Skinny, freckled one," he grunted as a response. Amelia had never considered herself freckled but taking that as a "yes" charged ahead.

"I'm calling to seek your expertise as a terrorist screening analyst. Seems my father may have had some trouble on his return to the U.S. from Central America, and knowing your status within the department, I immediately thought that maybe you could help us."

"Listen, honey," he huffed. "My job ain't helping lawbreakers out of messes. Individual responsibility is what I'm all about. If your dad done got himself into a mess, well he'll just have to get himself out."

"You're right, of course, Mr. Goldfield. The problem is that he's my dad and he needs my help. What can I say? I just remembered learning so much from you on the trail that I thought for sure you'd be able to give me a hand. It's only a little favor, really."

"I probably got carried away with the brandy, but I'm of sound mind and body now and don't plan on making the same mistake."

"I only need to know where he's being held. He was arrested in Houston, but I can't find a record of his charges. I was thinking that the TSC would have some information on him. I was hoping you could just look him up on your database or something and find out where he is."

"No can do, missy. Not my kind of work. You'll have to figure some other way out of this problem your daddy's got. Now, I gotta—"

"Ever been to Lake Tahoe, Mr. Goldfield?" she blurted, a lure tossed in desperation.

"Lake Tahoe? Never been. Why?" he asked, poised to bite.

"Well, I got this friend who has a cabin on Lake Tahoe, and I thought if you'd be able to help me out with this, he could put you up for a few days," Amelia offered.

"That's not a bribe you're offering," he said, wrestling with the bait.

"Of course not. Just my way of thanking you for doing this small favor for me," Amelia responded.

"What's your father's name?" Caught.

After feeding him her father's identification information, she clarified what she needed from him. "I need to know where he's being held, why he was arrested, and what they plan to do with him. If you're able to give me extra information, I'll see if my friend will let you stay an extra day or two. Do I need to repeat anything?"

"Yeah, give me that social security number again," he sighed, a fish out of water.

Amelia hung up the phone exhilarated. Bull would come through for her, she was sure. A few days at Lake Tahoe for a wannabe was a big payoff. Russ was going to kill her, but she'd cross that bridge when she got to it. In the meantime, she was relieved to know she had set the ball in motion. She couldn't wait until Bull put it back in her court.

Chapter 64

Two days later, she was back at Jonathon's office. He had called her that morning to tell her he had more information. When she saw his grim face, she knew it wasn't good.

"Listen, Amelia," he said as they seated themselves at the desk in his office, "let me get right to the point. This isn't the cut-and-dried case I thought it was. Turns out there are some inconsistencies in the evidence. Between that and your missing father, we just don't have a case."

She wasn't surprised by the death sentence delivered upon her case. She had known that without her father, sooner or later the pronouncement would come. But there was another reason he had cited that she hadn't expected.

"What do you mean, 'inconsistencies?'" She questioned in confusion.

"Well, the evidence isn't as straightforward as the final report suggests. In fact, there's contradictory evidence around the cause of the explosion. On the one hand, the findings suggest a diffuse explosion, like the natural gas one we are pursuing. But on the other hand, there is also evidence of a concentrated one, which points to pre-placed explosives."

"Excuse me? Pre-placed what?" Amelia interrupted, aghast.

"Explosives, Amelia. Part of the evidence suggests that other explosives were used."

"How can that be!" The implication of this new information ricocheted like a pinball against the other absurdities already amassed in her brain. She could only cover her face with her hands in an attempt to stop the wild lights and buzzers.

"Amelia, I'm not saying that's what really happened. I'm just saying that the evidence is contradictory. Amelia," he repeated, reaching across the desk to draw her hands away from her face. He left his own on top of hers as he continued.

"Please Amelia, don't take it like this. I'm just saying the evidence isn't conclusive in either regard. I believe it still points to company negligence, but I don't think I can prove that with the evidence as it is. You see," he went on, stroking her hand and looking with concern into her near-vacant eyes, "ordinarily a natural gas explosion will cause an outward explosion since the gas is lighter than air and rises. The explosion would push out the walls near the top, and the ceiling would collapse. A concentrated explosion, on the other hand, will usually result in an explosion first and then a consequent implosion, resulting in a crater and more thoroughly pulverized debris. The explosion at your house had both the high concentrations of natural gas present, originating in the area around the valve, and the crater and debris descriptive of a concentrated explosion. They didn't discover any residue of other explosives, but with the inconsistencies present and the fact it was a loose valve rather than a faulty one, I don't think we have a strong enough case. I'm sorry Amelia," he sighed, "I really wanted to win this for you. You deserve more than this. I'm sorry."

He continued to hold her hand tightly as if squeezing it would bring back the life to her eyes. When it did not, he decided to try another tactic.

"Amelia," he said softly, which got him a flicker of recognition and a bit of a sigh, "would you give me a chance to take your mind off all of this? Maybe Saturday night after you've had some time to yourself to digest it all?"

"What did you have in mind?" she finally answered, looking up in acquiescence.

"How about an outdoor concert in the park? It's the last outdoor concert of the season."

"Why not?" she agreed, with none of her customary enthusiasm. But Jonathon took what he could get.

"I'll pick you up at 6:00, then."

He led her to the door of his office, but instead of opening it, he simply leaned against it and took her in his arms. She didn't struggle, nor did she succumb. She simply stood rigidly in his embrace. "Take care of yourself," he said, finally letting her go and opening the door. "I'll see you tomorrow night."

She nodded and left him standing there, his hands in his pockets, watching her float lifelessly from the suite.

Chapter 65

"You're quite the popular girl today," her grandmother chided as Amelia entered the house. She took the note her grandmother held out to her but barely reacted even after seeing an international number for Honduras upon it and Simon Goldfield's name below. She had driven back to her grandmother's in a stupor, the words from her dream repeating over and over in her head. *Seek the truth. Seek the truth. Seek the truth.* She had never imagined the truth could be something like this, that they could have been, murd— she couldn't even let her brain form the word.

"There's another on the back," interrupted her grandmother's voice as Amelia was about to leave the room.

Turning the paper reluctantly, she saw his name, not in her grandma's simple script as it appeared but as one would imagine it upon a movie marquee: "Donovan Real Bird!" Her heart sank almost more quickly than it jumped. Had the sofa not been within arm's reach, she was sure she would have fallen from the dizziness that washed over her. *This is too much*, she thought as she squeezed her eyelids shut in an effort to reestablish her equilibrium, feeling the knot in her stomach bubble into nausea. *Too much.*

"He sounded so urgent," her grandmother explained, interrupting her thoughts yet again. "He said he called every Kingston in the book to find you. Someone you met in Montana?" she implored.

"Oh, Grandma," Amelia sighed, her emotional exhaustion keeping her tears at bay. "Someone who broke my heart. Maybe someday I'll call him back, but not today. But I do need to call this other person back. Mind if I use the phone?"

Pushing her nausea down and Donovan from her mind as best she could, Amelia picked up the phone and dialed the first number, though her fingers ached to dial the last.

Her Honduran contact quickly updated her on her stepmother and stepbrother's conditions, then spent the bulk of the phone call negotiating the bill. It was cheap, by American standards, but would still take a healthy chunk from the money Amelia's mother had left her. *What the Lord giveth, he taketh away*, Amelia recited in her head. Of all the biblical teachings, this was by far the one she had learned the most deeply. In the end, she would use a money transfer service to send the money directly to the hospital's banking institution. And because their conditions had changed very little, her stepbrother's somewhat more than her stepmother's, she could expect to make similar transactions for some time to come.

By the time she dialed the second number, she was somewhat curious to hear what he would say, of course the expected gouge to her bank account after this call kept her from being too excited about any particular outcome.

"Yeah, this is Simon Goldfield," Bull answered after the first ring. "Listen, I checked out what you wanted me to, and we do have a Robert Kingston in the system. Seems like a real live terrorist. Glad we got one more off the street. You should be ashamed to have a father like that."

"You have info on him? What can you tell me about him?" Amelia asked, ignoring the bait, Donovan all but forgotten.

"Looks like he's had some pretty heavy Al Qaeda contacts. But I'm not going to give you any of that. Let's stick to the deal. You do remember our deal, don't you?" he demanded.

"Of course, Bul—, I mean Mr. Goldfield. Lake Tahoe. I'm good for my word. What do you have?" she continued, trying to keep the urgency from her voice, sure that if he heard it the deal would be off.

"January's best for me," he continued. "Get me something in January."

"Sure, Mr. Goldfield. I'll let you know what I work out." She paused. "Now, what do you have?" she repeated, on the edge of losing patience.

"He was picked up in Houston, as you said, and held at the Houston Federal Detention Center as a material witness. There's been more information added since then. Seems he's been transferred, but that's all I got clearance for. Make sure to get me that place in Tahoe," he declared and hung up, leaving Amelia holding a receiver that held no sure answers but only the echo of yet another question.

Chapter 66

Connie had been right. Her father was being held as a material witness. As she drove to Connie's the next day, hoping to make sense of yet another layer of complexity—insanity, rather—she tried to understand what it meant for her dad to be a material witness in light of what Jonathon had uncovered. Was it all a mistake? Or was he really in league with terrorists? No matter what his faults, and Amelia knew they were many, she knew, too, that he was utterly incapable of such violence. His apparent detainment had to be the result of his journalist activities. There was no other plausible explanation. And given his detainment, he must have posed a significant threat to the U.S. government. How significant a threat? Jonathon's contradictory findings suggesting the possibility of pre-placed explosives gave her room to entertain the unthinkable. Yet, at this point, wasn't anything thinkable?

This time she didn't even wait until she was through the doorway, let alone seated, before she blurted, "Could someone have bombed our house?"

"What?" Connie exclaimed. "Why would you think that?"

Shakily, after Connie had insisted on seating her at her usual place at the table, which the accoutrements of her surroundings now knew better than to occupy, Amelia filled Connie in on the information Jonathon had given her. Although Connie wasn't convinced by the evidence, she didn't completely discount it.

"I don't know," Connie sighed, rubbing a hand across a face that Amelia noticed looked even wearier than the last time they had met. "I really don't know. Maybe someone rigged the explosion somehow. It seems so coincidental, the death threa—"

Amelia gasped. "Death *threats*? Is that what you were going to say?"

Connie twisted uncomfortably in her chair contemplating her response before facing Amelia.

"Yes," she finally admitted, quickly adding, "but your father wasn't exactly new to death threats. He always covered controversial material outside the mainstream media."

"Right. Nothing out of the ordinary. Just a few death threats," Amelia muttered.

"Okay, so he got a few more than usual, several calls, and a number of threatening letters. But in classic Robert Kingston form, the threats actually fueled his investigation, making him more resolved than ever to unveil the truth."

"What did they threaten to do, exactly?" Amelia insisted, leaning forward so far that she could see the gold flecks in Connie's eyes.

"I know what you're thinking," Connie sighed, rocking back in her chair to rest her head upon its back, "and I can't deny that I've gone down that road many times myself. It's probably just coincidence. In fact, I think I've been able to convince myself of that until you showed up." She sat back up, meeting Amelia's imploring stare. "Several threatened to burn down his house. One even mentioned you all by name and how you'd all be dead if he continued writing his lies. Nothing specifically about a gas explosion, though one threatened to make the London bombings more real to him."

"Did he ever try to figure out who was making them?"

"For the most part he assumed that they were listeners of the Patriot talk radio station, which sometimes used, or rather misused, his material to ridicule the anti-war movement. But he did tell me he had a heated argument—he didn't say anything about a threat—with his London bombing informant. Come to think of it, I remember your father being quite anxious about it."

"Did he know the guy's name? Where to find him?" Amelia asked astonished.

"I'm pretty sure your father knew him and maybe even his whereabouts since they had been in communication for quite a few years. But as far as I know, he never believed him capable of following through with his threat."

"Even after our house blew up?" Amelia asked incredulously.

"Well, maybe after, but he didn't stick around to find out, now did he?"

"So, turns out he'd rather run away and save his own skin than find the murderer of his wife and child. He disgusts me," Amelia spat with vehemence.

"Now hold on, Amelia. We don't even know if the explosion was intentional. Okay, maybe it could have been one of those Patriot Radio listeners or maybe some terrorist informant. Your dad stepped on a lot of toes. It could have been anyone. Or, more likely, no one."

"Oh Connie," Amelia said, succumbing to tears. "I never once imagined it could have been anything other than an accident. And to think my fa...a...ther," she sputtered, the word catching in her throat, "could have done something to provoke it... or prevent it!"

She let her last statement fully register. Her father, her brother's father, her mother's husband. Not only was he guilty of running away from the truth but possibly allowing their deaths to happen in the first place. Years of bitterness reached their boiling point at that moment, and she rushed to the bathroom to expel it into the toilet. *The bitterness of bile,* she promised her father as she stared into the yellow, phlegmy mixture that lay fizzing in the bowl. *That's what I'll taste every time I think of you.*

"Amelia," Connie was at the door. Worry stretched taut across her wide face, seeming to radiate even to the ends of her spiky hair.

Amelia stood up slowly, wiping her mouth with a wad of toilet paper.

"Well, Connie," she finally sighed, "maybe when this is all over there'll be a story in it for you."

"You would say that," Connie admonished, closing the distance between them with one large step and hugging Amelia close. "I don't much care if I ever get to write this story. All I want is that it have a satisfactory ending," she said, stroking Amelia's hair. "Man, I'd like to say a 'happy' ending, but given where we've started, I'd settle for 'satisfactory'."

"I'd settle for any ending at all," Amelia lamented, lifting her head from Connie's shoulder. Then looking straight into her eyes she added, "Any ending that'll lead to a new beginning."

Chapter 67

Amelia looked at the profusion of products that stretched in front of her upon the Walgreen's shelf, last night's date a blur as she tried to decipher the labels through glazed eyes. In spite of the overwhelming nature of the past two days, she and Jonathon had a wonderful evening enjoying the music of O.A.R., stretched upon a blanket on the damp October grass away from the livelier crowd below. They had spent more time kissing than listening, perhaps, but such multitasking took little effort for either of them. Amelia had barely thought about any of her past, let alone worry about Jonathon discovering she had borrowed her fall jacket from her eighty-seven-year-old grandmother.

What she needed today, however, couldn't be borrowed, nor could she borrow more time for continued denial. There was no coffee to smell or salmon to blame. There was just her memory of an incredible experience and the queasiness in her stomach that brought her back to it. Finally, she just grabbed a box and after paying for it, walked the three blocks back to her grandmother's.

It was Sunday, and she had turned down an invitation to church with her grandmother. She needed the time alone. Three minutes was an eternity, yet like that last block she and her father had driven to their home thirteen years ago, she wished the end would never come. But like before, the answer was inevitable, for it had already happened regardless of the last block or the last three minutes. She dropped the stick from her hand as if it burned and clutched her head in her hands to stop the truth that pounded against it: *pink means yes, pink means yes, pink means yes.* She crumpled upon the floor.

Pink meant yes, but what did 'yes' mean? That is what she could not figure, what did not compute. How could one who played with fire so little get burned so often? What or who had condemned her to a cursed life? Why was she powerless to fight it?

She spent the rest of the day in bed, complaining to her grandmother of the stomach flu. She needed a plan, but before she could make a plan, she needed to understand what it meant, what it would mean. Just weeks before, she had discovered her future was open: new money, Jonathon. Jonathon—who had helped her forget, who had begun to needle his way into her heart and nudge at its captor. And then just like always, the past came and snatched it away. Why did her past have such control of her future?

Monday passed in much the same way. She was immobilized. She declined to take Connie's call and then Jonathon's. The third call she declined, however, catapulted her even further into her darkness.

"He called twice today. He asked me to tell you he just needed to talk to you one last time. Then he'd leave you alone for good. Can't you just talk to him for a minute?" her grandmother pleaded and then added, "He sounded so sad."

Amelia had refused and then rushed to the bathroom to throw up. Why had he called? He had betrayed her, and now she knew he had betrayed the life she held within her too. They could have been a family, her family. Though she knew that was too simple, too ideal, in the cold, cruel nest of reality, she cried for the loss anyway, despite its ideality. Break it down to its cold bone, she demanded. She had had a fling, he had betrayed her, and now she was pregnant. What fairytale ending could she devise for such a romantic beginning?

On Tuesday, she forced herself into the car and drove to the one person who could offer her solace. Crouched upon her mother's grave, she wept for her misfortune. She cried for the lopsided grin and the white hanky he had proffered. It had become the real deal, security and support in a world that threatened to upend her with each step she took. And now, it was simply a luxury she had touched but could not hold.

Soon the startling contrast between her situation and her current setting worked its way into her mind. She had come here before to bemoan the taking of life, and now she had come to bemoan its giving. How could she grieve for life being given?

She began to cry again but this time for the clarity that once again was hers. Not for the ramifications it had upon her future or for how it had shattered the ideals of her past, but for what was and would be. Everything else would have to be molded around the simple truth that she would be a mother. *A mother*, she repeated to herself, as she hugged the ground that now held hers.

There was no rainbow when her tears subsided, but her clarity gave her resolve. She would move forward, she always did.

"For you, I'll do my best," she promised, and from her crouch she bestowed a kiss on one headstone and then the other. As she ventured to stand, she noticed something peculiar between the stones, a perfect square of mounded grass, as if someone had stacked upon the ground extra layers of sod. She placed her hands upon the mound and found it to be no softer nor harder than the ground around her. Yet, unlike the mounds of her mother's and brother's plots that had settled and leveled with the surrounding earth, this mound appeared to be less carefully contrived to return to its original contours. *A soft place to rest*, she mused.

"Dibs," she called softly to Scottie, placing her hand upon the mound to claim her place for their next family picnic. And with that, she got back to her life, ready to make modifications for the new life growing within.

Chapter 68

Her first step to getting back to her life was to retrace the first step she had taken to reclaim her past. She wasn't quite sure why she had come. Of course, she had promised Toby a visit nearly a month ago and hoped she wouldn't be too upset that she had waited so long. But she also wanted something more. Maybe she felt that Toby could tell her something more and lead her one step closer to her father. Maybe she just wanted a reminder that she did have a family here, a hodgepodge of sorts, like a collection of rare china that, however mismatched, would serve her child the world upon each of its ornate platters.

Amelia smiled as she stood at the information desk, watching Toby help the less-than-enthusiastic teen find resources for his research paper. Toby made up for any enthusiasm he lacked and joyously shared with him her investigative expertise. Her plump fingers went whirring across the keyboard yet again searching another website of interest when she caught sight of Amelia. How she managed to get out of her chair and around the counter so quickly without toppling the whole thing over, including the boy, Amelia had little time to contemplate as Toby's exuberant hug nearly squeezed out her life's breath. Didn't appear she was too sore with Amelia for her delay after all.

"Toby, you really have to be a bit more tender with me!" Amelia wheezed, when Toby finally let her go. "Remember, I'm one of those sickly, skinny types that blow over in a breeze."

"Ah, you don't fool me. You're not skinny, just small boned!" Then with barely a pause to hear Amelia's chuckle, she yelled over her shoulder to anyone it concerned and everyone it didn't, "I'm going on break!"

As Amelia sat across from Toby in Dunn Bros, she was reminded of the lighter side of life, the optimism that came with nature, not circumstance. She knew Toby's past was as tragic as her own: a son killed in a car accident, a husband that bailed on her and her grief. Yet here she sat in front of Amelia, the silver lining draped over her robust shoulders. It was so comforting to sit within its glow.

This time Toby had foregone the brownie and cappuccino and sat sipping black coffee. Amelia wondered what number diet she was on. Poor Toby, she just never gave up, yet always did.

"I was thinking the other day about that book list I gave to the FBI," she declared, after having shared a number of lively anecdotes and clever musings over the past ten minutes. "I have to admit I took a peek at it myself as I printed it off for them. Your father sure was interested in some obscure topics. Take time capsules and safes, for instance. *The Art of Time Capsules, Weathering the Storms of Time: Building a Time Capsule to Last, Is Your Safe Safe?* Anyway, something like that. Do you think the FBI would have reason to worry about someone making a time capsule? I could understand if it were books on bomb-making. But safes sound pretty safe to me," she added, wincing at her own pun. "Come to think of it," she laughed sheepishly, "I wasn't ever supposed to say anything about it. A 'gag order' they said. Suppose thirteen years later it doesn't make any difference!"

In spite of her confusion, Amelia had to giggle to herself. She never even asked the question, and Toby had given her exactly what she came for: more information about her father. She didn't say that, however, and instead responded, "I can't imagine the FBI being interested in any of that. I can't imagine it being of interest to my father either, for that matter. He's never been one for collecting memorabilia or safeguarding for natural disasters," *or unnatural ones*, she added to herself bitterly.

"Then again, your father never seemed to be one who did what was expected. Seemed to have a knack for setting the ordinary on its ear." Toby frowned at her empty coffee cup as she set it upon the table. "Well, that was completely unsatisfactory," she declared. "I better get out of here before I go for some real satisfaction."

As Amelia walked Toby back to the information desk, she couldn't shake the image of safes and time capsules. Finally, she laughed at the futility of finding relevance in a few books that shared a list with *Harry Potter and the Chamber of Secrets. And anyway,* she thought, *he could be the 'Prisoner of Azkaban' for all I care.*

Chapter 69

"Hi, Jonathon? Yeah, it's Amelia. I've been sick. I'm sorry I haven't gotten back to you. No, I'm feeling better now, thanks." She wondered if he could tell from her voice that she was different. She wondered if he'd tell from her face when he saw her.

She really had no idea why she was enlisting him in what she was about to do. She knew that she needed to break things off with him face-to-face, but this had nothing to do with that. This was for a far more selfish reason. She wanted him with her. In a way, he had been there from the beginning of this journey, and she wanted him to be with her for this next strange step. She would tell him later. Soon…but later. There was still a little time, and maybe she would find a way to do it that wouldn't hurt him so much. Hurt *her* so much. So, the subtext was left unsaid and instead, by the time they had finished their conversation, she had convinced him to meet her despite how crazy it sounded.

It was drizzling and nearly black as they made their way forward with the flashlight. The slope was slippery, but Jonathon's arm kept Amelia from falling. When they reached the top, he let the flashlight lie limp at his side, and in spite of the near blackness, his mouth found hers. His lips felt sweet, but as all sweetness in her life came with a price, she paid for it with her guilt.

Then as suddenly as the kiss began, it ended with a flashlight beam to her eyes.

"Okay, Amelia. What do you have up your sleeve? Please tell me we're not here to exhume any bodies."

In spite of the gruesome thought, especially since they were standing directly above her mother's and brother's grave, Amelia laughed into the beam of his flashlight.

"At first appearances it might seem that way," she admitted, producing a trowel from her grandmother's coat. "But we're actually here to exhume something else. Now get that out of my face so I can see what I'm doing."

He pointed it at the ground, and she pushed his hand until the beam shone between her mother's and brother's headstones.

"Do you see that mound?" she declared. "That's where we're exhuming." And with that, she crouched between the stones and began to dig with the trowel.

"This is just way too creepy, Amelia," Jonathon confessed, shivering less from the cold than from their current occupation. "Maybe if I had known you longer, I could find some humor in this, but I'm beginning to think you should be locked up next to your father."

"Just be patient. You'll soon see only my father should be locked up, but maybe not in a jail. It shouldn't be too deep."

It took another ten minutes of rooting around, and Jonathon's threats to leave her there alone, before Amelia's trowel hit the metal safe. Within minutes she had it entirely dug up.

"This is entirely too bizarre!" Jonathon lamented. "Before I met you I was an ordinary lawyer in an ordinary life. Now I'm standing in the rain in the middle of the night, digging up metal boxes in a cemetery. And inside I suppose we'll find the head of Jimmy Hoffa!"

"Nothing so glamorous," Amelia confessed, opening the lid wide so Jonathon could see there was no head, only stacks of money. "Just a little cash saved for a rainy day. And imagine that! It's raining!"

Jonathon raised the beam from the safe to her face.

"Please tell me that's not stolen money," he moaned as she smiled even more broadly.

"If only my father were that romantic. No, Jonathon, just some insurance money my father couldn't trust to our financial institutions, or to me, it would seem. Now shine the flashlight back down here so I can cover this hole up. Then we'll haul this down to the car."

But before she closed the safe, she caught sight of something that made her think her father was more of a romantic than she had given him credit for. She closed the lid quickly and covered her puzzlement with a smile as she looked up at Jonathon. He didn't need to know about that.

Within a half hour they were warming themselves inside Jonathon's car, the safe oozing mud all over the back seat. Jonathon sat grinning across from her. Suddenly, she wanted to spread kisses across that crooked grin and erase the past that prevented her from doing just that, but his smile quickly turned downward in an expression of earnest.

"I'm sorry about that," Amelia apologized, indicating the backseat. "We'll take out what we need to get it professionally cleaned."

"I'm not worried about that, Amelia," Jonathon replied, his face frowning under the dashboard lights. "I'm worried about me. Tonight, in this creepy setting, doing this crazy stunt, I felt more alive than I've ever felt. And it's not just tonight. It's every time I'm with you. You are so real, so raw. I touch you, and I feel life vibrate in my hand. I feel a genuineness that has been groomed out of my life until it's become a sterile shell of what life should be. When I'm with you, I feel my spirit again."

He was holding her hands in his and looking at them instead of her eyes.

"To be honest, I'm afraid to lose you. I know this is so fast, but I want to know, I *need* to know what you feel about me." Finally, he looked up at her. "I think I'm falling in love with you," he confessed.

She stared at him. She didn't know what to say about anything he had said. She wondered what she would have responded had her situation been different, had she not been carrying Donovan's child. She knew he was the perfect boyfriend, and eventual husband, not to mention the answer to all her grandmother's dreams. But in spite of all that, regardless of whether he could ever accept the baby within her, she suddenly knew she could not accept him. Donovan distorted his face at every turn, interrupted his kisses, and took his place in her dreams. She adored the image of him next to her, but it was Donovan who nestled within.

Her silence told him more than he was prepared to hear. He shook his head and silenced her with his hand when she decided to finally speak.

"No," he said. "Don't say it. I got your answer. Just answer me one more. Do you think you could ever return my feelings?"

Amelia swallowed and through tears that began to pool in her eyes she answered.

"Even if I could, Jonathon, there's so much baggage to sift through. I haven't even begun to organize it myself. The girl from the other side of the tracks would get old pretty quickly. And I'm from way on the other side of the tracks."

"That's not what you are to me," he objected, "but I suppose that doesn't matter now. I have your answer." He looked away into the rivulets of drizzle that coursed down his window to meet as a stream at its base.

"I better get you home," he said, putting the car in gear. She remembered another time he had said that, and like that time it carried with it regret, but this time also loss and fear. But the fear was not his. That was hers alone, and as they drove back through the darkness, it wormed its way inside her. She worried it might claim her womb for itself.

Chapter 70

Just wait 'til I show you—." Amelia began.

"You won't believe what—" Connie interrupted. They both laughed.

Upon seeing the safe Amelia held in her arms, Connie's curiosity got the best of her. "You go first!" she exclaimed.

"Well," Amelia continued, heaving the safe over to deposit it with a thud on the table. "I found something.

"You don't say," Connie remarked. "Should I even bother asking where...or how?"

"Suffice it to say it was sheer coincidence that I found it. Just a few pieces of the puzzle fell together and a little graveside digging later...*voilà!*"

"Don't even tell me," Connie winced at the thought. "I don't even want to understand what went on inside your dad's head. And I'm a little worried that you figured it out. But since we have it, let's have a look inside!

"Pretty much what I thought," Amelia said as she opened the lid and began to finger the money. "About two hundred thousand dollars. There are some documents in here accounting for the money. This receipt shows that twenty-five of it is my father's share of mom's life insurance. And this document shows the home insurance payout for the equity they had in their home. That makes up the remainder. Doesn't look like my father was involved in blackmail or bribery, only general mistrust of the government and our financial institutions. However..." Amelia paused for dramatic effect, as if Connie's google eyes at seeing so much cash suggested she needed even more drama, "seems like his general mistrust extended beyond protecting one's money." With that, she opened her hand, and in it lay a USB flash drive.

"Curiouser and curiouser," Connie murmured, taking it from Amelia's outstretched palm. "Have you listened to it yet?" she stammered, her voice taking on a high pitch in her excitement.

"Believe me, I wanted to but I didn't have any way to play it. Grandma and I are both still caught in the twentieth century, and I didn't feel comfortable taking it to the library."

Five minutes later, Amelia and Connie sat at the table, heads cocked, ears straining to hear the conversation emanating from Connie's iPad. It was obviously a phone conversation, and the voices echoed and broke, indicative of cell phone interference. Regardless, they were able to make out most of the conversation that appeared to have started in the middle.

"Wait a minute," Amelia heard her father's voice say. "You can't think I had anything to do with that. How do you even know they were surveilling you?"

"You think I'm stupid?" demanded a British voice with the hint of a foreign accent. "I know when I'm being followed. And they were American. You're American. And you wonder how I know it was you."

"There are millions of Americans—"

"And you're the only one I've been talking to!" You're the only one mentioning me in the papers!

"Anonymously! I've never breathed a word. Never. You know I wouldn't. This relationship, our relationship, has been mutually beneficial. Al Qaeda gets recog—"

"You talk of our relationship? You're an idiot. You used me; I used you. End of story. And I mean end of story. *Your story!*" He bellowed.

The loud "click" that followed caused both Amelia and Connie to jump in their chairs. It was another ten seconds or so before Amelia and Connie had the nerve to look at one another.

"Well," Connie sighed, "like I said, he stepped on some toes. Sounds like this was his London bombing informant. The British accent gives us a pretty big clue."

Amelia wasn't sure what to say, what to feel. Could that cold, British voice have taken revenge on her father? And how could that other voice, of the person she had loved and admired, have goaded him on? They were co-conspirators, she decided, equally responsible for the deaths of the two people she loved most in the world, but in her heart, it was her father who took on the true brunt of the blame.

"This doesn't prove anything," Connie reminded her. "He doesn't say he's going to do anything; he just intimates it. A lot of people have done that without anything ever coming of it. We can't jump to any conclusions."

"Why bury this flash drive after the explosion if it's so benign? And alongside the money? It must have had something to do with it."

"You've got a point there," Connie relented. "Or maybe he knew the FBI was investigating him, and he wanted to continue to protect his source? Or protect himself by keeping it as leverage against his source?"

"Or protect himself from being affiliated with a known terrorist?" Amelia suggested disdainfully. "It would be just like him to continue to protect himself."

"Well, the next question seems to be What should we do with this new information? I think this time, we leave it up to someone else. How do you feel about turning it over to the FBI? I know they're involved in your father's disappearance, but maybe they're the best people to handle this."

Amelia shook her head vehemently.

"But I don't just want to hand this over. I want someone to tell us what it means. The FBI won't do that. They're not going to just call us up and say, 'By the way, that audio you dropped off for us? Well, the guy is this terrorist wanted for the such-and-such and he confessed to killing your family. So glad we could help.'"

"True," she conceded, "but you're not going to go to Al Qaeda and ask them whose voice is on the tape, either."

"Maybe a private investigator?" Amelia suggested. "We've got evidence from the explosion that suggests it was intentional. Maybe a private investigator could help put the pieces together?"

"And how will they link this to the explosion? Even if you discover whose voice is on it, that doesn't prove anything, only that he threatened your father."

"Well, that's something, isn't it?" Amelia exploded. "I mean, my mother and brother are dead, the gas company won't take responsibility, the government and Al Qaeda are out of reach, so what can I hope for?"

"Okay, okay," Connie acquiesced, softly capturing Amelia's hands in her own. "It's a possibility. But before we figure that out, there is something I'd like to share with you. Are you up for some good news?"

Chapter 71

Amelia wasn't quite ready to drop the flash drive but decided good news would be a welcome interruption, so she simply leaned back in her chair and watched Connie tug out a newspaper from underneath the corner of the safe. It was the *New York Times*. Connie thumbed to a page and set it on the table in front of Amelia.

"Not the front page, but I think it'll do the trick."

Amelia had not even taken it in her hands when she saw her father's picture and under it the heading "Missing Newspaper Reporter: Victim of USDHS or Bodily Harm?" In a second, Amelia snatched it up and began to read.

Former newspaper reporter Robert Kingston of the Free News Press has been missing since April 12th. He was last seen at the Houston International Airport in the custody of TSA agents. Family and friends believe that Kingston may have been detained as a material witness due to his political views and contacts with Middle-Eastern informants. Kingston was best known for coverage of the London Bombing in 2005. If you have any information regarding Robert Kingston's whereabouts, please contact the New York Times, c/o Ana Kowalski.

Amelia looked up at Connie in stunned silence. She knew she was supposed to be pleased, but all she felt was bitterness.

Connie smiled back at her before saying, "Sealed case or no, this article gives someone a chance to anonymously let us know where he is."

"This is fabulous," Amelia said with forced excitement. "How did you do it, Connie?"

"Ana's a friend at the *New York Times*. We went to school together and have worked together on a number of stories. She covers the immigration beat, so I thought this was a good tie-in."

"Do you think someone will respond?" Amelia asked, half hoping Connie would say "No," and her father would be lost forever to the brutal throes of injustice that were turning out to be more just than Amelia had first believed.

"We'll have to wait and see. In the meantime, why don't I send your flash drive," she said picking it up and waving it at Amelia, "to the *New York Times*? Maybe someone can identify the voice."

"Connie, you're a genius," she declared, with real enthusiasm this time. "But not because your idea is any good," she clarified. "You just made me think of an even better one!"

"Humph. Is that how it is?" Connie replied with feigned hurt.

"Yep. So, *I'll* take the flash drive," she said, standing up and taking it from Connie's hand. "I know just the person who can figure it out for us."

With that, she gave Connie a quick hug. Then depositing the flash drive in her grandmother's coat pocket, she walked out the door.

Chapter 72

She was waiting with her ear to the receiver for someone to pick up, but unlike last time, with little anticipation. She looked forward to hearing his voice, yet she dreaded what she would have to tell him.

"Weiland Ranch," she finally heard and in spite of herself, she felt a burst of enthusiasm.

"Russ! It's Amelia. It's so nice to hear your voice!"

"Hey, Amelia. It's good to hear yours too. What the heck have you been up to?"

They bantered for a bit, but it was Russ's news that would open the door to her inevitable confession.

"I just got back from Tahoe," Russ announced. "It, and he, was fabulous. We really hit it off. I'm going back out in another month or two, this time for a few weeks. We want to see if we can tolerate each other for more than a week at a time."

"Wow, Russ. That's fabulous. I'm so excited for you. I truly hope everything works out between the two of you."

"You don't sound that excited, Amelia. What's up?"

"Am I that transparent?" Amelia laughed. "Well, Russ, I made a super big promise to someone in exchange for some super important information, and that super big promise involves Jason and Lake Tahoe."

"Okay, wait a second. Can you start from the beginning?"

So, Amelia gave him the briefest possible version of her missing father story.

"It even got written up in the *New York Times*," she said, giving him the information he needed to find the article. She then went on to explain why she had needed Bull's help and how she had gotten it.

"Russ, I'm sorry. I was desperate, and it just came to me. I know it's a big ask, but is there any possible way you can help? I could pay your friend for it. Turns out my father left me a lot of money."

Russ was more sympathetic than Amelia could have hoped for. He insisted that Jason would understand and would go out of his way to make Bull's stay memorable.

"Anything to help you out, Amelia. But Amelia, why didn't you tell me any of this before? I never even knew your mother and brother had passed away. I thought we were better friends than that," he admonished. "But that doesn't matter now. I know now and I'll do what I can."

"Russ, you really are the best. I'm sorry I didn't confide in you earlier. And now, at the risk of pushing my gall to the limit, I need to ask for your help with one more thing." She winced as she said it, but Russ's "Sure!" was so immediate she knew he was not put off.

"I need another favor from Bull. Can you think of any way I could convince him?"

They discussed the problem for a while longer, and when Amelia hung up, she was ready to dial the next number.

"Yes, Mr. Goldfield, it's 'that freckly girl' again. And no, I'm not calling to renege on our agreement. In fact, I'm calling to sweeten it, but I need something in return."

Hanging up the phone, she fished the flash drive out of her pocket. She pilfered a padded envelope from her grandmother's desk, addressed it, and then slipped the drive inside. Who could have ever foretold what a helpful figure Bull would be in her life. *Absurd*! She mused.

Chapter 73

Before dropping the envelope off at the post office, Amelia purchased a round-trip ticket for Bull to Lake Tahoe for a two-week January vacation. Then she dropped the tickets in the envelope to consort with the flash drive before she sealed it and sent it on its way. The other envelope she mailed to Jason held a four thousand dollar check for an escort and friend of Jason's, Hannah Lee. Though formerly known as Harold, Amelia decided what Bull didn't know wouldn't hurt him, and what he did know would certainly help her.

So now it was time to wait.

She didn't have much time to wait, however. By the time she got back to her grandmother's from the post office, she already had a message from Connie to get her butt over there; they had gotten a bite.

"What did she mean by that?" her grandmother asked, having overheard the message and not sure whether to be turned off more by the word "butt" or the enigma, itself.

"Just the lawsuit, Grandma. We're following a couple threads, and one just paid off. I promise when I know more I'll fill you in on everything," she insisted as she planted a kiss on her grandmother's forehead before rushing towards the door.

"Oh yeah, Grandma, can I take…"

Her grandmother just waved her on from the kitchen. "You're in luck dear," she answered, "I'm being a homebody today. And when are you getting that license so I don't have to worry about you driving around illegally?"

"Oh yeah, that," Amelia said sheepishly. "Sorta been on the back burner."

"Well, let's move it to the front, shall we?" she replied. "What about a game of Scrabble when you get back?"

"Only if you accept Spanish words too, Grandma. Otherwise I haven't got a chance!"

"Alright, but that means Latin, French, and Yiddish are free game as well," she countered.

"Yiddish?" Amelia laughed. "Since when do you speak Yiddish?"

"Since my Jewish hairdresser has been teaching me for ten years," she bragged.

"Okay, Gramma. You win. English it is. I'll see you later."

"L-A-T-E-R," she called after Amelia, "worth seven points."

"Fourteen, Gram," Amelia called back. "I'm on a double word score!"

Chapter 74

Although Amelia had her own news to share, this time she would let Connie lead with hers. She could see that Connie, in her excitement, would have it no other way. Amelia had but barely opened the door when Connie was already propelling her towards the kitchen table. Bypassing her customary cup of coffee, she began to spill the news before Amelia touched her butt to the seat.

"We got it. The tip. Ana just called me this morning. She got a call from a guy that claimed to be involved in some way with your father's case. Ana got the feeling that he was his attorney, but she couldn't be sure. Anyway, this is going to print tomorrow." She thrust Amelia the draft of the *New York Times* article.

Missing Reporter Held Secretly at MDC

Robert Kingston, a newspaper reporter of the Free News Press, who has gone missing since April 12th of this year, may actually be found among the ranks of hundreds of others who have suffered the misuse of the material witness statute.

The material witness statute allows for the involuntary detainment of witnesses until which time their testimony is presented to a grand jury or in a criminal trial, provided that they both possess information 'material' to the case and pose a flight risk. Since 9/11, however, the government has employed an expansive view of this statute in its War on Terror, using it to indefinitely detain and question hundreds of persons without due process. Only a handful of those detained ever testify in a court proceeding. As a result, the practice has been under fire by civil liberties organizations for violation of Fifth Amendment rights. In spite of a recent ruling by the federal appeals court in New York that found the misuse of material witness warrants unconstitutional, the case of Robert Kingston may demonstrate that this misuse continues.

Robert Kingston, was last seen on April 12th when he was detained by airport security at the Houston International Airport. An anonymous source with ties to Kingston's case claims that Kingston was first held as a material witness at the Houston Federal Detention Center and later transferred to the Metropolitan Detention Center where he is now being held. According to the source, the US government has not charged Kingston with a crime and has not offered 'sufficient and compelling' evidence that warrants his indefinite detention as a material witness. The source insists that Kingston's legal team is doing everything possible to "overcome the obstacles and stall tactics" the government has placed before them. "We are optimistic," the source reports, "that we will soon be able to reunite Mr. Kingston with his family."

"Of course," Connie jumped in the moment Amelia's eyes lifted from the page, "being held in this legal limbo is no laughing matter. We have no idea what will happen next. We assume your father's legal team will continue to challenge his detention, which may lead to his release, or his being charged."

"Charged? On what grounds?"

"That's hard to say. All I can say is that since most material witnesses within the context of the War on Terror never actually testify, I doubt that your father will, either. Typically, they are either released or charged with a crime. The crimes can be as sensational as terrorist activity or as mundane as opening a social media account for a suspected terrorist."

"So, all we can do is wait," Amelia conceded. She knew that Connie wanted her to feel excited that they had found him, but excitement wasn't among the crowd in her bag of emotions. Relief?

Okay, she'd give him that, to know he was okay. Worry? Maybe, for what he had to face. Frustration? Absolutely, for there he was, a location attached to his name and no way to hold him accountable for his real crimes, crimes the government lacked the imagination to trump up. Anger? Always.

"In the meantime," Connie said, interrupting her introspection, "I'm sure this will create a few waves. Maybe enough of them to pressure the U.S. government into making a different decision."

"Oh, God," Amelia exclaimed. "If this creates waves like you think it will, my grandma will never again be able to hold her head high at the Governor's Tea!"

Chapter 75

Only after Amelia left Connie's did she realize what finding her father really meant. She realized he held so many of the answers she had sought, and although she felt vindication in his captivity, she needed him to release her from hers. She needed him to tell her the meaning in all the bizarre twists and turns his life and hers had taken. What had he really done? Who was the man on that recording? What had really happened that spring night that had turned their lives to winter?

In spite of her every pore that cried out for the answers she knew he could provide, she would have to wait. And though her grandmother did not need another advantage in the game of Scrabble that poured across the dining room table, Amelia's mind, on the verge of knowing the truth, distracted her from finding an adequate place for the 'X' she picked on her second turn. In the end, she subtracted it from a score of fifty-two, along with a 'J' and an 'H'.

That night even Donovan could not visit in her sleep as the 'X' in *executive* power and *explosion* danced through her dreams like some sadistic episode of *Sesame Street* that *excommunicated* journalists and took the *axe* to the U.S. constitution.

Chapter 76

The weeks that followed as she waited on the outskirts of her father's legal purgatory seemed to drag on and on. Amelia was also a spectator on the distant sidelines of the Honduran saga that continued to play out thousands of miles away. She discovered that her stepbrother had finally been released from the hospital, but it had become clear that his mother's coma was permanent. Until someone made the more permanent decision to end it, that is. In the meantime, the two hundred thousand dollars her father had buried took the sting out of the hospital bills she continued to pay and the start-up money she transferred to her stepbrother.

She was somewhat a bystander in her own life as well. After weeks of hurried discoveries into the hidden aspects of her past, this new pace of waiting left her detached and restless. Her nausea had increased, and she could no longer pretend that it was only her past that mattered. Yet, only closure, she knew, would release her to move forward.

There was the constant pall of sadness, too, as she waited. Her changing body and the dreams that came at night—and those that infiltrated her days—were a constant reminder of Donovan. She had pushed from her mind her romantic illusions of the nuclear family, but the ever-present waves of his memory tested her levee of resolve, exploiting each weakness.

And there was Jonathon. Now that he was no longer in the picture, she realized how much she missed him. She knew, if given the chance, they would have loved. Maybe not with the same intensity as she had loved Donovan, but she felt sure that under the tenderness of Jonathon's love hers would have responded. It was a moot point, she knew. How could he have continued to love her knowing she was to have another man's baby? It wasn't a question she needed him to answer and, more than anything, she was relieved that she would never have to explain to him a stomach that was already bulging and a father held in legal limbo.

Amelia knew, however, that she would have to explain both of these counts to her grandmother sooner or later. She couldn't expect her to stay in the dark forever. But before she could prepare for this inevitability, the need to explain one of the situations came about sooner rather than later. Amelia was just descending the stairs when she heard voices at the front door. When she got to the kitchen, she saw her grandmother's back and through the opened door the pencil and pad of a reporter.

"Is it true, Mrs. Kingston that your son is being held as a suspected terrorist?" Amelia overheard as she made her way to her grandmother's aid.

"What? What are you talking about?" her grandmother sputtered, a mixture of confusion and indignation upon the wrinkled face that would appear in the paper the following morning.

"Hey, hey!" Amelia shouted, wedging herself between her grandmother and the reporter. "Leave her out of this. If you need to talk to someone, talk to me. Now Grandma," she gently commanded, "let me deal with this. I promise to tell you what it's all about after. Please, Grandma," she pleaded when her grandmother showed no signs of moving, "just go into the living room. I'll be there in a few minutes."

She watched as her grandmother reluctantly made her way towards the living room, looking back over her shoulder to shake her head.

Amelia stepped out the door to meet the reporters. She wasn't sure how much she should say and then decided that she would be as forthcoming as possible. Anything that would help her fath…the cause for civil liberties.

She answered a plethora of questions, mostly corroborating the articles that had appeared in the *New York Times*. She also shared her personal opinion.

"My father had sources from the Middle-East who helped him get information about the 2005 London bombing. But that's as far as his connections went. Any ties he had with Al Qaeda, if he even had any, would have been to get information for his stories. He simply was a reporter doing his job."

When they had driven off, Amelia took a deep breath and headed towards the living room. Her grandma was staring blankly into the television.

"What has my son gone and done now?" she asked softly.

Chapter 77

"Kingston's," Amelia announced answering the phone. "Mr. Goldfield. I'm delighted you called." She nodded over to her grandmother, who looked up expectantly from a crossword puzzle that remained untouched.

It had been difficult for Amelia to share the events of the past two months with her grandmother. Not only was the information painful and confusing, she knew her grandmother would be resentful for having been left out. That was an understatement. Amelia tried to explain how she had not wanted to upset her.

"Since when does being old mean I deserve to be treated like a child?" Her grandmother had responded. "I've buried three children, a husband, a daughter-in-law, and a grandson. What exactly are you trying to protect me from? At least I could have done some damage control. I could have leaked a little of the story out to the gals so I wouldn't be a leper to them now. Do you know why bridge and tea at the country club and brunch at the Governor's mansion are so important to me? Because they distract me, engage my mind so I don't have to think, to remember. Now even that is sullied. You should have told me."

She had sulked away then to her bedroom. Amelia had let her go, not wanting to hear the crying she knew would follow.

But her grandma had softened somewhat by that afternoon, enough to say, "This must have been difficult for you, Amelia. I can see you're strong like your father, but I hope a bit smarter."

Now at the mention of Mr. Goldfield's name, her grandmother had abandoned all pretense of doing the crossword puzzle. She had a vested interest in this conversation.

"You've identified the speaker?" Amelia repeated for her grandmother to hear. "I never doubted for a moment your expertise," Amelia flattered him. "No, I'm not familiar with the name. Yes, I'm sure I should be. Yes, he did have a very distinct voice. So British-Pakistani. Al Qaeda. Yes, I am familiar with the London bombing. And the Liquid Bomb plot too? How do you know? I see. Arrested…okay. CIA…I see. Killed in 2008. Yeah, I remember how you mentioned those before. Yes, they sure do the trick. I really can't say, Mr. Goldfield. Just journalism, I guess. Yeah, I agree. Not someone any decent American should be involved with. Couldn't agree more. Thanks, Mr. Goldfield. Keep in touch."

We're almost getting to be buddies, Amelia mused as she hung up the phone. Talking about the CIA, FBI, Al Qaeda. Yep, just like ole high school chums. And even though she got the answers she needed, they were far from the ones she wanted.

"According to Bull," Amelia began reporting back to her grandmother, "I mean Mr. Goldfield, he's been identified as Rashid Rauf, a dual British-Pakistani citizen. He was arrested in August 2006 as a suspect in a foiled terrorist plot to blow up ten transatlantic flights with liquid bombs. Apparently, a top CIA official traveled to Pakistan and had him arrested. He escaped in 2007 and was later killed by a US Predator drone in Pakistan in 2008. In 2012, Al Qaeda documents surfaced that verify his role in both the London Bombing in 2005 and in the foiled Liquid Bomb Plot in 2006. That's who my dad was talking to."

"Yep," her grandmother sighed, almost nonplussed. "Pretty shady dealings, your dad had. Al Qaeda and liquid bombs. Not something I would boast to the gals at bridge about. 'Did you know my son was good friends with high-level Al Qaeda leaders? A real pride and joy, my son.' My point, Amelia, is that if he was willing to be involved with someone like that, I don't think he much cared what, or who, he risked." It was justified bitterness—the bitterness that comes with birthing a son and raising him to be a man that jeopardized his family and maybe even supplied the means to their deaths.

"I can't help but feel the same way, Grandma. But maybe when we're able to talk to him, we'll know what really happened.

"Well, let's just say his FBI interrogation will seem like summer camp at a country club when I have my turn with him." With that she stood up abruptly and headed toward her bedroom.

Under lighter circumstances, Amelia would have pictured her grandma wagging her finger at her shamefaced son. But for this situation, Amelia put her in charge of his waterboarding. That was a better fit.

Chapter 78

Connie stared at the timeline Amelia placed in front of her. Neither of them could deny that Rashid Rauf fit neatly within its scope: April 2004-Abu Ghraib; May 2004-Beheading; May 2004 to June 2005-Journalist slump; July 2005-London Bombing; July 2005 to March 2006-Rauf as informant & Rauf's threats; April 2006-Explosion; August 2006-Rauf's arrest.

"It's possible," she finally surmised.

"If you think about what he said on the tape, it's clear that he was giving information to my father in exchange for the publicity. He also thought my father was jeopardizing his operations. That's motive. Finally, he loves to have people blow up things, so fits his modus operandi as well...Hello, Connie. Are you listening?"

"Angel," she finally said, "I'm glad you have a plausible scenario. I hope that gives you some closure so you can move on with your own life. I've watched you for over two months now on this great quest, but really, other than the money you found, where has it really gotten you? I mean you, personally? Sure, your dad probably has a little more backing to help him with his legal issues, but are you really going to put your life on hold until his issues are resolved? That may not be just months; it could be years."

Years. Would she really have to wait years to confront him? She had followed all the leads she had, and now all she could do was wait and wonder whether the one person who held the answers would ever be able to provide them. So much for seeking the truth. No, so much for *finding* the truth. Seek she had. *It would be cruel*, she mused, *if that were all I had been meant to do.*

"It's time to move on, Angel," Connie crooned. "Make a plan for yourself. Go to school. Make some friends. Travel. You have your freedom now. Only your mindset is holding you in captivity."

In a way, she was right, although she didn't know about the baby on the way. Amelia could still do most of those things with or without a baby. She couldn't convince herself, however, that she had accomplished what she had set out to do for her mother and for her brother. It was more than a mindset; she had made a promise. And until she made good on that past promise, there was little she could do to advance her future.

Chapter 79

Amelia came to learn that the future advances with or without one's consent, so instead of fighting it, she became its somewhat willing passenger. In the months that followed, she finally got her driver's license, to her grandmother's great relief. She also listened to her baby's heartbeat and counted his ten fingers and ten toes, as well as other appendages. She had grown fond of the lump that everyday took up more of her body and the space around it. She had frequent visits from both Connie and Toby, who both showered her with the gifts and attention her own mother would have loved to bestow. Her grandma, too, had not tired of nursing and coddling her, giving up morning brunches and afternoon teas. She hadn't judged Amelia and had questioned her only once.

"Is he the father? That sad man who called for you?"

Amelia had nodded then turned away, her tears falling as if they had never stopped.

"Amelia," her grandmother had continued, "I hoped it was that lawyer, but since it's not, wouldn't it be just as well to follow your heart?"

She had looked up at her grandmother despite the embarrassing tears and shook her head.

"I've grown up, grandmother. I no longer believe in fairytales." Then she paused to smile. "Only the wicked stepmother part, I guess," she laughed wiping at her tears. She had shared bits and pieces of her Honduran childhood, just enough for her grandmother to sympathize but not enough for her to vow revenge.

"Are you sure there's no room for fairy godmothers?" her grandmother had coaxed. "Maybe if you just followed it through? You did that for your father. Don't you deserve to do it for yourself?"

Amelia had no answer for that—only sadness that kept her mute.

But that night she had dreamed. She had dreamed she was slithering upon his bed as if a viper. Her head a crown of silky black hair. As she neared her prey lying upon the bed, a hiss erupted from her long, thin lips. "C'mon, Donnie," she had hissed. "Just one for old time's sake."

Her prey had opened his eyes, and through them, they recognized the viper. And as Brenda's venomous fangs lowered towards Donovan, his shiny, dark eyes widened into discs that burst into shards of glass to scatter upon the rumpled sheets and the surrounding floor. Clutching his empty eye sockets, he sprang from the bed shouting, "No! Never!" Blind to the shattered glass that pierced his feet, he tripped over the empty beer bottles strewn across the floor and fell savagely to his knees. Amelia left him in her dream: he wailing her name, rocking back and forth on his knees upon the shards of his eyes.

It was an image she could not shake and for the first time she felt real doubt. What had happened that night? Had she gotten it all wrong? Was her grandmother right after all? If she could search for closure for her father, couldn't she find it for herself?

Yet even the path to her father had stubbornly resisted her appeals, and as her baby grew, the information she sought did not.

Chapter 80

"Amelia!" She heard her name called from behind, and there was no mistaking its tenor. She saw, even before she turned to look, his tawny waves and lopsided grin. She could make a dash for it down the aisle, pushing her half-full cart with the wobbly wheel. Or she could feign deafness and casually finish the aisle she was on, leaving the cart behind to race from the store. Instead, she turned her head to greet him, even as her mind pictured her clumsy, but clean, getaway.

She had to admit her heart fluttered when she saw him. He was truly breathtaking. Though less tan than in the fall, the contrast between his skin and hair made both all the more alluring. And his eyes. She pulled the cart tighter against her middle, and keeping her back to him as he approached, she responded over her shoulder in kind, "Jonathon! What a surprise!"

That was an understatement. It would have been more accurate had she called out, "Jonathon! How mortifying!" Yet, she didn't look half bad that day. A recent shower, a new outfit to replace those she had outgrown, and even a dusting of makeup. It wasn't a total catastrophe. All this she thought as she pulled the cart more snugly against her belly.

In a moment he stood somewhat awkwardly beside her, halfway leaning in for a hug and halfway extending his hand. Had the cart not been there, a hug would surely have been the result, but instead Amelia extended her hand and tightly clasped his. He placed his other hand over hers as well and stared into her eyes in true delight, despite the awkward greeting.

"You look as radiant as ever," he remarked. It was a funny choice of words given the current situation and Amelia couldn't help but laugh.

"I appreciate the exaggeration," she said through her laugh. "But I can truly give you that compliment with no exaggeration at all. I'm glad you're well."

"And how would you know that I'm well?" he quipped. "Who's to say I haven't been locked up in some crazy ward waiting for my heart to mend."

She laughed again. "I doubt very much someone like me could ever set you back that much, Jonathon. I knew you'd be fine."

"Don't be so sure about that, Amelia," he said more seriously this time. "You both underestimate yourself and overestimate me. But I am glad to see you again."

"Me too, Jonathon. Really."

As they looked at each other smiling, Amelia thought for a moment that she had managed to escape the mortification she had dreaded. But instead of the goodbye she expected, he said,

"You know, you do look different. Happier, maybe? Yes, there's definitely something different about you."

She may have been able to keep up the charade long enough to avoid detection, but suddenly she just wanted it over.

"I think you mean fatter," she replied, stepping out from behind the cart, no longer willing to hide the truth that he deserved to know.

The shock on his face couldn't have been more evident as he took in the bulge of her belly. Not only was he at a loss for words, he seemed to be at a loss for breath as well. Amelia stood waiting for him to gain composure, color rising to her cheeks as his gaze finally broke away from her belly to look at her face.

It wasn't quite a smile that found his lips and it definitely didn't reach his eyes, but at least he tried for a modicum of humor.

"So...you roofied me?"

"I know," she sighed. "It's a shock. It was for me, too, when I found out. It wasn't something I had planned. It wasn't anything I imagined could happen."

"I think you know how it *could* happen," he blurted, and then recovering added, "When did you know? How long did you know?"

She had dreaded this question, but here it was. With a sigh, she forged ahead. "I found out a few days before we went to the cemetery together. I wanted to tell you, but...but...I don't think I really believed it myself."

"All I remember," he said this time with bitterness in his voice, "was telling you that I was falling in love with you. And you basically telling me I was too good for you. I took that as an assumption of my arrogance, a critique I didn't believe I deserved. Had I known this," he said gesturing to her belly, "I would have walked away knowing it was simply the truth. It looks like I *am* too good for you."

It stung, but Amelia didn't doubt she deserved it. None of it had been planned. None of it was fair, for either of them. And even if it had been something less catastrophic than carrying another man's baby, like having a dad connected to terrorists for example, her circumstances would always have tainted his.

"I'm sorry, Jonathon," she said closing her eyes and taking a deep breath. "None of this is how I would have planned it." She smiled sadly. "Our relationship would have been a lot different had it been up to me."

"Don't be so fatalistic, Amelia," he admonished. "We all have choices. I just don't agree with yours." It may have been the tears that began to pool in her eyes, but suddenly he softened and reaching for her hand he said, "I don't mean to be cruel. I guess I'm just really surprised …and angry. I think what I really want to say, what I really feel is that I had the right to know. Ultimately, the result would have been the same. You're right. I wouldn't have gotten past it, but at least I would have known…"

"That you dodged a bullet," Amelia finished for him.

He laughed sadly. "That's not exactly what I was going to say, but yeah. I wouldn't have had any illusions about what could have been. It's not that I deserve someone better than you, Amelia, but maybe someone in better circumstances. Life is hard enough without inviting the unexpected to your door at every turn. Hell," he laughed with actual mirth this time, "you had me turning in circles with one revelation after another. I think this last one is just a bit of overkill, wouldn't you say?"

"I know," she agreed, trying to laugh as she swiped tears away with her free hand. "That's why I ended it. I'm sorry I didn't tell you. I just wanted to keep some of my dignity. But ultimately," she said with regained composure, "what's important is that I'm in love with this baby growing inside me, whatever the circumstances."

Jonathon nodded and giving her hand a squeeze said, "I wish you the best, Amelia. For you and your baby. I truly do."

They exchanged a long sad smile until Jonathon reluctantly let go of her hand and walked back down the aisle and out of the store. Amelia looked at her half-full (or was it half-empty?) shopping cart. She didn't have the energy to finish her list, but somehow, with one foot in front of the other and one wobble of a wheel after another, she worked her way toward the check out and back into the reality of her life.

Chapter 81

Connie was visiting Amelia again, and Connie, who had hated shopping her whole life, was presenting Amelia with yet another gift for "Angel Baby," as Connie had taken to calling the growing bump of Amelia's stomach.

"You have to stop this!" scolded Amelia. "Before you know it, you'll have to mortgage your home just to keep this little boy in trendy duds."

"I know your mom would have loved to do this for you and Angel Baby. It's the least I can do, considering I'm the next best thing! Now isn't that sad," she said smiling sheepishly at Amelia, "I'm the next best thing. You truly are unfortunate!"

Amelia whipped the onesie she had just removed from the bag at Connie. "The only thing that makes me unfortunate," Amelia complained, "is that my baby is going to be dressed a lot snazzier than I am! Maybe my 'next best thing' to a mother should start getting clothes for me."

"That would be no fun," Connie proclaimed. "They don't make cute onesies in your size."

Their laughter was interrupted by Connie's cell phone that began chirping some inane tropical birdcall. Connie's eyes got big as she looked at the caller ID.

"This one I need to take," she said, fixing her gaze steadily on Amelia. "Hello, Ana? How have you been?"

Over the next five minutes, Amelia tried to piece together a conversation from Connie's one-sided questions and exclamations. By the time the conversation was over, Amelia could barely keep herself from jumping across the table and grabbing the phone.

"What? What? What is it?" She demanded when Connie finally ended the call. "What's going on?"

Connie looked at her with the same big eyes she'd worn since reading the caller ID.

"I can't believe it. I really can't believe it," she said shaking her head.

"What? What?" Amelia repeated, about ready to strangle the answer out of her.

"Your father, Amelia. It's over. I mean the *major* legal stuff is over. It's just small potatoes now."

"Really, Connie? That's how you're explaining this to me, using vegetables?"

Connie laughed. "I might as well explain it using dingle berries for all the sense it'll make." She took a long dramatic breath. "They charged your father."

"Oh for God's sake, Connie! With what? What did they charge him with? Conspiracy? Treason?"

"With tax evasion! Isn't that the darndest thing! What they won't think of next! Let's just hold someone in jail without charges for eight months and then charge him with tax evasion!" she laughed shrilly, and then suddenly she was out of her chair pulling Amelia up on her feet.

"It's over!" she said, jumping up and down, her hands on the sides of Amelia's shoulders, making her bounce up and down as well. "It's over!"

Amelia didn't feel the exuberance Connie felt. Nor did she feel the truth in her words. It wasn't over. It wouldn't be over until her father looked her in the eye and took accountability for what he had done to them. To her. Even to those beat-up bodies left in Honduras. To all of them. And even then, she couldn't be sure it would be over. How could the damage this man had delivered upon so many ever be over?

Chapter 82

When that day finally came, Amelia didn't know what she would feel more at the sight of him: anger or the sense of retribution. But when he entered the room on the other side of the safety-glass partition, she was stunned to realize that all she felt was pity.

He was so thin, and now that she saw him without his cowboy boots or hat, she realized he wasn't much taller than she, this giant of a man she had tried a lifetime to reach. Today she not only reached him but looked at him from the summit beyond.

Her imposing father, a little man in an orange jail suit, smiled at her in a way she had never seen before, surprise and joy radiating from every angle of his face. How she would have loved to see him look upon her with that smile just once before in her life. It seemed it was the first time he ever really saw her. Yet she felt no joy.

He picked up the receiver as he sat down in front of her, so close she could not remember a time he had been closer. The lines on his face were so deep they mimicked the furrows he had plowed upon their Honduran mountainside to prevent the rains from washing away the fertile topsoil. His eyes were a watery blue, like the Honduran sky minutes before the sun burned away the morning fog.

"Hi, Dad," she finally said into the receiver that felt so cold against her ear.

"Amelia," he sighed. "I can't believe it's you. And look at you," he said seeing her belly for the first time, "I…I didn't know," he stammered. "You're going to be a mother. You look beautiful."

He was wiping at his eyes, and it took Amelia a moment to realize they were tears and not mountain raindrops. The only time she had ever seen him cry was after the explosion, and then only once. But here, he was like their mountaintop home—vulnerable to the elements, exposed to the stars, his only barrier the transparent safety glass between them.

"Daddy," she consoled before she could stop herself. "It's going to be okay," she intoned, unconsciously stroking the glass between them. "I found you."

"Amelia, I can't believe you're here," he repeated, the morning sun finally drying the mist from his eyes. "When they took me away in Houston, I thought it would only be for a few hours. Weeks later I was still there, wondering what they were planning to do with me. I didn't even get to make a phone call, if you can imagine. Then they transferred me to the MDC. They said I wasn't actually being charged with anything, that I was a 'material witness.' I didn't even know to what crime. They said since I lived in Honduras I was a flight risk, so they couldn't let me go. They assigned me a lawyer, but I only got to see him at my first and only court appearance. I didn't see him again until I got here to Minnesota nearly eight months later."

He was shaking his head as he relived his story, running his free hand through hair that loosely covered his pale scalp. Amelia waited, patient for the first time since she had returned to Minnesota.

"I got my lawyer back when they charged me. I was surprised because after weeks of interrogation, I was sure they were going to charge me with terrorism. But no, tax evasion. My lawyer tells me they have a pretty tight case. Seems like I wasn't too good at keeping the books for the newspaper. I don't know. Might be so. I've always paid more attention to the journalism. Funny thing is, they set bail at two hundred and fifty thousand dollars, something unheard of for petty tax evasion. My lawyer says it's because I'm a flight risk. I need ten percent to meet the bail bond, but I haven't had anyone who could help me out."

"Until now, Papa," Amelia said, interrupting for the first time. "I have the money."

"Yeah, I know. I wanted you to know about it before, Amelia, but I was worried that things would still be too dangerous for you. I got so many threats, and even after the explosion, they said they'd come after you, too."

"Who daddy? Who said that?" Amelia implored, her face nearly pressed to the glass.

"I figured that after so many years things had cooled down, that it would be safe to visit," he continued, ignoring her question. "I had already missed thirteen years of my little sister's life, including her yearlong struggle against the cancer that finally took her. I couldn't miss her funeral as well. And it was time for you to have your own life. I had protected you too much already. It was time to let you go.

"There's other money too," he continued. "I hid it because I was afraid the FBI would confiscate all of it under the guise of 'terrorist assets' or something of the sort. I wanted to tell Connie, but I was afraid to implicate her in any of this. I was sure they were just waiting for an excuse to bring her in. Luckily, she's steered clear of the whole conspiracy thing and most of the more controversial anti-war reporting. I don't think she's even on their radar any longer, and I want to keep it that way."

"Hold on, Papa," Amelia interrupted. "You're talking about the safe, aren't you? I already have it. I figured it out and just like I thought, you decided to bury it rather than keep something that important in a corporate institution."

He was smiling at her.

"That's my Amelia," he chuckled. "You've gone and figured it out. So now tell me, how did you find it?"

"Let's just say not even a gag order can keep Toby quiet!"

They smiled at each other for a moment, and Amelia remembered suddenly this same moment repeated so many years before. She had just shown him the article she had written for her elementary newspaper about her favorite librarian.

"I used to wonder," she had written, "why God gave Toby such a very big body. But now that I know her, the answer is easy. How else could she have room for such a very big heart?" Her father had smiled up at her afterwards as he smiled at her now. Though Amelia wanted to stall, extend that moment in both directions, she knew that a moment shared, or perhaps repeated, is only that. So, she let it die like so many other moments she had wished to covet.

"Who killed them Papa?" she nearly whispered into the receiver, placing her hand upon the glass as if it could penetrate both the pane and his resolve. "Please tell me the truth."

His smile disappeared as he sighed and looked away. "The only truth is that they're gone," he replied softly. "All other truth is irrelevant."

"Not to me. I have to know. They would want me to know," she insisted.

"Let it go, Amelia. Let them go. I, as well as anyone, should know it is not always noble and courageous to seek the truth, not when it condemns others to die. You know it too. I see it in your eyes."

"You could have never seen it coming, could you have Daddy?" Amelia pleaded, wanting more than anything for him to proclaim his innocence. But he could not.

"Oh yes, I could," he declared, nodding his head vehemently. "With all my knowledge of the evil struggle for dominance, I knew best of all what could happen. I knew and yet..." he stopped, looking around wildly for some answer other than the one he knew. "Yet," he finally cried, "I didn't stop! I kept digging deeper and deeper! Even after the threats on both sides, your mother pleading for me to stop... I searched on," he confessed, his voice now a hoarse whisper, "for some elusive gem coated in gunpowder. But you Amelia," he continued urgently, "can stop. Let it go. The truth is they are gone. Trying to find meaning in their deaths can only bring you closer to yours." He looked down at her stomach then, as it pressed against the glass. "You and my grandchild have a whole life to live. Let that be your truth."

"I can't, Papa," she cried. "I've come too far not to hear it from you. Don't you owe me that much? Was it Rashid Rauf, Daddy?" She stared into his eyes for his answer, but all she could see in their milky pools besides her own desperate reflection was his resolve.

"I owe you a lot of things, Amelia, but a death sentence is not one of them. I'm sorry. I can't tell you. I love you too much."

As he continued to hold her eyes with his, his last sentence penetrated her consciousness. She had searched years for the knowledge it professed, and she finally knew the truth: he loved her. Why had he never told her that? Why had he kept her at a distance with such indifference all these years? Why had he abandoned her, too, when her mother and brother already had? Now was her chance to ask those questions.

But looking straight into his eyes, she knew he did not have the answers. He was not a mountain of a man; he was this small man in an orange jumper, imprisoned in a life that had more questions than answers. Without the answers, he had forged ahead like she had, seeking them—sometimes following an illusion, other times gut punched with the truth but forging ahead nonetheless, creating fissures that could not be mended, breaks that could not be healed. She had come so far to find the truth in these and many other unanswered questions, but the real truth had been simple: an answer to a question she had not thought to ask.

As he moved to stand, Amelia drank in the power of the answer she had received. And as she watched the guard grab her father's upper arm and lead him away like so many months ago, a feeling of loss overwhelmed her. She knew this time she would not abandon him. She had learned a truth from him that mattered more than all those he would never reveal, and she had discovered one about herself: she loved her father, and she had forgiven him.

"I'll post bond, Daddy!" she shouted through the glass as he and the guard approached the door on the far end. "You'll be out of here tomorrow. I promise!" As the door slammed shut behind them, she stared at the space into which his slumped figure had disappeared. All too soon, the knowledge of the other suffering he had caused a thousand miles away would press upon his already burdened shoulders. This would be his journey, she realized, but he would not face it alone.

As she turned to go, she felt it for the first time. It hit her lowest rib like a sledgehammer, though it was but a gentle nudge. She rubbed her hand across her protruding belly, the past and the future intertwined within her womb, co-conspirators in an enigmatic plot that prodded her forward all the while it called her back. She finally knew which direction she would choose.

Both.

Epilogue

The chimes that announced Amelia's entrance were a far and much fairer cry from the whistles and bells of her earlier visit to the casino. She had wormed her way through the dense smoke of the gaming lobby, each ding of a fortuitous wager and the rattle of its subsequent release of coins making her jump, until her heart was palpitating even more than her mission warranted. The woman she had asked had been unwilling to cooperate at first, but upon seeing what Amelia carried, had softened and written the information on a scrap of paper. Amelia was both relieved to have the information and disappointed to learn she would have to spend another day in the rental car.

But finally, she was there, and the chimes that welcomed her made her heart flutter as much as the din of the casino had made it palpitate. She found herself surrounded by eagles, buffalo, and beautiful dark people peering at her from behind frames and from sculpted eyes. But she did not return their stares. Instead she found herself moving to the back of the gallery, towards the silhouette of a woman seated upon a pedestal, her tarnished iron form bowing a head of molten hair that flowed down the length of her back, her arm gently cradling the rusted metal of an enlarged belly, her plaque unabashedly proclaiming her title: *Amelia.*

Amelia stood in front of the statue, unable to breathe, so tangible was the sadness, loneliness, and tender regret emanating from this symbol of motherhood. *Her* symbol of motherhood.

She knew even before she felt the lock of hair lifted from her neck that he was there. And as he entwined the tendril between his longing fingers, she embraced a new chapter in her life. *And your new chapter,* she thought, smiling upon the bundle that slumbered in her arms, *will be authored as it should be, with the wisdom of our pasts guiding the tender pen of your future.*

About the Author

    I grew up in rural Northern Minnesota, raised on a small, dysfunctional farm under the direction of an eccentric father. My subsequent life experiences were equally unique (and dysfunctional!). Little wonder I was not at a loss for real-life, made-for-fiction material from which to create my debut novel, *Authoring Amelia*.

    During high school, my father moved to Mexico and later Honduras. The few letters I received from him fostered within me a fervent desire to know Latin America. I got that chance after college, first traveling through Central America to visit my father and his new family in Honduras, and later living for a time in Mexico. As many Americans traveling for the first time in a developing country, I was struck by the rawness around me, confounded by the concurrence of intense beauty and vitality alongside gut-wrenching ugliness and despair. The image of the foal sucking the teat of its dead mother in the novel is an image that will remind me forever of the interconnectedness of these two extremes.

Once back in the States, I decided to utilize my Spanish skills to teach Spanish-speaking adults English. Soon after, I became a full-time educator, teaching English and basic skills to adults from all over the world. I am in love with my profession of twenty years and equally in love with each and every student who passes into my classroom.

To further my abilities to both teach English and teach others to teach English, I earned my Master's in Education in 2014 and went on to earn a PhD in Post-Secondary and Adult Education in 2017. I also have several professional publishing credentials to my name: *What's Next?* (New Readers Press, 2012), a phonics-based reading series for adults; *Bridging English Language Learners to GED Prep* (New Readers Press, 2017), a set of teaching guides for GED teachers; and the *Future Advanced* student book (Pearson, 2020), that I designed from cover to cover and for which I authored several pieces.

Though my own life provided substance for the novel, *Authoring Amelia* is a work of fiction in its entirety. Through this strong, vibrant young woman, I was able to explore the coexistence of the callous nature of life alongside its deepest moments of grace. And Amelia? Well, she rose to the challenge, determined to reconcile these opposing realities and make from them one reality all her own.